DISCIPLINE'S WORLD

E.L Discipline

Andrea Johnson Books Publishing

Rave Reviews for E.L Discipline Books

This book is absolutely a mix of fantasy and reality! The way it's written and the context that seems to have been carefully chosen could not have been better. – *The Seduction of Discipline*

This Book is AMAZING, I can't say it enough... The passion in his words is something out of this world –
The Seduction of Discipline

This is the second book I have read from this author and again, I am extremely impressed! His first book was incredible and now this! This book is definitely a page turner especially for someone who is in the process of going through some sort of change in their life. –
The Importance of Discipline

Discipline is the most important aspect in such a lifestyle, this book will absolutely let you into the mind
Of a REAL MASTER, a REAL KING, and one hell of an author. –
The Importance of Discipline

There are so many key points in this book. It's very well written as well. Love chapter 4 the most. Healing and vibrations. –
The Importance of Discipline

Excellent book, nothing like you may think. Not a gender-based book. Highly recommended. –
The Importance of Discipline

<u>Acknowledgements</u>

I would to thank the fans of E.L Discipline. Whom have been patiently waiting for this one to drop. Would love to thank Andrea Johnson Books Publishing. They have an absolutely amazing team.

Shout out to Andrea Torres, for her hard work and dedication into these projects and future projects to come. I work quick, and she matches my work ethic.

Shout out to the people that want me to fail, but, deep down are rooting for me to succeed. Shout out to the silent enemies, that watch everything I've done, but, you never see them or hear from them.

My motto for 2018, "let's fucking win!" There will be more projects in the works, for the near future. Keep on a look out for more work of E. L Discipline, coming soon....

Discipline's World

Cover art designed by Andrea Johnson Books Publishing.

First published by Andrea Johnson Books Publishing. 03/28/2018
6565 N. MacArthur Blvd, Suite 225 Dallas, TX. 75039
www.Ajbpublishing.com

This book is a work of fiction. Names, characters, places, and incidents are the product of the author's imagination or are used fictitiously. Any resemblance to actual events, locales, or persons, living or dead, is coincidental.

Because of the dynamic nature of the Internet, any web addresses or links contained in this book may have changed since publication and may no longer be valid. The views expressed in this work are solely those of the author and do not necessarily reflect the views of the publisher, and the publisher herby disclaims any responsibility for them.

ISBN-13: 978-0692093948
ISBN-10: 069209394X

Contents

Chapter 1: Her New Life

"This is your new life, and with this life it will consist of; loyalty, dedication, sacrifice, commitment, complete openness, respect, obedience, consistency, philosophy, guidance, Discipline (when need be), punishment (when need be), elevation, love, passion and challenge beyond the body."

She never experienced something so primitively strong. She's never been challenged, but the look in my eyes made it seem as if I invaded her every thought. I knew she could feel me, no words need be exchanged. Just a look, a gesture, made her blood rush and her heart beat faster. Gave her goosebumps down her fucking spine. My gaze gave her chills, made her damn legs weak. Watered her flower, igniting a flame within her soul and leaving a feverish dampness in her pussy that was uncontrollable. It inspired a desire for her to get on her knees and please me. An undeniable wish for my strong chocolate man hand to grasp her throat and command her to fulfill my deepest and darkest desires. These things that I would provide to her, become the only things that feed her cravings. Constant wetness between her thighs become worse with growls from me in her fucking ears. I spoke soft, but forceful.

"These feelings that I inspire within you are natural. I am your Alpha and Omega. Your beginning and your fucking end. Prior to me you were incomplete, after me you will desire none. Once I have you, no matter the time frame, I will ALWAYS have you. As of this moment you are mine. Matter of fact, you will always be mine. You will witness the complete alteration of your mind, body and soul. You will witness how they run to get to me at my command."

I pointed my strong index finger to the ground, downward. She knelt immediately. I then grasped her precious long black sleek hair. My fingers curled inward, grabbing a fucking fist full. I spoke sharply.

"You will come to me, you will always come to me. When I need you, when I want you. I will use you however I please, for pleasure, for pain, for as long as I please, wherever I please. As this life becomes a life of your choosing, you need to understand what you are giving. Your independence belongs to me, as you choose to give all of yourself to me, I intend to claim just that. Every fiber, cell, breath, movement and thought in your entire being."

She said to me, I'm the best in the world. And I replied to her.

"You're a smart girl, but flattery will get you nowhere. However, you will get more with sugar than you will with vinegar. You still think I'm the best when you're furious with me? Am I still the King when you're in your moods? I want to see how you get when you're not in your comfort zone."

She is aggressive on text, in person she kneels and begs. She kisses my tattoos slowly, I'm biting the back of her neck aggressively. I'm riding her next. Bring out the latex. She's fitting to blow, no not that white, I'm referring to sex. Once I've had my hands on her, I could always have her. In her eyes all I witness is lust. Once she was CONTROLLED by this Powerful Chocolate King, she would look at regular men with disgust. The need to touch me was deliciously excruciating for her, and not being able to invoked a divine conflict where she both wanted to be free yet never wanted to be let go.

The sense deprivation made her palms damp, as her fists alternate between clenching and unclenching. I bet I make her crazy while she lay wonderfully ensnared beneath my blissful torment. I stuck one of my big fingers in her slick, tight opening and she clamped down on her pussy lips. Fighting back her moans because she knew she wasn't allowed to until I said so. She already teetered on the brink of climax and knew it wouldn't take much more to push her over the fucking edge and just cum and cum and cum again. I rubbed a slow teasing circle over her clit with a wet fingertip. Her body convulsing.

"You know the rules, ask me! You know the rules, don't cum until I say so. You may moan now." I commanded sharply. Bringing about more gasps and breathy urges for me to continue before I replace my drenched finger with my Dominant tongue. Squeezing her eyes shut, straining against her tight binds as she cries out to the ceiling. What was she doing? Looking for God to help her? He's busy. She was going to beg for 'Discipline'.

Oh yes, I found a good rhythm that made her legs convulse and widen further. I knelt down, my head moves in as my tongue pursues her drenched pussy.

"You've come here because you do not want mediocrity. You've come here for pain." I said sharply. "For pleasure. For Discipline. To be Dominated. To be taken. To be devoured, overwhelmed, destroyed and then loved and protected."

I take her mind everywhere, so I can take her body everywhere.

"You go through the motions with me. I will have you wherever I please. I've given you the case of Vincilagnia. To be controlled is the only thing you know. The only thing you feel comfortable with. The only thing that makes sense. The only thing that turns you into a dripping mess. Erotic. Aesthetics. Euphoric. I will not physically punish you because you love it. So I will punish emotionally and psychologically, which is more effective. I will not fuck you hard if you've been bad, disobedient, overstepping or challenging. But when you're good to me, when you're good for the both of us, I will give you every ounce of this pain. You will feel every impactful delicious slap. Grasp. Grip from the flesh around your throat as you are throttled by me. Power coursing through your veins, leaving you craving more and more and more. Insatiably driven. A passionate, loving, Big chocolate cock hungry nymphomaniac, pain slut for me. Fuck your 'shhhh" world. Your, 'they might hear us, see us world.' You're now in My world. Discipline's world. You trigger my voracious appetite. Pull your skirt up, take your lace, nylon sheer cut panties down and get up against the wall, now I fucking take what belongs to me. In.... a.....Dominant fashion. Where we are is irrelevant. I will have you when I want, how I want."

When I gave her that first kiss back when we first met....
I knew she would be anything, give everything. But when
I am in that pussy I go dummy in her walls, like a fucking
crash test. I want to see her when I want. I want to touch
her when I want. I want to sex her when I want, not when
she wants. Not when it's convenient for her. She is here
for my use. When I call her that means she comes to me
and makes herself available. This isn't vanilla (regular)
and no, I am not a switch. She's very familiar. I am
adamantly Dominant, and she is my bitch. My submissive.
My whore. My pleasure palace. My everything and
anything I want her to be. She is mine. When I say mine,
it is in all the sense of the word. I take completely.
Reality for me is, if I can't control her...Mind, Body and
Soul, I can't have her. I won't have her. I told her
straight...

" Perhaps vanilla men do not care to admit it, but I will.
If I can't control you, I don't want you. My body, my
mind, my soul will never allow me to give anything
phenomenal. There will be no great sex, nothing that
exceeds physical pleasures, no connection. No aftercare
and I will take away everything you desire, love and want.
I won't allow it as well. I only believe in TPE, the acronym
I go by meaning, 'Total Power Exchange.' It's a price to
pay for Dominance, as I pay a price for your submission.

An 'exchange.' I know it's not fair. It's not fair, but I really don't fucking care. This is what you signed up for. This is what you want. An unequal, yet powerful bond and dynamic. Love. Domination one sided."

"Now on your knees, face down, ass up and keep that arch for Daddy. Give me everything, show me everything. Don't question, don't hold back. I know what you need, and it isn't what you think you want. It is to do what pleases me, when I fucking tell you to do it. Without my guidance and commands, you are lost. Without my Dominance and strength, you feel incomplete. I'm going to control you in every way and you will fucking love it, believe that."

I slide my big chocolate dick between those feverish begging pussy lips, Dominating her drenched hole. My slow yet deep and intense strokes had her creaming immediately.   "Daddy, may I please cum? Please, pretty please." I smirk, she was begging nonstop. I replied. "Yes, you may." Only because I knew I was going to make her cum way more than just this once.

"That's only the first one. Now this second one, you will work a little harder to earn. Your orgasms belong to me and you will earn them. All of them."

I flip her over, I don't ask, I just fucking did it. I pin her hands above her head with my massive chocolate man hands. They grasp her wrist and I pin her fragile hands against the mattress. I slide in once again, thrusting even deeper and faster. The ferocity had her breast moving in rhythm and her moans got louder.

"That's right, beg whore, beg!"

I could feel her walls closing in on me. Her pussy wetter than Niagara Falls. My strokes made it seem like I was stirring macaroni and cheese or kids smacking water down there. I love when her pussy talks to me. She was crazy fucking wet. The sheets were soaked, and she was dripping from her pussy down to her crack. Nothing better than missionary. My lips pressed against hers while I'm inside her. Mouth and tongue in complete Domination with hers. Exploring the depths of her mouth. Multitasking. Managing different sets of tasks efficiently. Eye contact. Controlling her body. Training her body. Mastering her soul. Testing her flexibility, pinning her legs back close to her ears. Heels in the air. Big muscular hand on her throat. Choke Stroke. Exhilarating just to stare into her eyes, observing her facial expressions as she loses herself in my madness. Going crazy from the things I do to her body. The things I do with my hips, she can't help but moan. Her moans are different. Her breathing changes. Her walls close in around me once again. I'm thinking, 'damn, this pussy is mine.' I'll show her those Kegel exercises. Toning those vaginal muscles. Training her pussy to take all of this Discipline thug therapy.

I place her legs on my broad shoulders, then I work her out. I spoke forceful but soft.

"I don't give a fuck which face you show the world, what you show everyone else. The nice. The innocent. The bitch face. The shy or quiet. I know your true face. I know the face you make when my thick long chocolate Dominant Dick is thrusting in between your begging, submissive pussy lips. When my big strong tongue licks and sucks on your clit. I know the face you make when you're drenched, or when you scream right before you cum. I know your face when you submit yourself completely to me. I know your face when you're on your knees."

My gaze demanded obedience. She adheres to my commands. Climbing her drenched and dripping walls like Spider-Man. Slow, hard, deep, strong, methodical strokes make her feel alive. Then speed it up. Brutal crime scene, my dick is the serial killer to her pussy. Dick murders her then it brings her back to life again. A new woman. A mix of intensity and passion. Dominance and aggression. My words capture her mind, trigger thoughts of desire. My voice and commands touch her heart and she utilizes those and follows. I claim every part of her being. Her submission is fluid. It came easy. All she could do was surrender. Her need, my hunger. My wisdom, her guidance. I said to her...

"The aftermath of me is, you will never be the same again. You're changed forever."

Then we both drown together in her pool of passion. Cum and cum and I growl so loud. She has such difficulty walking to the bathroom. I tell her, "when you come back to bed, we need to discuss some shit......."

Chapter 2: Responsibilities

"You must constantly stay on top of your responsibilities. As my submissive, you have a right and duty to fulfill my desires, at all times. Understand, I am no ordinary man."

I gazed squarely at her, she stares at me. She did not bat an eyelash. She listened to every word carefully as they came out of my mouth.

"I require more than the ordinary man. I will give you nothing but the things you earn. The things you work hard for. Complete obedience will highly be rewarded."

She views a side of me not many get to see. Tender and soft, while she knows I can be brutal and callous as well. Calm, to only be interrupted by destructive acts and vicious behavior during play of misbehavior. Dominance and Discipline are not exempt in good times nor bad times. She's good to me, therefore I treat her like gold.

"You will suck my big chocolate dick. You will kneel when I step into the room. No need to ever impose my will. A word, a gesture, a soft touch inspires more and more surrender. Your pussy is mine to devour when, how, wherever I please. Your mouth is mine to play with however I see fit. Your ass is mine to mark with whatever I choose. Your breasts are mine to grasp, slap and bite. I want what I want, and your job is to make yourself accessible to me. I do not want to take you by force. When I say, 'strip', that's what you are to do immediately. However, I do not have an issue ripping that shit right off you."

I grabbed her forcefully by the hair.

"Face down and give me your ass up. I'm going to show you why you are mine. Don't fucking move and stop running."

The moment I shoved my thick, long, muscular chocolate cock inside her drenched hole, through her begging pussy lips, it was a snug fit as her walls grabbed my big dick perfectly tight. Thrusting inside and out, back and forth, she was begging to cum for me instantly.

"Damn, kitten is eager huh?"

This is what her pussy has been longing for. Starving for. Addicted to. My strong, big hands grasp her waist, pushing and pulling her into and away from me. Her round soft ass bouncing off my pelvis and huge dick.

Vibration like an ocean wave. Her tits bouncing in rhythm. The slapping of flesh was like background music, as her moans took over. I don't care how fucking loud she gets, she was going to do as I commanded. No exceptions. I yanked her back towards me.

"Can I cum daddy, please?!"

I ignore her and go about my business. My business was that pussy of hers at this moment. I then continued to yank her hair towards me, anchoring her head so she was staring at the ceiling. My big muscular hand slithers from behind her just to grasp her throat. That choke stroke, I control her movements and I do not need rope. I give her the business, I work her out like physical fitness. She is crying, whimpering, damn she's so fucking adorable when she's suffering. Okay, okay, she's earned it.

"Go ahead, cum for me!"

She releases all over me, letting me feel her sweet lustful juices. "Give me that orgasm that belongs to me." She took her last deep breath before she was drenched like Niagara Falls. This was just the beginning. She was gonna cum a whole lot more than that. Within minutes she was begging to cum yet again.

"Fuck, shit, can I cum again Daddy, please? You feel so fucking good. That big dick is stretching me out, getting me wetter and wetter for you!"

I allowed her to cum once again. Orgasm number two. She took these back shots like a queen. Power and Dominant strokes, she released more powerful than a .480 ruger. She took my magnum bullets, I murder that pussy. I command, "cum for me now!" Her walls, so fucking tight, closing in around me. Her pussy drooling all over my meat, my chocolate dick. Our tormented souls find comfort in the way our demons play well with each other. In the moment when the lights are fading, and my fat cock is rock hard inside her. When I'm trying to destroy her pussy from within. When my strong fingers curl inward grasping a fist full of her sleek, luxurious hair. Firm grip is tight around her throat, squeezing the flesh around it. Whispering ownership terms, vulgar, nasty and fucking disrespectful shit in her ear.

"You worthless slut, give me my pussy bitch. Mmmmm, just like that. Show me why you're nasty for me. Give me that good pussy, gripping my fat dick...whore! Let that dick stretch that shit open." I flipped her body over. "Turn around now!" I said sharply, while I look down at her flickering consciousness, prior to me slapping that pretty little face. When her pussy is screaming from the wetness I've created, when her soul slowly abandons her body, when blood from her brain has stopped and rushes to her throbbing pussy because my big chocolate powerful fingers pinch those arteries shut. When she is floating in deeper love than ever before. When my huge savage dick is thrusting into her, pounding her into a dripping mess. That moment I hate her, and she loves me.

I drain her energy, I have complete control over her body. I whisper to her once again.

"You are the monster I've created. Now I destroy it before I build you back up again." I provide non-stop orgasms. I feel it again and that's when I command her.

"Beg me now, beg me again. Beg me to gush!"

I roared this command in her ear. I feel her walls tight around my thick cock. Her eyes begging, her mouth begging, her body begging. Her legs shaking.

"Daddy, please?!"

I reply, "please what?" She answers so breathlessly.

"Can I cum please, again?"

There she goes, that's what I wanted to hear. I allowed it. The third orgasm was more powerful. She squirted like a water gun, raining down like a busted fire hydrant. The sadist in me is present. The beast is unhinged. She takes deep and short breaths before her loud moans take over the entire room. Complete surrender to all of me and the damage I've caused. I allow her to cry and then catch her breath. It turns me on even more. Her eyes shut, back arched, crying out to the ceiling. Not even God himself can save her.

"Don't cry, 'oh god', cry for Discipline. Beg for more of this thug seduction and passion. Whether it's pain or pleasure, beg for it slut!" She loves the gentleman in me, but hell, does she love the Savage when he is released.

We clean up, we cuddle and then went to bed. The following day I made plans.

"Get dressed. You can be dressed casually."

It was a hot summer day, so I told her to wear one of the sun dresses I had picked out for her.

"I want you to wear that nice sun dress I picked out for you." She replied, "Daddy, where are we going?" I grasped her jaw with my index finger and thumb. My stone grip kept her mouth shut.

"Don't ask, just do." Her eyes popped wide.

"Yes Sir."

I planned a nice day out. I had the whole day planned. First, we were going to the movie theater. I selected the place, which movie, snacks, etc. So we pick our seats and I pick the highest seats towards the back. That way we were watching down below us, but no one was behind us. We sat comfortably, the seats reclined as well. The fifteen-minute previews were over and now the movie was starting to begin. The lights now dimmed…. I whispered in her ear immediately.

"Take off your panties and give them to me, now!"

She did just as I instructed her to do. I took them with my left hand, moved them to my right hand and placed them in my right pocket. I was sitting on the outside and she was sitting on the inside. I changed my position a little bit. My lips move towards her earlobe and my right finger goes in her already drenched torrid hole. I whispered to her.

"You're so fucking wet." Her eyes were shut, and her mouth open wide, gasping for air. "Fuck are you thinking about? Open your damn eyes. Watch the fucking movie. Who told you that you can enjoy this shit? You know who you belong to at all times, and you know who and what you are to me...."

Chapter 3: My Queen, My Slut, My Bitch, My Good Girl

"You are my good girl, my bitch, my slut and my Queen. I will have you wherever I please and you will always be ready for me."

She continues to breathe heavily, however, her eyes are fully open. Damn, she was so good, she just became wetter and more wet. My fingers were soaked, as now I had two in her pussy hole. Her walls closing in on my fingers.

"Don't you fucking cum without my damn permission!" I growled in her fucking ear. Her face looked hot, she did not cum. Her breathing sped up and an ache began to throb between her fucking legs. She was shifting in her damn seat trying to alleviate it. She leaned in and pressed her lips toward my ear.

"Can I please cum, please, please, please?"

I smirked.

"I am about to eradicate the word 'cum' out of your damn vocabulary because you're always begging to do that." She gasped loudly, "no, please don't!"

I was joking, I love to watch and feel her cum, but I love to watch her suffer as well. But, was it about the ability to come when she asked? Was it the ability to cum on command? Was it the ability to cum? Is that all she cared about? Therefore, I asked her...

"So what do you want more? To no longer use the word or to no longer do it? You know, the actual act?"

Speechless, she didn't know exactly what to say. All I could do was snicker.

She replied, "I'll stop doing and saying it, because all I want to do is please you."

That was the perfect answer. Of course, I want her cumming and asking my permission to do so. But, it's the principal, and I did not want her to forget that.   I then allowed her to release all over my strong muscular fingers.

"You may cum now Precious." I smirked. "Cum on my fingers. Let me feel it." As I whispered that in her ear, she was gushing all over my fingers. I placed my other hand over her mouth, shutting her up. Then I took my hand off and placed the fingers I had in her, the fingers she had cum on, by her face.

"Open your mouth, taste yourself."

She did just that. Man, I had her literally wrapped around my fingers. She made love to my fingers with her mouth and tongue. She was licking slowly, sucking roughly and sipping quickly. I love her unguarded, vulnerable and helpless. Just exposing her damn weakness. I wasn't finished with her though. I wanted her to cum some more. I don't even remember what movie was playing. Fuck that, I wasn't watching the damn movie, I was watching her.

My tone was more savage now, whispering softly but so forceful in her ear, radiating from me like a beacon.

"Spread your fucking legs wider!"

After a few minutes I was getting annoyed with her and then I became a little rough with her. I grabbed her and pulled her towards me. Away from the safety of the chair's arms. My angry mouth sucked and pulled at her breasts until one freed itself from the decollate bra. I pounced and sucked on her exposed nipple and with my other big muscular hand, I began groping her under her sundress making a beeline straight for the honey pot. I could tell by anguished moans, the fondling made her feel real good and that warm tingle was coming back, working its way up her thighs and radiating through her. Her body just always surrendered to me. Her mind, her eyes, her lips, her. She loved suffering and hurting for me. She enjoyed every fucking minute, every fucking time. She must have cum like three different times. After all this time I still get her nervous. Dark rumbling tones cascaded down her spine alongside an involuntary shiver. Goosebumps erupted along her arms and legs. Such compliance. A regular man wouldn't know what to do with her. I was just sinfully lethal. I constantly bring out her demons and I play with them very well. Her body jerked in response. A few murmurs sounded as I touched her again, this time a little differently. Stroking a few inches down her arm.

Amazingly, she remained still except for the closing of her eyes and the muscles of her face going slack as she relaxed onto the experience. Her head swung from side to side with the most amazing expression of bliss curling at her lips. When she began to moan, she notices her own bra and panties suddenly draws tight. The sensitive tips of her nipples rubbing against the fabric. The constant need, the absolute need, to fucking strip out of her restricting clothing clawed at her damn gut. I then pinched one of Mia's, aka 'Precious', nipples. Her fucking back arched, and a low sultry wail came out. I loved watching my submissive and her reactions to the way I, her Master, teased, tempted and tormented her. This was definitely more than she ever anticipated.

I grabbed both her legs and pushed them roughly apart. Precious held her breath in anticipation. She leaned back in her seat and allowed her legs to fall apart. The sudden desire flowing through her was more than she had ever experienced in her entire life. I bet she's grateful for the darkness in the room, her pussy wetter than Niagara Falls. She whispered in my ear," Daddy, please fuck me!" and I smirked, "I will fuck you when I want, not when YOU want."

A low but forceful gasp slipped out of her. I was stroking her inner thigh and pussy nonstop. Soft pleas fell from her mouth.

"Please Daddy, if you won't fuck me, may I at least cum once again for you?"

For me huh? She is slick. She wanted to cum for herself, but she throws in the 'for YOU' pitch. I spoke soft but with authority.

"NO!" I slid my fingers and pushed through the sopping folds of her pussy straight to her throbbing clit. Her eyes focused on me. She did not take her fucking pretty eyes off of me, not for a second. Well shit, I fucking stared back at her. My gaze told her I took great pleasure in seeing her twisted up and on the verge of losing it in front of me. It drove her even more crazy. Perhaps it's the way my lips curled slightly at the corners that clued her into the enjoyment that I derived from this. She fucking belonged to me, every fiber in her being said so. Every cell in her body said so. I finally allowed her to cum. She released, and she was relieved. Never in her wildest dreams would she have thought she would enjoy this type of public play before. Yet her fear of discovery dissolved a little more with each passing second. Her mind swirled with my deep and masculine voice. Every fucking thing I demanded, she yearned to give me. Her pussy squeezed.

"Let me feel it. Cum for me now!" I whispered forcefully. She bit down on her lower lip to keep from crying out, while her muscles clenched and spasmed in pleasure. A ball of heat gathered and exploded, flooding her body until the overload of sensation left her in a mindless state of euphoria. Oxytocin dripping from her pituitary gland, she shut her eyes then opened them. Her hands between her legs, her lungs screamed for air and tears stained her cheeks. She managed to pull down her sundress, tuck her boobs back into her bra before the lights in the auditorium came on, but that was the extent of movement she could handle at the moment.

As the rest of the people in the theater began to move towards the exit, I told her, "don't move, stay where you are. Follow my lead. We are not leaving yet."

She struggled to find her composure. The overwhelming sensation felt so good, she didn't want it to stop, well at least not as of yet. She couldn't even remember feeling this damn good in a while. Prior to me that is. I held her hand while people were moving and passing by us trying to exit. Most of the people cleared out and now I said, "let's go."

Still holding her hand, I guided her out of there. "Let's get you some fluids." I said urgently. She grabbed my arm tightly and firm, "I'm fine, really." She tried to assure me. I could imagine butterflies doing acrobats in her stomach and a bee buzzing in her head.

"I'm sure you are, but you still need fluids and that's not up for discussion or argument." I said firmly. We got water.

"Here, drink up. It's essential that you constantly replenish." She stares at me and laughs.

"You forgot I'm in the medical field?"

I laugh as well. "You're constantly taking care of everyone else, you forget about you. But don't worry, that's MY job."

She gazed at me again, squarely. "You know, I don't need taking care of." I grabbed her hand firmly, "Shut the fuck up and let's go!"

I held her hand with the perfect amount of pressure. Another subtle sign of confidence and power she always appreciated.

"Are you nervous Precious?" She loved the sound of the nickname I gave her, rolling off my tongue. "Do I make you nervous?" I asked once again, this time more detailed and specific. I already knew the answer. Hell yeah I made her nervous. I'm a MASTER in a lifestyle she craved for so long but had little to no experience in, not to mention I'm able to get her turned on without touching her. To have that type of power over her was dangerous.

"Yes Daddy, you make me very nervous. I'm constantly on edge. I never want to make you angry or upset, I only crave to make you happy and proud."

I lifted her hand to my lips and I kissed the back of her hand. "I have so many other plans for today. That's the greatest thing, the day is far from over."

I grabbed her ass so firmly as we walked to the car. I placed the key in the ignition and started up the vehicle to drive off. I had planned a picnic with her in a nice park I knew of. While we waited at a light, I tell her...

"Now you're going to please me." I unzip my pants and took out my big, long chocolate cock. I grabbed her by the hair and push her head down onto my big dick. Her eyes aligned with my cock, my meaty chocolate cock.

"Start sucking." I commanded, but she already knew what to do. I started to drive as the light turned green. Windows tinted, therefore, no one could see what was inside. Her full lips wrapped around my girth, and her petite hands held onto the long shaft, and she then began to suck on the big tip head of my cock. Her lips of sin, so eager and anxious to sip me up. She was sucking and licking the big tip, while she slid her hands up and down. I placed my hand on the back of her head, slamming her deep into me. So deep I could feel the back of her throat. I crave to take what is mine, and if she is all talk, I have something to shut her up with. I will fill her mouth up, until she gags, swallowing all of me, she would make sure to leave no clean up. She is grateful, of such things.

To some women, masturbation may be a 'touchy' subject. They dread to speak of it or admit it. Oral sex is a matter of 'taste.' I used her, and guess what? She loved to be used by me. Gagging on my cock, tears running down her cheeks, we hit the highway. I loved that she chose my dick over the damn air to breath. I could hear every slurp, gag, drip, lick, suck and moan because she was so turned on. Her pussy was drenched. I held the steering wheel with my left hand and my right hand was playing with her clit. I placed a finger in her drenched hole, then took it out to play with her clit once again. She paused from sucking, just to moan so loudly.

"Keep sucking, I didn't tell you to fucking stop." I pushed her head down with the hand that was playing with her wet pussy. She was so wet it sounded like I was stirring macaroni and cheese. So wet she was fucking dripping greatness. The wetter she became, the better she sucked my big thick dick. Filling her hole had her in a euphoric state. Her lips opened wider for me and her throbbing drenched hole began to close around my strong fingers. She was anything for me. Did anything for me. I literally had her wrapped around my fucking fingers. Her head game was so good, however, I didn't cum. I controlled it, I didn't want to, not yet. Not while I'm driving, but I demanded her to orgasm on my damn fingers once again, just like in the movies.

"Cum on my fingers, NOW! I want to fucking feel it, cum for me baby girl. Cum for me now!!!"

I watched where and how I completely controlled her whole body, mind and spirit. She came right on command. It was beautiful, well my leather seat on her side was soaked but I'll get it cleaned. We finally arrived at the park. I found great parking and turned off the ignition.

"This is where we get out baby girl." I opened the trunk and took out a big blanket and I brought out a big basket of goodies filled with fruit and consumable delicious things for us. I found us a nice spot by the trees, and we sat down but not before I set the blanket and basket down. We sat, we laughed, we ate. Then I said, "get up. Let's take a stroll around this park." I didn't really want to take a stroll around the damn park, I had other plans in mind......."

Chapter 4: Fuck You Here, Fuck You There, Fuck You Anywhere

We went to the park for a stroll, and I found a tree where no one was around. I then stopped, and she stopped as well. I pushed her up against the tree. I kissed her passionately and roughly. I pulled out some rope I had placed in my pocket earlier, because I am constantly planning ahead. I then began to bind her body against the tree. I wrapped the rope underneath her tits and around the tree to keep her body still. I placed her hands and wrists above her head and then started to bind them to the tree. She was nicely restrained, prudently restricted. Helpless and vulnerable just like I loved her to be.

I lifted up my shirt a little, so I can unzip my zipper on my pants. I pulled out my big dick and lifted up both her legs as if I were pushing her thighs to touch her chest. I slid my cock inside her waiting pussy. She let out a big gasp of air. I held her legs up and began to thrust into her pussy, leaving a big heaping, dripping mess. I fucked her slow, I fucked her quickly. I fucked her roughly, I fucked her passionately. I fucked her so hard she could do nothing but moan loudly. I covered her mouth with my hand. I thrusted and thrusted and thrusted some more. My stroke game was very strong. My dick game was so potent, so hard, I had sweat pouring down like it was game six, Michael Jordan. I came inside her pussy, my cum shots were so powerful. I untied her and told her to get on her knees. She knelt immediately.

"Finish me off. Suck and swallow every drop. Let's go." I said urgently, "I have more plans for us. Our day is not yet finished."

I booked an art museum for us. We arrived, and the place was packed like a damn zoo. My hand was on her ass the entire time we had some privacy. Sometimes when our backs were up against the wall, I would grab her pussy, and no one was the wiser. I took her hand and we went through this maze of art for a stroll. I found us a private place where no one was walking through. Not in, nor out. I lifted her up against the wall and put my dick inside her and began to fuck her once again and again and again. I whispered in her ear....

"I want to fuck you here, there, everywhere, so when you are ANYWHERE, all you will think about is me."

We finished, and we went back to the crowd of people to enjoy the rest of the museum. She was looking at a painting she was intrigued by. Standing in a crowded room, I came from behind her, and made my way to her. I pushed my erect, bulging chocolate cock from my pants against her ass. Just two fucking layers of fucking material was between us. That separated us, I leaned in from behind her, and went close to her earlobe. "Baby girl, tonight I am going to do some shit to you, a lot of shit to you. But first I will rip that thing off you, just to get to that addicting flesh of yours." She gasped in anticipation.

"Oooh, can we go now?" she asked.

I turn her around, and just gaze into her eyes, I do not make a sound, I do not even answer her question. I just look into her eyes. I know where we are, I really don't care. I corner her, so our eyes can relish in each other's. Her entire existence throbs for me. Her entire body begs for my prominent touch. She aches for only me.

I then pull here even closer just to feel her heart beat, to see the intensity in my gaze. To witness her sense of helplessness. The fear of being caught, called the cops on, or thrown out, ties our wrists like there was invisible rope. Even though I doubt that would occur, these boring vanilla (regular people) would probably be filming and enjoying. Bringing some intense and excitement to their boring lives. Don't worry, I was not going to give them a show. I wouldn't be putting my woman out there like this, we were not porn stars, no world, you do not get the pleasure of us, what have you deserved? What have you earned to do so? Therefore, we just gaze, we continue to use our eyes, and our eyes speak volumes. It talks to one another in secret code, eyes slowly undress and uncontrolled ravish. Eyes explore, and eyes explode. Eyes caress, eyes gently and slowly trace along all curves and edges. Our eyes get the pleasure to participate in the lust and desires that our bodies so eagerly crave. Yes, our eyes get to experience, and now we must leave, because at this point I cannot take it.

The exhibit was not through, but I told her it's time to fucking go, and we both got ourselves together and left. So calm and cool like two innocent little devils. We drove and drove until it was dark out. I stopped and parked the car in a dead-end street that I found. It was a hot and beautiful summer night. Beautiful stars shining bright.

"Get out." I said, as I got out as well. I met her on her side of the car.

"I love these stars." I said as I took her by the hand and helped her out of the car. I lifted her sundress. She had never had this much sex in one 'fucking' day. I loved watching her lick her lips at the sight of my big, rock hard, muscular, chocolate dick. Gasping for air from slamming into her round ass so hard. Smiling at me, knowing damn well I won't take no for an answer, when Daddy says he needs that pussy now! Fuck your 'shhhh, let's keep it down!!' This night is ours. Soon, the night was over, and we both had to get back to our vanilla jobs in the morning.

***

The next day, I sent her a text.

"Good morning Precious, how do you feel?" She replied,
"I'm sore. My entire body is sore." following a, "lol" with her text back to me. I get to the board room and I'm bored. All I could do was think about her. I text her.

"You have that toy I gave you?" She replied, "the vibrating ring thing?" I smirk, "Yes." She answers, "yes, I keep it in my purse, I don't leave home without it. I never know when you're going to tell me to take it out and put it on."

I laugh to myself before I reply back. "You read my mind, go fucking put it on." I commanded via text. She did exactly as I expected, because she was feeling the vibrations. She was twitching. Now I could control the vibrations with my phone when I was not near her and the vibrations were stronger when I had the remote close by. She felt the vibrations so strong.

"The vibrations are stronger than ever." She knew I was near. "Shit, are you here? Are you at my job? The nurses are here and so is everyone else! Please tell me you're not here!"

I smirk to myself and text back, "I am here!" I knocked on her door at her office. "I told the nurses not to tell you I was here." She responded back, "well I will be having a word with them." I then cut her off. "Do not be harsh with them, they were in a tough position. If I didn't get through they knew I was going to get them in big trouble, and they knew how you were going to discipline them as well perhaps. But they rather you get to them instead of me. After today you might forget to ever want to reprimand them."

I shut and locked the door and shut the blinds as well. "Take your panties off." I demanded. "Wait Daddy, I thought you said in your rules work and family are my only excuses, and they are off limits and you would never interfere with them!"

I smirk. "Yes, that's true but two things; one, I'm allowed to break my own rules a little, not you. And second, is this not MY pussy?" I then grasp that pussy of hers with my hand firmly while I say it. She answers, "Yes this is YOUR pussy and ONLY your pussy Sir." I smirk once again then stop and give her one of my darkest stares and with a menacing tone I tell her...

"Then do exactly as I say." She took them off and gives them to me. I lift her up but before that, I push aside whatever papers she had on top of her desk. I put her on top of the desk. "Fuck your office, now it's OURS. Now it's the place where I destroy your body." Now it's my mirror that I use to watch her eyes roll back while my cock massages her insides. Now it's MY playroom as she rolls her tongue around the tip of my big dick, and behaves like the perfect little slut for me. I take her clothes off; her breasts are out like a good whore. Fuck being quiet, naked in her damn office because of me. Now she's creaming all over my big dick, in OUR room. OUR office. OUR playground. Fuck the world, she's MINE. Fuck being quiet, she yells IF I tell her to. Sorry world, she is with me, she belongs to me. Okay, I lied. I'm not sorry. Fuck your public places, fuck your, 'they might see or hear us.' Fuck your 'shhh' world and people. You're in MY world, Discipline's world.

She came all on my dick and just kept cumin and cumin, nonstop. "Yes, just like that. Drip for me, let me feel all those juices. Am I sorry? No, not sorry. Anytime, Anywhere, you are mine. You belong to me." She was flushed, hair a mess.

"How am I going to function for the remainder of the day?" I gave her one of my sly smiles. "That's your fucking problem, not mine. Pull yourself together and get it done, like you always do." I got dressed, fixed myself up prior to leaving her office. I then left her with, "text me when you finish work and are heading home. We will speak later."

Chapter 5: Kiss You Like I Miss You, Fuck You Like I Hate You

After my book came out, 'The Seduction of Discipline' I was so successful and people from all over the world were intrigued. I had to go to Miami for a book fair and to promote the book. I was going to be gone several days and I wasn't going to see her. She knew to behave and to remain patient. I never needed to tell her that. Miami can be very tempting, but I was going strictly for business not pleasure. Laying in my hotel room before the book fair...

"Show me that pussy!" I demanded, while we were facetiming. She placed the phone downward and I gave her further instructions. "Rub that pussy for me, let me see how wet that shit gets for Daddy." She was so wet. That pussy misses her owner, you can tell. I was licking my damn lips. "Don't cum, don't cum or touch MY pussy until I get back. I want that shit so fucking wet and juicy that when I slide my dick in it, you cum instantly and often. I want to drive you insane."

She gasped loudly over the phone, "damn Daddy, that just made me wetter. The thought of you just handling me, taking what is yours makes my pussy so fucking happy she wants to explode already." I then cut her off. "I don't give a fuck how good it makes you feel. Do you understand my instructions?" She replied, "yes, Daddy. But I'll be a good girl and wait for you Daddy. I'll always wait for you my King, and I will wait for as long as you want me to."

That's my bitch, that's my good girl, that's my whore. Loyal to the damn core! She's fiending for when I finally arrived back to New York. No matter what, I always put her noisy mind and quivering body into a state of lechery and quiet solace. She has a high sex drive, a huge appetite for MY sex. I have a huge sex drive myself and when we're together, it's like an explosion. Like fireworks on the fourth of July, a volcanic eruption.

The book fair in Miami went very well and as soon as I arrived back to New York, I booked a hotel room. I told her I was home, but I wanted to do something entirely different. Not her house nor mine, and I gave her directions to the spot. I had arrived there before her and placed rose petals on the bed, a blindfold and some nice lingerie for her to change into.

"Precious, here are the directions to the hotel. I want you to get there before me and get ready." That was all I texted her. I left the extra key with the clerk at the front desk. I put the room under 'Mr. Discipline'. I warned him she would be arriving and instructed him to give her the key. She arrived and asked the clerk for the key. He handed it to her and she walked towards the room. She opened the door and entered. Deja vu, just like the first time we ever had sex. She steps further in and notices a note on the dresser.

'Take off your clothes and change into this. Put the blindfold on and then the handcuffs. I will be there shortly.' Meanwhile, I was there the entire time. Hiding in the closet. She did exactly how and what I instructed in the note I left. I watched her get undressed. She unbuttoned her blouse exposing her beautiful breasts. I saw everything, all of her but she could not see me though. I watched her every move with a passionate hunger deep in my eyes. I could smell her scent, feel her energy and soul. I could sense her anticipated vibrations for me as she continued to undress. My big chocolate cock was already hard knowing what I was going to do to her. All my muscles were tense, and I was ready to pounce like a Lion on a zebra...It's fucking dinner time! However, I did not move an inch. Instead, I devoured every move she made with my eyes. I was ravenous, and she was exactly what I wanted to consume.

I continued to watch as she took off the rest of her clothing and placed them politely on the sofa of the room.

Now she removed her nylon sheer lace panties and her dainty, very feminine, lace bra. Those juicy plump breasts popped out. She brushed her hair back with both hands. She then took off her heels, bending over as I watched, tantalized with the most delicious view of her pussy from the back. She walked over and placed her heels next to the sofa on the ground where all her other belongings where. She now walks over to the bed and I got another view of her juicy, delicious beautiful breasts. They were so firm, so sensitive. Her nipples were erect, and I bet it was from the sheer anticipation she felt. She was undeniably aroused. Her hands went to stroke her own breasts, but she faltered midair. Does she dare? No. She's good, she knows the rules. No touching without Daddy's permission. Plus, she wanted to follow my orders and instructions on the note to a "T". That's what I would assume.

She slipped into the attire I had picked out for her, lays on the bed and places the blindfold over her pretty eyes. She then puts on the handcuffs, locks and ensnared her wrists in. She now waits, patiently and quietly for me to arrive, not knowing I am already there. I come out from the closet area slowly and quietly. Not making a single sound. Last time I had her completely naked. This time I thought I'd switch things up and have something to get into for me.

I walked up to her and the first thing I touch is my pussy. She let out a big gasp of air and I whisper in her ear. "Daddy's home. Did you miss me?" She let out another big gasp prior to replying to my question. "Yes Daddy." I kissed her lips roughly, tugging on her bottom lip as if I needed it so much like I needed air to breathe. My big hands caressed her beautiful breast. Kissing her lips so passionately and aggressively, my tongue Dominating hers and exploring the depths of her pretty little mouth.

"Keep your hands above your fucking head and do not move them until I say." My lips moved from her lips down to her neck. From her neck down to her breasts. I sucked and tugged aggressively on her erect nipples. I lifted her whole breast into my waiting mouth, I was using my tongue in a circular motion around her nipples. Damn, that drove her nuts. Her back began to arch off the bed. She moaned so loudly for me.

"Daddy, that feels so good." She murmured. My tongue down her navel, then her inner thighs, I stopped at her clit. I placed my tongue on it and flicked it back and forth then in a circular motion. I sucked on it like it was a starburst candy or a skittle. I was tasting her rainbow. I then tongue fucked her pussy hole. I lifted her legs up and stuck my tongue in her asshole. I placed a finger in her pussy while I did that and as usual, she soaked it. I moved my finger to her mouth and she opened immediately to taste herself off of me. I spoke softly but forcefully.

"I kissed those lips because I missed them, now I plan to fuck that pussy hole like I hate you!" I took off my clothes and ripped the lingerie she had put on, quickly and aggressively. My erect big chocolate dick popped out of my pants ready to conquer, ready to Dominate, ready to take what is his. I shoved my big hard cock inside her drenched, begging pussy hole, sliding back and forth between her saturated pussy lips. Shining my dick, blessing me with her juices, creaming on my thickness. Every thrust she took a deep breath. Already begging me to allow her to cum and I've only been inside her for like ten seconds. "Please Daddy, may I please cum for you?" Of course, I'm going to say yes. She was a good girl while I was away, plus I wanted her saving herself for this very moment, right now. All these juices, all this cream, all this pleasure of hers, for me.

"Yes baby, give it to me." She came all over my cock, all over the sheets, gushing nonstop and squirting like a busted fire hydrant. "Daddy, I can't stop cuming, oh my,

I'm squirting so much for you." I yanked the blindfold off from over her eyes.

"Look at this mess baby, look at this dick going inside you." I grabbed her head pushing it towards me, just so she can watch all this dick going inside. Slamming into her soft yielding wetness and she loved it. Thrusting so hard into her, her breasts moved in rhythm to the way I took her over and over again. Imposing my will, my Dominance, my demands upon her. Complete surrender made her wetter.

"Who do you belong to Precious?"

"You Daddy."

"Whose pussy is this?"

"Yours Daddy."

"And when will I have MY pussy?"

"Whenever you want, wherever you want and however you want, Daddy."

She is so good, she's so wise, she's so obedient and she is so MINE. I was continuously driving my hard, thick, long, chocolate cock into her, taking her soul and Dominating her orgasms. I love her, but she loves me more. She said...

"if it turns you on to hurt me, then I want to give you all of my pain." Pussy was so tight, I had to slow it down, control my mind and then I continued to grind. She came like five times. I flipped her over, placed her on her knees. Face south, ass north. I put in work, I stare down just to watch her ass twerk. Slapping of flesh was like a standing ovation. Turned into background music as her moans took over. I pulled her head up. My hand slithers from her back. To her throat. Choking her throat from behind. My muscular fingers in her mouth. Then I push her face back down. With my massive chocolate man hands, I spread her ass cheeks, then penetrated deep with my beast. She had that Niagara Falls pussy. It just continued to rain all over me. She came a sixth time. I then was going onto my first. Prior to my explosion from my thick long chocolate monster, I growled loudly. I growled ferociously. And it made her even wetter. I busted more powerful than a .44 magnum or a desert eagle .50 AE pistol. I spoke nasty shit in her ear, while I worked her body to complete surrender. I told her...

"Do not ever beg for my attention, I will purposely not provide it. I'm not here to give you what you want, I am here to provide you with what you need; structure, stability, love, Dominance, Discipline, more love, orgasms, pain, guidance, strength, and handle you better than any vanilla(regular) man would ever dream of."

My appetite for her is insatiable. There are three things I will do to her pretty little face; whip it, slap it, and kiss it. With my thick, long muscular chocolate beast. With my massive muscular hand, and with my full lips. She may suck, but she would never bite the hand that feeds her. But I will suck on her titties, that pussy, those toes, that ass and leave hickies, excuse me, 'battle wounds,' on her thighs. The type of love that I provide is beyond physical. It is prestigious. She will never obtain a kind of love like mine from another, as long as she lives. I don't need to remind her, she knows where she belongs. And that was just round one.

Her lips wrapped around my girth snugly. It felt so good I almost came, so I had to slow down and control myself once again. Then I got back into a rhythm again. Fast, deep strokes, then slow half strokes. I took my cock out just to see how hard I had stretched her open. Then I placed it back in and her gaping pussy queefed.

"Yeah, talk to me baby, I love it when that pussy talks to me." The more I spoke to her, the more my big hands and strong fingers grasped her throat, squeezing the flesh around it, the wetter she became. The more her pussy spoke to me, the more accepting her body was for me. She could not stop cuming, and I allowed it. Every pleasure comes with the price and she deserved it. Yes, she fucking deserved it.

"I'm not going to hold this from you. I want you to keep cuming for me. Consider it your reward for today."

She was more than relieved. "Thank you daddy, thank you." Following a huge gush after another, she was on her fifth orgasm. Damn, she was soaking up the sheets. She had some control man. All those times when she held it for me and now, she's like a water fountain. She is a damn faucet dripping nonstop as I sink my fat, long dick into her aroused, slickened pussy. She loved it hard, she loved it rough. She loved it gentle and then she loved it so aggressively. She was panting heavy with excitement, with lust. Her pussy was throbbing and starving for Discipline.

"Keep your hands above your head." I ordered, as I grabbed her legs and placed them on my broad shoulders. Her thighs almost touching her chest. Then I began to hammer her. "Look me in my eyes when I fuck you. Look me in my eyes when I make you cum for me." She gazed into my eyes and didn't look away nor did she shut them.

Her pupils were dilating, and her mouth was open wide. The ferocity of my thrusts made her gush again instantly.

"Oh, thank you Daddy." she purred. She has never cum so much in her entire fucking life. I was a god to her, I was a King to her, I was a Master to her.

"No one will ever do your body like I do your body, for as long as you live." I said firmly, while staring straight into her. I pounded the fuck out of her. My big hand whipped across her face and slapped her cheeks. I slapped each side and that made her even wetter. I choked her so firmly, I had a stone grip on her throat, and that was it for her. Her walls were closing in around me and I was growing weak. I knew I had a few more pumps left, then I was done for. I pounded and pounded and pounded as hard and as fast as I could. She was reaching her seventh orgasm, and I was about to have my first. We both drowned in her pool of lust and desire. "Grrrr" I growled in her ear before I let out a huge nut inside her. "Ugh, ooooh, ahhhh," as she came for the seventh fucking time. She was a dripping mess. I ran the shower, so we can clean up. Damn, there's nothing like that 'I miss you, I hate you sex'!

Chapter 6: On Your Knees

We had just cleaned ourselves off. "Get on your knees." I demanded. I wanted her to always be on her knees. "This is how you will always be for me. No exceptions, ALWAYS. This is exactly how I will always want you. No exceptions, Always. This is how you will always greet me and accept me at all times. When we are in public it's different, but when we are in private, you will always be on your knees for me, your Dominant, your King, your Master, your Daddy. On your knees is the proper way to show me gratitude. To show me devotion, loyalty, appreciation and respect. It is not the only way, but it is the most nonverbal and subtle way. It is a powerful gesture and the most profound way to ever get my attention. Completely surrendering yourself to me and immersing in submission would not take away from the Alpha, independent woman you are, it would only make you stronger. Submission filled you with a peace and serenity you never felt before. The discontent of life melted away as you became fully mine."

I stood above her as she knelt before me and grabbed her chin with my thumb and index fingers and say to her, "look up at me. Look up at me into my eyes and say, 'I am your slut. I am your baby girl. I am your queen. I am your devoted bitch, no matter what.'" She did and repeated word for word what I ordered her to say.

  "I've said this once, baby girl, and I'll reiterate it again, once you've had a taste of a real Dominant, the rest of the world simply does not taste the same. Once you've had Discipline, the rest pale in comparison. To be frank, I am proud to own you. All of you. Always. I am pleased with you and all that you do for me. Our souls connect on a totally different level than any vanilla (ordinary) beings. Our connection is strong, and the power I have over you is something that will be hard to obtain with someone else because of who you are. The things that you do for me will become like second nature, if you're not doing them it will feel abnormal to you. It will feel like something is missing, and therefore will be this strange feeling of uncertainty and a feeling of loss within yourself. This becomes a need and a lifestyle for you. You will never lack, and without it you will feel incomplete. On Your Knees......"

Chapter 7: Crawl To Daddy Beautiful Girl

"That's it, kneel and crawl to me baby. Crawl to your King and show me what I deserve. Show me what belongs to me. Show me your passion, your dedication and hard work. Show me your willingness, determination and drive. Show me, show me like you have never shown me prior."

She crawled to me slowly, erotically. "That's it, look up at me. Don't worry about your step, look me in my eyes. I'll watch your steps, trust Daddy to guide you to where you need to be. Come to me, I will take your hand and go into the fire and we will come out unharmed, unphased and prevail. Come right into the darkness and I will lead you out into the light. Crawl to Daddy and I will fulfill all your deepest and darkest desires, my beautiful diamond."

She was waiting on all fours for my next command, as I was gazing into her begging, 'fuck me' eyes. Watching her completely submit, surrender, waiting for me to give her exactly what she needs. Exactly what she deserves. I lean over, my hand slithers behind her just to whip my big hand on that soft round ass of hers. Slapping each cheek hard. The impact my hand creates as it kisses her flesh firmly. A loud gasp escapes her soul. Her journey is here.

Patience is not about how long one can actually wait, it's about how well one behaves while waiting. I asked her...

"What are you willing to provide, so you may receive? Is it good thick, muscular, long, chocolate dick you want? Is it Domination? Just pleasure or pain? To be owned by a powerful man? Never fall in love with the shit I provide to you. If you came here to only fuck, I will fuck your whole life up and have you falling in love. If you came here to just give, I will have you giving everything. If you came here to just be, I will have you willing to be anything. If you came here for slight Domination, I will fucking destroy you. Gradually dismantle you piece by piece. If you came here for pleasure, I will give you pain and you will learn to appreciate both. I will be honest with you. One hundred percent, I... want... to... control... you. In every way, in every form. No exceptions. ALWAYS. I want you constantly helpless. I want you vulnerable. I want to overwhelm you, overwhelm your senses, and if you are unwilling to give all, which consists of your mind, body and soul, I will gladly take nothing and gladly give nothing as well. However, you being here, in this moment, like this, on your knees, says a lot to me. I will devour, conquer, destroy, man handle and Dominate. I will never provide you with what you want only what you need and what you earn. You need this, you need structure, Discipline, stability, accountability. You crave this. Train your mind, body and soul to embrace this.

Now open your mouth, Daddy is going to show you exactly how he likes it. Be grateful, be appreciative of the sounds, the feelings, the extremes, the depravity. Do you know how many women are deprived of these types of pleasures because their men are inadequate, therefore, these women suffer mundane lives. They are single and have to pleasure themselves. Be thankful, be humble, feel lucky and feel blessed. Embrace your desires and your fantasies, those strong urges that constantly come back. If it pleases me to have you on your knees, YOU WILL KNEEL reverently. If it pleases me to have you crawl, YOU WILL CRAWL to me. If it pleases me to have you feed me in public, you will do so. If it pleases me for you to be good, you will be just that. If it pleases me to choose your hair styles, hair color, nail color and nail styles then I will, and you will do as I instruct. If it pleases me to bind you, then you will offer your arms, hands, wrists, legs, ankles, waist. If it pleases me to Discipline and teach you, then you will learn, follow and you will grow. If it does not please me to punish you (because it does not) you will never piss me the fuck off, nor get in trouble or make a mistake...ever again. However, if it pleases me to whip you, you will not make a single sound. If it pleases me to touch you, I will touch you everywhere. If it pleases me to have you serve, cater, worship me, then you will do so with loyalty and grand devotion. Chain of command is I say it, YOU do it. End of chain. A man that is a woman's escape will always have her running back to him. A woman that touches a man's soul and is his peace, will always be the one he turns to. A pet that has no leash will try to roam the streets and rub on and attempt to get the attention of everything in sight. But a trained pet, you can always allow it to roam, and it will always come home. Why? Because it knows no other familiar bone. It knows where it's heart and soul lie, and the flesh follows the soul. How loyal is a hungry pet? Does it attempt to bite the hand that fed it in the past? Because it's not fed in the present? Does the pet bark back because it's not fed when it wants to be fed? How loyal is it? How loyal is it when it's hungry?"

She could not answer the question. She had no answer. She didn't want to say the wrong thing, so she remained quiet.

"I'll tell you. A loyal pet always waits for its Master to feed it, no matter what." I spoke to her forcefully but softly. "You are not in control here. You are not here to ask for things. You are not here to be fancy, and I don't give a fuck who or what was before me. That was, or they are, irrelevant. After me, there will be none. Before me, you were incomplete. I am the Alpha and the Omega, your first and damn sure your last. You're here, once again, to be blessed. Show me your soul and the magnitude of your worship. You will be better for me, better than you ever were for anyone. All the distractions, talks, looks, uncertainty, the foolery, the gossip in the world, you will not partake in. Focus on one goal and one goal only. Pleasing me. My job will be to make sure you focus on nothing but that. You require my strength, my powerful hand, my Dominance, my Power, my body, my mind, my control, my spirit and my great vibes. Now, show me how bad you need to be away from this world and I will grant you what you deserve. You are mine. That means all your uncertainties, your fears, your doubts, and insecurities vanish when you're with me. I will show you the strength you always had."

I loved the way her breathing altered as I placed my hand on her flesh.

"You're nothing, worthless until I make you priceless. Don't ever forget that. I know you are ready for evolution. You are ready for immortality. You are completely ready to leave this world, this vanilla world, behind and step into Discipline's world. A world full of endless possibilities. You are ready to step into phenomenal. Are you ready to be a Goddess, or would you rather remain a mortal? Out of all the chains you are bound to, the strongest one is wrapped around your soul."

She was not a submissive when we met, now she's a submissive for me. Never shy to speak her mind but is quiet as a mouse, and only speaks when spoken to in MY presence. She's an aggressive woman, a shark in her life and daily duties. However, she is meek as a kitten with me and to my face. Too much for a regular man to handle, just right for me. My invisible collar and leash reach so far. She wants no limits, no safe words. The tighter my grip the more she lets go. Her surrender is her greatest power, my control is her release. So, once again I say to her, "open your mouth. WIDER!!"

Chapter 8: I Want It Nasty and Sloppy

On her knees, mouth opened wide. "Stick your tongue out and leave it just like that." I pull out my already firm, burly, long, chocolate dick. I tap the big tip of it on her tongue. Then I whip it on her face. Left cheek, then the right cheek. I finally place it in her mouth. "Spit on it." She does, like a good girl, and I put it back in her waiting mouth. Her hands remained behind her back.

"Lick, suck, deep throat it." She coughed. I shoved my fat cock in her mouth once again. I placed my thumbs on the back of her neck and my four fingers across her throat. I kept pushing my cock in her mouth as I pressed downward with my thumbs at the same time. I was going to fuck her face to a whole other dimension. I could feel her throat expanding in my hands. Tears and mascara running down her cheeks. Shortness of breath, her begging pussy vibrating and her clit throbbing. I am her first of everything. I kept moving my cock in and out of her pooling mouth, and when I looked down I could see her anxious pussy dripping. Her throat suffering but desiring for more pain, begging for more of this huge, monstrous, chocolate dessert, to Dominate her mouth.

I know when she's mine, I can see when she's been a victim of the world for too long. When she's tired of the norm. When she's tired of pretending, life can't be what she knows now. It can't be clean and proper all the fucking time. She needs filthy and slutty. Dangerous and intrinsic. She needs 'out of control'. She needs spit coming from her lips down her chin, onto her breasts. She needs her throat spasming from being face fucked. She needs her face red from being slapped from dick and hand. She needs her ass punished. She needs to walk with a limp for a few hours because I was pounding her pussy out and her legs pinned back. She needs the memory of me dancing in her fucking head all day long, the following day while she's bored at work, back to her vanilla (ordinary) world. They can have her temporarily, but I demand her back, so I can do it all over again. She needs to experience my insanity to keep her own sanity. I knew she was mine before she did.

The first time we "met", her face in her fucking book. Her proud, snotty attitude...

"Hello there Miss. What's that mind like?" The look in her eyes when she finally looked up at me with her, 'I haven't been fucked right and handled properly in a long time' eyes. Like I said, I knew she was mine before she did. I could hear her cry before she made a damn sound.

She begged me without saying a word. Now she begs for me behind closed doors. She is mine, and the world can have her for a moment when I'm fucking done. How do you think she feels? Used? Slutted? filthy? loved? taken? appreciative? Thankful and fucking free?

"Get onto the bed," I said sharply. I reached in my drawer and came out with some toys, restraints, handcuffs, rope, vibrating wand, and I begin to tie her up. I start with her wrists and ankles. I reach for the flogger and proceed to slap her clit two times with it, very intensely. I slap and whip her breasts with it as well, roughly and she took it reverently. I took the vibrating wand, set it to the highest setting possible, and place it on her clit.

"Don't cum yet." I ordered. I knew she was going to cum right away, I could imagine how that shit feels. I covered her sweet tiny mouth with my massive hand. She was humming loudly as the vibrations were coming off my palm. She wanted to cum so bad. She was squirming all around. However, she did not. She's so good. She definitely deserved this big chocolate cock, she deserves to cum. I let her.

"Okay, you may release." I said. She was gushing so much. What a pretty sight, like a damn geyser. She was drenched like Niagara Falls. I removed my hand from her mouth. I slowly shoved my heavy cock between her yielding, begging lips and into her saturated hole. Thrusting back and forth inside her, stretching her walls further and opening her up to a whole new world. She's addicted to me and can't keep her kitty off me. Now I'm going to kill that pussy softly. I slapped her face, "look me in my eyes when I'm fucking you." I growled at her. I grabbed her breasts as my thrusts became more powerful. Her lips parted, and her mouth opened wide. I grabbed her throat with my big hand. My strong fingers stone gripping and squeezing the flesh around her neck. She became wetter, I could literally feel it. As I grip tighter, she lets go more and more and her pussy opens further.

I turn her around. I don't ask, I just flip her whole body over. Her hands and wrists still bound to her ankles. Now she's in doggy position, face down and ass up. I grab the flogger but before I use it on her, I drive my stiff, long, fat chocolate tool in her pussy again. I thrusted, then I lashed her with the flogger. Every time I thrust, I lashed her. Her ass was bright red, punished, and her pussy was pounded. She was pleading...

"Daddy please...may I cum?"

"Let me see if you can take some more lashes before you cum."

I thrusted and thrusted then gave her another lashing. I throttled and stroked some more then gave her yet another lashing. She was pleading.

"You can't take it huh? If you cum without permission right now, you know what will happen. Take that shit, show me what you got."

I lashed her again for the third time and I drilled into her some more. A fourth time, as I rode her rougher and rougher. Then I lashed her for the fifth and final time giving her the, "okay, go ahead and cum all over me." She could not stop or control how much she was cuming. I swear this woman was fucking spoiled.

"I'm going to fuck you how I want, as deep as I want, in whatever position I want. Front, back, upside down. Tied up. Blindfolded. Roughly, softly, brutally, ferociously. Until your pussy is sore, until your legs are useless, until you forget where you are. Until you leave your body, until you are out of breath, until you can't even speak. Until you aren't sure if you even exist."

Her mind, body and soul were not made for just sex or play. It wasn't made for fumbling hands and sloppy hurried insertion. Some may have seen her shape and didn't see its purpose. They saw themselves in her body and this is the difference with me. I saw art, I SEE art. The purpose of her curves were for passionate words. The silk texture of her skin was for inspiration in all its glory. Not a thing to be pawed at, not for amateur hands or part time worshippers. She was made to be touched in meaningful ways. To change the artist while being changed by the art. To be molded from clay by the skilled hands of a sculptor. To be sketched properly and expertly on a canvas by the hands of a painter. To be written on a scroll by the hands of a poet. She was made for more. Many couldn't see this. She was made for art. I squeezed her ass cheeks then flipped her over onto her back. She gasped, then licked her lips as she let out a satisfied moan.

"Look at me bitch," I growled, "I want to see the exact rotation around your clit that makes your fucking eyes roll back in your fucking head. You look high as hell. Eyes drooping, head bobbing, body convulsing. If you weren't yelling and screaming, I'd swear you were on some type of drugs. What, is my dick like heroin? Cocaine, morphine? Shit, it must be. You're addicted and go crazy for it and when you don't have it, you go through withdrawals."

I could feel her thighs shaking and her toes curl. I'm thinking, 'here we go again, she can't stop.' I command her to orgasm.

"Cum for me baby, I know you want to. Cum for me now!" Here it comes, her walls close in on me tight. Her grunts and moans turn into whimpers of bliss and screams of explosive release. She's crying as that orgasm rips through her entire body. Wetness all over the fucking sheets as she's trying to catch her breath.

"Look at Daddy with those drugged up eyes." I say with a smirk. "What do you say?" She catches her breath and says, "Thank you Daddy." I reached now for my butt plugs. I grabbed a special one and showed it to her right before saying...

"Turn around. Face down and ass up." She did as I ordered her to do. I then slowly slid the plug inside her but not before I lubed it up. Butt plug in, I then reach back for the vibrating wand. Double the sensation drove her insane. Her pussy would not stop dripping. I took the butt plug out, she was gaping then I shoved it back in. I removed the wand that was vibrating on her clit and shoved my thick cock in her pussy. Now she has double penetration. She feels as if she is now being taken by multiple lovers. I'm driving her completely insane with all these fickle emotions.

Chapter 9: Bend Over Now

The first lick was the fucking beginning. It sent shivers up her spine, brought out her veins, proceeding down back to her stomach, to the nucleus of her pussy. I could feel it. it had been a long time since a man that had strong dominant hands and character, laid a tender touch upon her flesh. I didn't just know that because, she told me. I knew that because her body spoke to me, more than her words. Slight pleasuring for self via masturbation was not enough. Come on, I knew it was not enough. Nothing can compare to the touch, I mean a real touch, of another.

She didn't care if I had others, just as long as she was one. All she cared about was this moment, our moments, in itself. To her, I was her only, and she was accurate. I was her one and only, no one else's. People she was not with and no one else's. She's not dealing with or was speaking with any other people. So, I guess I was her one and only. But frankly, her number one job is to please me and that's it, my job is to make sure she focuses on nothing but. Everything else was irrelevant to her.

I placed kisses up and down her bareback, and then her front. I suck that pussy like it was my last Capri Sun drink. I eat that pussy like it was my last real meal. I sucked on her clit like it was a Starburst candy. I stuck my finger in her pussy as if her pussy needed filling, that it needed proper filling from its master. She then begged me...

"King, may I please you?"

I allowed it. "Yes, you may." She then continued.

"But can I do it myself, pretty please?"

I see she wanted to suck my big chocolate cock, but she wanted to control how she sucked me. It was a while, since I allowed her to do that. I then said...

"Yes, I'll allow it."

I wanted to see what she had, I wanted to see what she got.

"I didn't stutter, suck that big dick, let me see the beast that I have created in yourself."

She got off of the bed, and then she dropped to her knees, she spit and then she swallowed my dick whole. Well, I was exaggerating, she at least tried to suck me whole. She could never deep throat me before. She ended up choking every single time. She practically inhaled her throat with my big dick. She tried to inhale me so deep that if my Organ had a bullet in it, it would have passed clean through her skull into the wall behind her.

She gazed up into my beautiful brown eyes, with an expression of immense pleasure in her own eyes. I cannot control how wet her pussy then became. She cannot control how wet her pussy became. I reach from behind her, and I slap that ass. Then I stuck my finger in there, then placed it on her clit. Damn, she was more soaked from giving me pleasure, than when I give pleasure, and she loves when I pleasure her.

"Get on the bed." I commanded. "Let's get this big chocolate cock inside of you."

She didn't want to stop sucking, I could see it in her eyes. Her eyes were begging. But she would never argue with me. She would never object to me. She would never have rejected me.

"Yes daddy, how do you want me?

She was already positioned in the doggy style. That must have been her favorite position, but her favorite position was going to be whatever fucking position I wanted her in. Missionary, I was going to make her love missionary.

"Get on your back." I ordered. She sat on her ass cheeks, then, she laid backwards. She spread her legs waiting for me to bless it. I took my big cock and I teased her, slapping it repeatedly on the clitt, then slowly sliding inside her then taking it right out. And then doing it over and over again. I did it over until I finally just remained inside, inside her begging pussy. I was sliding inside and outside of it slowly. I wanted her to feel every fucking single inch of me.

I went in so deep, and just stayed there. Her mouth wide open as her lips on her face parted, even as her pussy lips parted as well. I could see it in her eyes, that oxytocin and serotonin. I could see the endorphins kicking in and all of these chemicals, they were dripping from her brain. I then begin to stroke, my slow strokes became medium speed full thrusts. Then they were a little faster. I could hear how wet she was becoming,

"You hear that Precious?"   I asked her. She was out of breath, and breathing heavy, Moaning and groaning.

"Ugh, Ugh, yea…ye…… yes daddy."

I then started riding and driving her, faster and faster. Transforming her pussy into an inferno hotter than hell, because at this moment, not even the devil was fucking with me. I place my massive chocolate man hands on her throat, and squeeze the flesh around it. Her little hand grasped my wrist, and pressed my fingers harder against her throat. She became wetter then a water fountain.

"Don't grab my wrist again!" I said to her. And I pushed her hand away, I slapped her on her cheek on her face, and she smiled at me. The sadist in me, feeds the little masochist she has in her self. But, I wanted her to know I was serious.

"Don't get comfortable, just because you get some type of physical freedom from me lately." And she replied...

"No, my king, I will not."

I tied both her hands above her head with both my massive hands. Grasping her with it.

"Now cum, cum for my big black cock. Come for my dominance, come for my commands, come for me."

She shut her eyes, then began to scream and cry, and her pussy closed in so tight around me. Therefore, cuming all over my big chocolate dick. She kept cuming and I kept thrusting, I didn't stop. I thrusted until she came like seven different times. I was heading towards my first ending the torture, as I thrusted harder into her and exploded. I then came inside her more powerful than a loaded desert eagle .50 AE pistol. I growled in her ear, "grrrr," and I stayed there for a good 10 to 15 seconds. Allowing my big cock to throb inside of her. She was laying limp on my waist, and eventually I pulled off away.

She protested immediately. "Nooooo!" She yelled and I looked at her, she looked back at me, then she let me go. She did not want me leaving from inside her at all, not one bit, not one inch.

"Let's get cleaned up, I have a meeting early in the morning tomorrow." We then cleaned ourselves off. I went to my place, she went to hers. I have to be up at the meeting around 8 AM. 5 AM hits and she was texting and calling me nonstop. I picked up my phone after the third ring.

"Hello?" My voice was deeper and groggy. She replied, "Oh Daddy you sound so sexy right now." I said, "so you called me at 5 AM to tell me my voice sounds sexy?" She replied, "well your voice is sexy all the time but that's not why I called you. I called you because your pussy is soaking wet and I can't control it. I'm horny." I didn't reply at first, then I said...

"Precious, it is 5 AM, I must be up in a couple of hours and you are calling me because you're horny?"

She then said, "well I'm not calling for you to come and give it to me right now. I'm calling to know if it is okay if you have Precious touch what is yours?" I then replied, "so you pleasuring yourself is more important than my sleep?" She responded, I waited patiently for an answer from her. "No, but your rules, at least one of them is, 'ask permission before you touch what is mine.' Those are your rules."
I then said to her, "you are absolutely correct. So the answer to your question, can you touch what is mine now?" I paused and she inquired again...

"Yes sir, what is your answer daddy?" I then said to her forcefully...

"The answer is no." And then I hung up on her. At that moment, she was not about to call me back. She knew she was probably in some type of trouble with me, and she was damn right if she was thinking this.

After my meeting, I texted her, 'come over now!' She replied right away. She always replied to Daddy no matter what she was doing. I mean, I gave exceptions like work and family, but other than that, she was as fast as lightning when it came to texting me back.

She came over, I greeted her at the door. Then she knelt before me immediately. I said, "no, get up. Earlier this morning you had a question for me, but I'm sure you knew after I hung up on you, you were going to be punished, correct?" She nodded her head. "Well go over to the bedroom."

She walked to the bedroom. "Go to the bed." I said. "Place your palms on the mattress. Don't fucking move." I walked out the room. I came back seconds later with a belt, the flogger, a whip, paddle, butt plugs, a wand and clamps, and the ball gag. "I'll be right back." I told her.

I didn't give a specific time or date when I would be back. I went shopping, I went to grab something to eat. More than 30 minutes had gone by. She knew she was going to get punished, just not to the extent of the punishment. I was headed on my way back. Now punishment begins. I walked back into the bedroom, she was in the same position as I left her.

"We shall now begin." I said forcefully. I walked towards her and I started with the butt plug. I slid the plug in her asshole.

"Don't move this, make sure this remains inside that asshole until further instructions by yours truly, me!" She then replied...

"Yes Daddy."

I then reached for the purple wand. This wand had about 20 speed in about 15 different vibrations. I used it as I placed it on her clit. I tied rope utilizing it to bind her wrists to her ankles. "Place your knees on the bed, kneel in the doggy position, ass facing me, face down now!" She did as I instructed her to. I tied her up, she could not move. Her pussy was pulsating and her clit was throbbing from the vibrations of the wand. Butt plug was still inside her asshole. I reached for my flogger. I was being thorough, and lashed her over and over again. She had lashes coming at her ass cheeks, her back and her legs. She had a butt plug in her asshole, and a vibrating wand that was on high on her clit, and I then   lashed her over and over again. She was screaming.

"Please, Daddy, can I cum? Pretty please? Please, please!?" The thing was, that's what she was asking for all morning.

"See Precious, you were asking for that all morning so no you may not." I love to watch her suffer, but this was not a time for fun. She needed to learn, she will not cum because she's horny. She will not cum because she needs to fucking release. She will cum when I say she may. Her body was shaking and she was crying. She was screaming, but she did as I commanded her. She did as I demanded. She did not cum. She held whatever outburst she had to herself. Yes, she held it in. Why? She knew if she did not she would suffer severely. This went on for at least fifteen minutes. And then I said...

"Now you may cum." She released a stream of cum all the way down from her pussy to her thighs. She soaked the damn sheets, that was beneath her. She gasped for air louder than she ever did before. I then untied her wrists from her ankles. She did not move until I told her she was able to move. She was a very good submissive. Fuck that, that was an understatement. She was better than good. She was a great submissive for me. It's just that this very morning she was very bad for me, and that cannot just be. That cannot constantly occur. Therefore, I must teach her a lesson and Discipline her when she is bad and she must know, she will get punishment.

"Now, you may lay down."

She quickly dropped onto her stomach on the mattress. Her ass cheeks were in my sights, and they were bright as red, and she had welts as well. Her pussy was so sore. Her ears were ringing. I could tell. She was in another world. Discipline's world. She could not move. She was fucking motionless and completely out of breath.

"Yes, I allowed you to cum, but for the remainder of the week, you are not allowed to cum. Don't even fucking text me or call me to ask me to overturn my decision, nor to ask me if you may. And, you are not getting dick tonight either. So, when you're ready and can feel your legs and pussy again, and you can walk to the restroom, get yourself cleaned up, put on your clothes and walk out of my place. We will speak tomorrow. Have a safe ride home and text and call me when you arrive safely. So I know you made it home safe."

I then walked out of the room. I went to go watch my sports and read a book. She took a shower, and she got dressed. She came into the room, I was in, and said...

"Good night Daddy."
I then snapped my fingers at her. "Hold on, where do you think you are going just like that? Come over here!"

She walked towards me, then I said to her, ordering her, "fix your face, this instant. And never leave without giving me a kiss good night, I don't care how upset you are." She did as I said, she kissed and hugged me good night.

"Good night Daddy!"

I didn't say a word, just looked over at the television and continued to watch my sports.

"Don't forget to text me when you arrive home safe. I love you!" I said to her, as she was walking away from me. She looked back at me, and my eyes didn't leave my book.

"I will Daddy, and I love you too my King."

The next few days Precious and I spoke via phone, via text, however, we did not see each other. Strictly my decision. We FaceTime , but we were not in each other's physical presence. Which was part of her punishment, having or better yet not having physical access to me until I said otherwise. So a week went by and I ordered her to come see me. It was like Precious and I had magnets in between us. Every time we were together, we could not help it, we fucked, we made love, we had sex. But, I could not keep myself from her any longer. I have to admit, yes I must admit I was an addict for her screams. And I love to see her drip with desire even more.   We fucked when she came over. There's nothing like, forgiveness sex. Nothing like being pleasured from someone sorry. Nothing like that, 'I miss you sex.' After we had great sex as we always do, she slept over. I then reached over and she was nowhere to be found. I called out for her as she was already making her way back to me. She had a tray full of goodies. She had scrambled eggs made, a loaf of bread, some bacon, orange juice and some fresh fruit. Just like I like it. Now, I'm very self-sufficient and I take pride in being so, however, I would never turn down being spoiled this way. I wanted to fuck with her head.

"Who the fuck told you to make me breakfast? I called for you this morning and you were nowhere to be found." She was frantic, "I'm sorry Daddy, I... I..." I cut her off. "I'm fucking with you, you're not in trouble." I love watching the look on her face and the worry in her eyes. Yeah, I know I can be an asshole but, she loves me.

I ate the breakfast she made for me. The lovely breakfast. "Can I suck your dick while you eat Daddy?" I smirked after I took a sip of some orange juice and nodded my head, my mouth was full. In this moment I gave her some control, to suck me, however, she knew just how I loved it. She began with the tip, playing with it and moving it in a circular motion, clockwise on her lips.

Then she used her tongue to lick along the shaft and counterclockwise on the tip. She carefully placed my big cock head into her salivating mouth. She opened her mouth wider to take and accept all of my manhood, every inch. She shoved it down her throat, well as far as she could possibly go, which was not that far. She paused to catch her breath.

I laughed, "Now, you know better than that, you can hardly deep throat Daddy."

She knew she couldn't handle all of this glorious meat in her throat, but she was so stubborn. I took my pistol out of the drawer, a Smith and Wesson .45, and told her she would be sucking on this for practice.

"So, let's see you deep throat this babygirl. Let's see how far you go then we'll see how far you go on my big cock."

She sucked my gun so passionately and with such enthusiasm. I gazed into her eyes a little jealous.

"Oh, so my pistol gets better treatment than I do huh? You love sucking that pistol more than MY pistol?" I said as I pointed to my dick. It was at this instant I saw how much she loved guns. I took it away, placing it back in the

drawer. "Suck my dick just like you sucked that piece."
She did just that, just as I instructed. She loved that cock,
my cock. She stroked that cock. She kissed that massive
cock. She made love to that big cock. She licked it and
gagged, happily, on that big cock. "Stroke the tip. Hold
the shaft with your other hand while you suck on me, all
at the same time." She was working for that nut. "Work
for it baby, get that cum right out of that beast. Suck
Daddy's big dick." I could feel it. The sensation was so
strong. "Keep stroking, keep sucking." I growled. "Here it
comes baby, open that pretty mouth of yours...grrrr!"
She swallowed every drop of my vanilla cream. Her
favorite. She loved how I taste, she savored it. She is
always ready to taste and take all of my amazing
greatness. She sucked me dry and she sucked me clean.
"Okay, good girl. Now let's get cleaned up and dressed.
We are going out today."

I had some afternoon reservations for us. We got into
my car and I put on some old school hip hop for the ride.
Some, Rakim, KRS-1, LL cool J, Biggie and Tupac. She's
over here singing the lyrics to some of these songs and I
was like, "Wait a minute, hold on. You know this shit?
Damn, there are some things I still don't know about you,
huh?" She giggled and gave me a proud little smile. I
intend to know all there is to know about her. I spoke to
the GPS, "Directions to Cafe......,"

"Sorry, I did not get that." It said. This bitch is worse than Siri on the iPhone.

"I said, the cafe BITCH!!!" This time I was a little more forceful. "Directions to the cafe. Here you are." Precious started laughing, and I followed laughing right after. "I guess she likes it a little aggressive as well, huh, Precious?" She smiled and shrugged her shoulders.

We arrived at the cafe. It was the first place where we actually had brunch. We were sitting at our table waiting for our meals. I whispered in her ear, "Let's go to the bathroom, you first. Get in there and text me. Make sure no one is in there." She got up quickly to do as I requested, and before she left I said, "I'll be there shortly."

She texted me when the coast was clear, and I replied, "I'll be right in." I snuck in swiftly and quietly. I opened the first stall door but she wasn't in there. I went to the second one and nothing. I moved to the next one but that one was empty as well. She was in the fourth stall, the furthest from the door...perfect. I opened it and there she was.

"The fuck you doing hiding from me? You could never hide from me. I'll always find you." She giggled. "Take those panties off and BEND OVER NOW!!!" We got in a good quickie and returned to our seats. A couple of minutes later our meals were brought out to us. I whispered to her, "the food took that long? They must have known we were taking care of some business and decided to have our shit ready when we came back." She snickered like a little girl. When the waiter left I said, "so, I need to know a lot more about you. You love so many genres of music I see." She replied, "well you did see me at a club the second time we met." "Yes, that's correct, but that doesn't matter. People go to the clubs all the time. From young to older individuals." I said. "Yes but, myself, I love music and I love to dance. Music speaks to me as it does with you. You and I have that in common." I smirked. "Indeed, we do, indeed we do."

Chapter 10: Face Down, Ass Up and Shut The Fuck Up

We took a trip to the library, the one we first met at, after eating. "I'm here because I am looking for a particular book." She was intrigued. "Well Daddy, perhaps I can help. What type of book and what is the name of this book?" I grabbed her by the hand, "It's usually back here." We walk all the way towards the back, where the last row of book shelves were. I said, "Oh, here it is." I pull her close to me and passionately kiss her lips. I tug on the bottom lip and play with her tongue. I begin to remove her panties and she stops me halfway. "Wait, can we just not do it here? There's so many people in here and I don't know if I can remain quiet in a place where WE ARE TO REMAIN QUIET." I push her hand back.

"I don't give a fuck where you are comfortable and if I want you to remain quiet, you will do just that. Understood? Now, face down, ass up and shut the fuck up."

She slid her panties off and handed them to me. She bent over, face down, and spread her legs wide. "Spread those cheeks for me, now." I commanded sharply. I stuffed my massive cock in that tight little pussy once again for today. "I didn't get to enjoy you back at the cafe. We had to have a quickie, but here? I'll not be interrupted at all, by any means or by anyone."

I fucked her harder than I normally fuck her. I placed my big hand over her mouth. She was to remain quiet. I didn't even want to hear a soft muffled moan.

"I will take that pussy of mine wherever I want. I will take that pussy of mine however I want. I will take that pussy of mine whenever I want, and you will do two things about it, nothing and like it. Your body is no longer your own. Your movements are no longer your own. They are mine, they belong to me and you already know, when I take, I take completely."

I made a perfectly good blockage corner for us so we wouldn't get caught. It was so good, and I know she enjoyed it as well, if not, I really didn't care.

As we left the library and got in the car, I said to her, "I'm dropping you off but before I do, understand something and understand it very well. I will never put you in a position where you might get caught or face anything detrimental to your mind, body or soul. I will always protect you, at all times no matter what. You're either going to trust me or you are not. So you understand?" She nodded and answered, "Yes Daddy, I understand."

"If there is no trust, we have no relationship. Our bond is strong because of it. I want you to know and learn everything I know and learn. I want you to follow without question just like you do now, but I want it to always remain consistent." She nodded once again and answered, "Yes Daddy." My index finger and thumb grab her chin and I stare squarely at her and say....

"Good girl."

I was consuming her, taking her over. She can feel me in her, on her, around her. I am as powerful as can be. I was a dominating figure, a dark shadow taking control of her senses. She is drowning in my overwhelming desire for her. My desire for her is frightening, but She wants it, she needs it, and can't live without it. Her body craves my expert touch, healing her shattered soul with every stroke. The world around us is black. There is only us and the passion that burns. I spoke to her softly...

"You love it when I abuse you. You love it when I use you. You find yourself lost in my insanity. However, you find peace in my chaos. I am your escape, the only thing that make sense. More than breathing, I am intoxicating. Your guilty pleasure, favorite sin. That even if you were to walk away, the urge would constantly come back. When I feel your leg begin to shake, your moans become louder, my strong muscular finger grip tighter, I thrust faster. I stroke harder. I push your body to its limits. I growl in your ear. You give me all your pain, and that's my pleasure. My pleasure becomes your pleasure, and now ultimately the pain becomes your pleasure."

No disrespect, and with all due respect, but I have no respect. Not even money can make someone a better lover. Real love doesn't cost a thing. Allow me to remind y'all. Once you've adapted to darkness, light feels mundane. Once you've experienced sadistic, nice is nauseating. I will show you real power, and program something in you, that makes you crave one thing. One way and only one way. And anything less will bore you. I am her perfect medicine. Cure for all her major symptoms of illness. However, I can hurt her in many different ways; my thick chocolate MUSCULAR DICK, my whip, or my powerful hand. Psychologically, or emotionally.

Have you ever made a woman a freak or a nympho? Prior to you, she was comfortable not being sexually active. A year, two years, three. Then you give her a taste, and now she wants it all the time. When sex is so bad for women, they give up on it. You can't trigger her erogenous zones. Increase her libido, of course she will feel this way. Let's say Lions copulate about forty times a day. But, we know it's not for a long time. It's usually one position and perhaps one to two minutes. Let's say, you and her go for four rounds, and it's about 10-20 minutes each. That's about 40-80 minutes. That's about as equivalent to the Lions. You're considered a beast. Now, if Lions copulate seven days a week, disregard that shit. Because then that's about, 280-560 times a week. No human fucks that many times, I don't care how high your level of testosterone is. It's not humanly possible. Even if they live together, they are not that sexually active for seven days a week, for that duration period. At some point, it may feel as if you both are living as roommates. Because, there's just no intimacy. The fire is diminishing. Lions do not work. What else are they doing besides, fucking, hunting, protecting their pride? They copulate, then they get hungry and then they hunt. They need to mate, and bare cubs, to carry on the legacy.

"Tonight baby, no love making. Simply back breaking. Not a soft kiss, but straight domination of those nice full soft lips. I will utilize my massive cock as a weapon to destroy you. Deeper and deeper, triggering all these fickle emotions you have for me. Savage of dick, which is inhuman, brutal, aggressive. Making your period come down early. Fucking with your monthly clock. Your body convulsing. Walking funny. Legs so numb. Reaching places inside you, your last never could reach. Touching the depths of your mind and soul no man wants to touch. I will fuck you so deep, you see me in your sleep. No question marks, I am here to take what is rightfully mine. Conquer and devour you whole. I own your soul."

Big, chocolate man hands wrapped around her neck, squeezing the flesh around her throat. Suppressing the blood to her brain. Endorphins kick in. Oxytocin dripping from her pituitary gland. Dopamine engaged. Blood rushing downward. Head swell with power, as I further open her flower. I eradicate whatever shyness that was inside her. Any fear, now transitions into desire. She's a different woman around me. She moans louder, she supplicates ferociously. She squirts brutally. Insatiable desire for me. I have an insatiable passion for her. She becomes the object of my unbridled lust. I fuck her slow, I fuck her fast, I fuck her quick, I take my time with her, I fuck her long. I fuck her round for round. I fuck her deep. I fuck her good. I treat her bad. I disrespect her kitty as if I hate it. I fuck her spirit, that after I'm gone, she continues to feel me. The slightest thought of me, leaves that tingle and that clit throbs like a heartbeat. Her mind races. Only I am capable of calming her storm. I am her escapism. This 'Discipline' therapy is her stress relief. Brutal sex and sweet love, go together like peanut butter and jelly. Some call it, 'domestic violence.' I call it, 'foreplay.' You see craziness, I see normalcy. You see, 'freaky', I see 'regular.' What's chaos to the bunny, is normal to the king cobra, viper or python. You see aggressive sex, I see her seventh orgasm before I had my first. You may see it as, 'it's against her will.' It's ironic because, every time my grip gets tighter, she lets go. My hand is suitable for her neck. Her throat belongs to me, as I grind her into the bed. In her submission, you see, 'weak.' In her submission, I see, 'strength.' In pain, you see 'fear.' In her pain, I see 'love.' In her pain she sees pleasure. My callousness behavior, takes her to eternal bliss. Her submission is her strength, my control becomes her complete RELEASE. Nothing like the first big gasp in your ear, on the first thrust.

I am the alpha and the omega.

"Your beginning and your end. I am your creator, and definitely your destroyer. Witness the evolution of yourself, as you become a brand new woman. Like a bitch, I'll let you roam. But this is your most familiar bone, and you'll always come home. I allow you to walk the street with no collar, but I keep my collar on your soul. The choke hold I have on your mental. No matter where you are, you know where you belong. I am the most powerful entity you will ever encounter. I will implement training that corrects, molds, perfects your mental faculties or moral your character. No one will ever know you like I know you. And you're so stubborn you won't allow it. If he's man enough and lasts. Has the patience, to explore the depths of your mind, then he deserves all of you. However, I've ruined you. I've Imprinted my essence in your soul, that anyone that tried to entertain you outside of me, would need to know me well, I mean fucking well in order to understand you. I am like your most potent drug. Even if you were to walk away, the urge would keep coming back. A song. Rope you see in the store. A movie. A word. A picture will always remind you of me. You would look for attributes in other men that I already possess. You then will realize it is perhaps a little similar, but the feelings will never be the same. I am your guilty pleasure. Your favorite sin. I am your escape. The only place that makes sense to you. I am your stress reliever. You feel the rush. Intoxicated from my touch. Drunk off my gangsta love. This Hennessy thug passion. Long lasting. I own you and conquer you in every way, and in such Dominant fashion. I've put you onto my nasty ways, and you will never care to go back to mediocrity ever again."

Women Choose...... "You came to me. You know why you're here.

Never assume anything baby doll, but the fucking position."

Let us all get something perfectly clear here, women choose. It does not matter if they are in relationships, married or "it's complicated. "Some, "sort of," "kind of," ones. They come to you, they are entertaining you, flirting, etc. However, wherever, whenever. Words, thoughts, eyes, hands, etc. They are choosing. Trust me on this fellas. A man only feels threatened by another man, and his insecurities will flare, when he feels he does not deserve his woman. It's when he knows he sucks as a man. It is when he knows he is inadequate. She does not want to hurt your feelings, she cares about you. Of course they will not say, "you suck. You are terrible! You're wasting my time." Women are nice, they are loving and nurturers.

Confidence is not built through social media, it's something within, same as Dominance. They go hand in hand. It is also not something you may learn in school, and you do not get a late start. Dick is everywhere, but big Dominant, savage Dick is not. Taking charge is not. Assertiveness is not. Connection is not. Love is not. Power is not. Sexual energy and chemistry is not. Two rules in life as a man; you either step up and show you have testicular fortitude, or you step the fuck aside and allow another man to conquer. Like I stated above, women choose. A sub chooses how she will be with, and to whom to be that to. Power is given. What you do with that great responsibility is up to you men. You either adapt or you perish.

I spoke to her forcefully, but soft..."When you learn to let go mind, body and soul you will learn there is free-Dom when you do. Now you are empowered. You feel like a real woman."

Now, if a woman cannot love a God or King properly, step the fuck aside and allow a Goddess, Slave or Queen to. Gentlemen, if you cannot fuck or love a Goddess or Queen properly, step the fuck aside and allow a God or King to simply show you how it is done...

"I will always keep you humble. Just to remind you, it is mine. Just to remind you what the fuck I can do. Just to remind you who the fuck I am. To remind you what this is, and who you are to me. When you're complaining about your legs, when you're struggling to squat down on the toilet, or in your chair at work. I will not apologize. You're fucking welcome. Why will I not apologize? Because, I want your soreness to be a constant reminder of where you belong. In my grasp, in my zone, controlled by my massive, chocolate man hands. Tamed by my massive, muscular chocolate dick. There is no flaw in your body. I love everything about it, because it is mine. My love does not exist without pain. It's not an option, you will be hurt. It's a requirement. By Discipline. By a real man. By a powerful King. By my hand. By my whip. By my chain. By my gifts. By my thick, long, muscular chocolate beast. The dick that is utilized as a weapon to destroy you. The dick that splits your flower open, as you bless me with your nectar" Slowly, sliding my big tip out of her, just to slam it back into her viciously, with no regard, no remorse. Big muscular hand covering her pretty mouth, as I feel her delicious kitty that belongs to me, embrace my girth. Drenched and torrid walls shut around my fat, long chocolate.

"Save your screams and moans for when I want you to scream and fucking moan." Slapping that pretty little face of hers repeatedly, as I commanded so sharply. Pinning her legs back. Legs convulsing from the intensified thrusting. Eyes rolling back in deeper love than ever before. I feel her drenched, torrid walls become tighter around me, as I continue to thrust my fat, long chocolate beast between those begging moist lips. Rearranging her cervix. As my big hands move to the front of her neck, just to squeeze the flesh around her throat. Cutting the supply of blood to her brain. All that blood seeping down to her kitty.

My strokes become more vicious. More brutal. She becomes wetter and wetter. I'm dragging all those orgasms out of her. All the ones begging to be released. My words are forceful...

"Leave those legs back and open them walls and embrace me. Don't shut them. Don't choke my dick, until I tell you. I want you squirting, like a busted fire hydrant. I want you drenched like Niagara Falls. Appreciate this greatness. This gift I give you properly. This rareness. I will not always fuck you like this. But today, I ravage your soul and body. You won't even feel any of this. At this point the endorphins, dopamine, oxytocin dripping from your brain are in full effect. But you'll feel this pain afterward. You'll feel this pain when you wake up in the morning. You'll relish these moments. Marks of my big hand print on your ass cheeks, when you stare into the mirror. I'm in your mind, reliving me annihilate your body. Dominating your soul. You will be trusting in my leadership. Destroyed by the extent of my sadism. Confident in my authority. Unburdened by my decisions. Ultimately, fucking appreciative of my Dominance."

Three things a woman will always remember; her most loved, and intense orgasm. Her strongest sexual pain, and the person that gave her both.

"I'll take you to subspace, a paradise so exhilarating and euphoric."

A submissive has four types of women in her. The LADY, which you are always to respect. The SLUT, which you are always to abuse, brutalize and devour. The LITTLE GIRL, which you are to always protect, and cuddle. And you will own the heart, mind, body and soul of the WOMAN. And you will never be forgotten. I love to pleasure the one I'm with. It turns me on to turn you on. If you are not one hundred percent committed in a D/s relationship, I suggest you never start, because both are equal in servitude. The true essence of submission is to bend at the neck, not ask, but give. It's a huge stroke to my ego to make a woman orgasm multiple times. Worship and devour her body. Stimulate her mentally. Cover her spiritually. I'll admit that. It's a power trip. What I do, and my lifestyle induces strong emotions. My sex, pain, pleasure, Discipline, my love is not just the most potent thing on this planet. It will always remain with you, even when I'm gone. It soaks into your skin. It floats through your dreams and has you silently smoldering with delicious remembrance for hours. It has you craving it for days later. And it has you aching for it when you do not receive it for a while. You will ache. Sob. Cry. Bruise. All desires fulfilled. Then you will be fucked, made love to and pleasures like a whore by me. By a powerful man. Complete trust in the fact that your body belongs to me and I will use it however I please.

This is what you've always craved. Wanted. Needed. No more hiding from yourself. It's been too long without me, and longer without this. Without the greatness that I provide. The love. The Discipline. The security. The passion. The guidance. The strength. The power. The pleasure. The total body stimulation by me. By Discipline. By my hand. I will hurt you. Without concern. Without remorse. Without hesitation. Without restraint. I will hurt you, because deep down that's what you desire. I will love you, without concern, without remorse, without care of others, without hesitation, without bounds. I love you, because that's what you require. Bdsm is just an acronym until a Dom or sub give it true meaning. Twenty four seven. Psychological, emotional and physical. You will never witness a bond, a deep connection, a sexual chemistry stronger than a passionate Dominant, and loving, giving submissive. I've ruined you forever. Now if you are not being controlled you will feel as if you aren't loved and protected. If you aren't being choked you will feel as if you are suffocating. If you are not under restraints, you will feel as if you are confined. If you are not being spanked, you will feel as if you are in pain. If I am not verbally abusing you, every 'nice' word will never seem as a compliment and you will not know how to take it. And if it's not rough, you will never be fulfilled. Your submission is your strength, my control is your release. Now you are fucking complete.

I love to build a connection with my submissives, or Slaves/Queens. We will engage in vanilla(regular) conversations, joke, perhaps laugh, but we never forget who we are, what the dynamic is, or what we are to one another. Be careful who you bring into your circle. You embrace their energy. Their energy remains within you, whether it's good or bad. Energy is contagious, either you affect people, or you infect people.

For women, the best aphrodisiacs are words. One of her G spots are located in her ears. And I happen to have a deep voice, I have no control over. The bass in it, I'm sure feel like it's vibrations on the clit. Until a man finds himself and understands himself, finds his true identity, he'll ruin every woman he comes across. Never being able to elevate her. Or rebuild what the past has destroyed.

When a woman is loved correctly, she becomes twenty times more the woman than what she was before. Sometimes you have to go deeper, and she will feel you after you're gone. Men do not understand, having a well fucked woman on your side and how beneficial it is. Her mood, her mannerisms. Her willingness to worship, all comes from her need. However, never allow sex to cloud your judgement, change your character. If sex or being physical is the only way you know how to connect, and build with a man, or woman, your relationship is on the verge of turmoil. You all may have had sex, but have no idea, what true intimacy is. Some utilize sex, as a way to connect more. Don't allow good sex to confuse your heart, and make you think you're in love. (I know, easier said than done, because once women get great sex, it's like they become dumb. They get extremely weak). How do you have a well fucked woman on your side? Keep reading.....She will never truly fall in love with a man she can't learn from. A man who can't elevate her. Some women are too much for some men. Undress her conscious and make love to her thoughts. Drink from her water fountain and touch her intellect. Watch how she breaks down those walls. Just so you can be inserted through those walls. Beauty without depth is just decoration. A woman's beautiful face will attract a flirter. A woman's beautiful heart will attract a lover. A woman's beautiful spirit will attract a King, and a woman's beautiful character will attract a real man.

A true alpha knows, exciting and pleasuring her body is easy. The question is, can you quiet her busy, and noisy mind? Can you lead her down, deep into the blissful stillness? Into the calm that she craves? Find and hit that special spot deep inside her............cerebral. Conscious women taste better. Women with a high emotional intelligence, cum plenty of times. It's a gift and a curse to feel everything so deeply. Sex is an exchange of energy and power. When you fuck with negative energy, that's what you endure. But remove sex from a lot of relationships, and you will witness, and discover that many people have nothing to offer. When it comes to me, I will imprint something so deep in your pineal gland, that anyone that wants to know you, will need to know me. Crave to study my skills in order to understand you. You can't be a sapiosexual fucking with niggas. That's like an oxymoron almost. Like 'big shrimp.' Or 'Biggy Smalls.' You speaking like them, behaving like them subconsciously, to be accepted, and now you're settling for mediocrity. Without that mental connection, I would be that selected Dominant to restrain you, and we wouldn't have a relationship beyond that. You would never know which side of the bed I preferred, or If I even drink coffee in the morning. You might be complacent and content. Because you're getting that good shit from me, but I'll get bored. And the boring that I provide, is the greatest thing for you. But a soulful individual requires more. I know what I provide, therefore I fucking demand what I demand.

Knowledge can make her moist. Give her a mindgasm by going down on her thoughts. Intelligence is the ultimate aphrodisiac. I don't fuck, I soul touch. That's why every woman I've ever engaged in any physical, mental, or emotional activity is never the same. And they will always remember me. A part of me is with her. Women look for attributes and qualities in other men that I already possess. The deepest penetration is of the mind. I happen to be the cerebral assassin. Words are a woman's weakness. I just happen to be the master of the seductive language. A Sapiosexual connects with me on a deeper level, because I have the ability to seek beneath the surface, and communicate soul to soul. Conversations could pertain to economics, politics, fine wine, sports, art, sex, race, slavery, bdsm, media, relationships, etc. Meanwhile, her mind will wander off without permission, imagining how big my chocolate dick is, or how great I am in bed. I've touched her pineal and pituitary gland, that has now ignited smoldering desires within her soul, because this is no confinement to you. Rope, and restraints feel like home. My hand completes you. The feeling of being taken. Being owned, is so hyperactive. Every conversation is craved. Every word soothes your soul, or cuts deep. You have a longing deep inside you, where only I can fulfill. Make me work harder, when you say my name. Give me all your rain, and I will give you this mixture of pleasure and pain. This passion as potent as cocaine. Lose yourself in my insane. As you find peace in my madness. Run my fingers through your thoughts, penetrate your heart. Your soul caged, long before your thighs part in opposite directions.

I never need to remind you where you belong. I never need to ask you, to whom you belong to. An exchange of energy and spirit. Your mind, body, and soul has been deprived of good loving for so many years. That stops immediately. I now show you how a true man, a King, a God, truly loves a woman. Something vanilla(regular) men are incapable of giving. Something vanilla(regular) men are incapable of showing. I want to drown in you. Indulge in you. Not because I lust for you, but because I want you to feel my passion. My love. My power. My thick chocolate Long cock. Climb your walls like spider man. Drenched like Niagara falls. To be ravaged by a Beast. Guided by a King. Cultivated by a Master. Disciplined by a Dominant. I am your escape, where the only thing that makes sense to you. In my presence is where you feel the safest. It's like time stops for the moment. You yearn for my elegance. My fragrance. My smile. My dark menacing gaze. My strength. My muscles. My power. My Dominance. My cold heart. My firm grasp. My assertiveness. My hate. My love. My slaps. My spanks. My savagery. My protection. My love. My marks. My bruises. And sometimes, you need my methods of punishment. My essence and my imprint in your entire being. To ruin you, and any possibilities of anything else. That anyone or anything that tries to entertain you outside of me, will need to know me well, I mean fucking well, in order to understand you. So when I'm fucking you so deep, so intense. So passionate. So painfully good, and you moan, and you cry, whimper and whine. I'm not just fucking your body, I'm fucking your soul. I create this loving, giving, bigdickoholic slut for me...

"It is between your legs, but it belongs to me. This is mine to do with how I want. To devour, to slap, to play, to tantalize, to leave drenched, to take. Whenever I want. However I want. Wherever I want, over and over again. Keep your fucking hands where I want them, bitch. Not on my face, nor on my head. Hold your legs up, until I am finished. I don't care how good I make you feel, hold them until I am finished. You may cry, complain, whine, scream, your legs can convulse. You can give those faces if you have to, but do not move those hands from where they are. And you will beg me to climax, and you will climax when I allow you to. And I won't tell you again."

"Turn around, face down, ass up and your hands behind your back. Do not speak unless you've been instructed by me to do so. Do exactly as I say, when I say it. How I say it. I'm going to take you, over and over again, like you've never been taken before."

I'm not a thirsty man, but I'm thirsty for her. She is the object of my unbridled lust. I want to love her. But hurt her at the same damn time. I want to stroke her hair so tender, and as my broad, confident muscular chocolate man hands grab a fist fill, and anchor it towards me aggressively. I want to fuck her so hard, she feels it in her dreams. I want to make love to her and cuddle her, that she feels it in her soul. I want to spank her so hard that she struggles, when she attempts to sit for a couple days. I want to kiss her luscious, begging lips, but leave bite marks all over her submissive body. I want to slap her, destroy her, protect her and care for her.

I know what you're thinking, 'love and hate' relationship. No, I just display my love in all different ways than the norm. This is special to me, so if you've never been dominated like this, or introduced to this, you're not special to me. And I have no interest building with you. The struggle between the beast, the Sadist, the Dominant, the Daddy, the King is real. I control them, but sometimes she makes me weak for her. I love them all, but hate the Sadist. The savage. Once he's released, he's difficult to tame. He's stubborn, and set on destruction and pain. He's heartless and he thrives off your suffering. War and combat. Love scares him away. Purity puts him back in his evil cage. The cage I've built for him to tame him. My love controls him. My hate fuels him. But not only is my love difficult to obtain. It is displayed. I don't want to be, and I hate to be angry at her. She should never see this dark, Sadist, evil creature, but only in bed. Only during playtime. I don't like to punish her, but I will never hesitate to hold her accountable, if I want to prove a point. Teach her a lesson. My love however, it is more than words. I want things of her, that she deemed unlovable. That she deemed unobtainable to a man.

I spoke to her softly, but forceful, the deep bass in my voice resonated in her thoughts, "I make it my business to know what you know. Everything about you is mentally documented. The memory is photographic. Numbers are well stored as well. Appearances, efforts, and time. If I'm doing my job, I know what you need, before you open your mouth to ask for it."

She makes my thick long chocolate beast, rock hard with her personality. Her clothes don't even need to come off. She's so submissive. It's in my DNA, I'm attracted to her. Her smile is light to my dark, menacing soul. She's always been in control. But all that changes. She thought she was in control, until I came along. How she was before me is irrelevant. What I see is an innocent, yet strong, confident woman.

Our emotional connection is fierce. Our sexual chemistry is through the roof. When I address her as 'slut', she's excited. 'Good girl', she gets wet. 'Bitch', so comforting. I know she feels me when I think about her. Because when I fuck her as rough as I can, I leave a part of me with her. She views a side of me, not many get the chance to see. Tender and soft, to only be interrupted as she witnesses my savage by her misbehavior. Or destructive and brutal acts, by my vicious behavior in the bedroom/playroom.

Dominance and Discipline do not just occur in bed, when we play. Dominance and Discipline are not exempt in good times, they are not exempt in bad times. She's so good to me, so I treat her like gold. The reality is, women only respect men that can Dominate them. Whether that be; physical, emotional, or psychological. It doesn't have to be the way I do it. I do not take pleasure in Dominating weak women. I Dominate what's strong. Submissive is strong, not built for the weak. Weak men, and weak women will never be able to understand this. Submission is to be of use, not used. To give, not wanting or what's done to you. I've fought her on leaving a dangerous, incorrigible man like myself. And she refused. She's told me...

"I just want to please you. Allow me to please just love you. My number one goal is to please you and make you proud."

She's hungry for power. Hungry for knowledge. Hungry for Discipline. Hungry for Dominance. A hungry woman is always obedient. I said......

"Do you hate love? Trust? Sacrifice? Loyalty? Honesty? Do you want to love, but do not desire to be loved in return? Do you really want love? Do you love, love? Or do you need to be loved? Huge difference. There are things you will do you've never done. You will get your nails how I like it. Hair how I like it. Dress how I like it. I will choose the proper foods for you to eat. I own every inch of your body. Your mind. Your soul. They are servants to me. I will ravage. Stimulate. Cherish, and Dominate how I see fit. If you misbehave, I will hold you accountable. Every fucking time. I'm not playing, this is your life now. I don't care if you've never been given rules, you will follow mine. I don't care if you've never chased a man. Catered to a man. Pleased. Worshiped. Knelt or crawled before a King. You will learn today. You will get adequate training resulting in you being the best woman for you and I."

"I can see things in you, that you've never noticed before. Your flaws, I see beauty. Where you feel weakness, I see and give you strength. Where you know doubt, I give you purpose. I look deep within your soul, and no matter if it's damaged, or broken, I see a woman that loves the hardest. And that type of love you possess is extremely powerful. I want that love, but not just any love, I want your love."

If she could love a lunatic like me. A maniac like myself, she deserves more than words. More than Dominance. More than effort. She deserves more than pleasure. More than pain. More than suffering. More than what basic society is willing to offer. She deserved greatness. I give her that gangsta loving. She warms my cold heart. She lights up my dark, menacing soul.

"Come to Daddy, he's going to give you that work." She wears my favorite thongs. Nylon sheer lace cut. Lift her up, and her plump booty coming out those jeans, but I don't want to pull her pants up. Good girl, but she's Daddy's slut. I have her doing things, she's never had the courage to get done. Her and I. It's pain, pleasure, intense and it's fun. All this testosterone is turning her on. Her legs wrapped around me, has my thick long chocolate beast hard as a missile. Before I hit her g spot, I rip off that g string. I'm like Winnie the Pooh when I see that honey. Dripping wet for Daddy. Licking my lips, before I lick both her lips. Salivating from the sight of it. Diving in head first. Swimming in that good pool of lust. No goggles. I work my big tongue how I only know how. Eat that cat like the only way I know how. Tongue does miracles. Her legs convulsing. I eat her lips, and make the others speak.

Music to my ears. There's no fear, no insecurities. I see all of that leaving her. No good girl, she's a different woman. Moans so loud, she has no regard where we are. She loses herself in my craze.

My tongue is out on her clit, moving my head back and forth, up and down. Then I pause. Just my tongue working circular motions on her. Clock work. Counter clock work. I stick a finger in between her begging lips, into her drenched hole. Her gift.is tight. It's warm, and juicy. She's having a difficult time maintaining her composure. She's moving. She's whining. I'm smirking. I enjoy her suffering for me. Her moans getting louder, and she's cringing. But I'm not going to let her climax soon. I command sharply...

"Keep both your fucking hands up, like it's noon." I pin her legs back. Her whimpering. Squirming. Whining. Just makes me work harder. She supplicates, "please, please, please", and I reply, "no, I'm not finished enjoying you. This is my pleasure right now, you will have your pleasure later."

I flip her over. I put her in sixty-nine. But she can't even get it in on her end, because she's constantly pausing to moan.

"Did I tell you, that you can stop?" I force her head down back on my big cock. I'm spanking her, while I eat her simultaneously. She surrenders what she is, for what she can become. I devour every inch of her, before I fuck her savagely. I spoke softly, but forceful.

"On your knees, face down ass up, and your hands behind your back. You have your rights, and your safe word. Do exactly as I say, or else. Keep that perfect arch just how I like it, no matter what, and she replies, "yes Daddy."

I am the most rewarding, yet dangerous lover to become involved with. It's how you push my buttons. Soon as she comes over, I tell her to take her clothes off. I don't want to talk right now, I'm horny as fuck. It doesn't matter how bossy she is. How Dominant or savage she may appear. It doesn't matter how self-sufficient she is. There's a little girl inside every woman. And she's not too grown to get her ass whooped. Today we test your savage. We test your flexibility. We push your body to its limits. She respects this big strong muscular hand. This thick long chocolate dick. Which is the most prestigious. Most prominent. Potent. Addictive. Thing. Drug. Pleasure in this whole world. I disrespect her body brutally. I'm very stern and I don't play.

Her body was like heaven, but I put that shit through hell. My big strong muscular, grasping hands on her waist and hips. Exerting my strength. Hands behind her back. Face in the mattress, ass up, kitty spread to embrace my girth. Pulling her into me, with a combination of powerful, intense, vicious thrusts. I make her "Elvis shake." Smashing her into me, like I'm trying to make my pelvis break. My strong hips control her. As she bounces on and off of me. Like a wave, and a slap simultaneously. Walls caving in, feels like she wants to release on me. I commanded her...

"Look back at it. Now look at me. Look me in my eyes, when I Dominate that kitty." Her moans. Screams. Whimpering. Cries. Fuel me. Make me work harder when she calls me, 'Daddy.' I train her body to handle me. To Take me. To Embrace me. To Please me. To grasp her fragile little throat, is invigorating. While the other has a grasp, of that luxurious hair. Gripping a fist full. I'm in complete physical control. I control all her movements. I flip her over. Put her on her back. Legs pinned back. Full penetration. I fill her up. Maximum stimulation. All the way to the back of the vaginal cavity to a point where the cervix is pushed aside. My strength is immaculate. From my chocolate man hand, to my thick long chocolate beast. Strong fingers squeezing the sides of the flesh around her throat. The brink of asphyxiation. I speed it up, then I slow it down. I speed it up again, then slow it down. Her facial expressions are priceless. I work her out, like a "ThighMaster." The tighter my grip around her neck, the tighter her walls close in around me. With every slap, she releases, and is left drenched. Rhythmic thrust, breasts bouncing in unison. Head swell with power, as I further open her flower. Begging me to allow her to release. Her legs convulsing. Like a leaf in the wind. She loses herself in my sin. I own every orgasm. I own every breath she takes. Slapping of flesh. The wonderful smell of sex. The pounding is like background music, as her breathing changes, and moans take over.

Tonight, we die together. Reborn as immortals. Powerful beings. Souls entwine. I blow her back out. Leave her a gratifying, dripping mess. Subspace. All the noise comes to a halt. Temperature dropping. Heart beats back to normal. Souls entwine. Everything reminds her of me. A song. A voice. A word. A scent. Imprinting my essence in her heart. She is no longer the same woman as she came in.

She gave me things, more precious than money. She gave me more than her body. She gave her trust. Her loyalty. Her dedication. Her devotion. Her hard work. Her honesty. Her doubts. Her fears. Her obedience. Her love. Some women will search the world for. Lie for. Plot for. Manipulate for. Do whatever it takes for, "Love." Then there are a separate portion of women who just crave to be called, "mine", "yours", "his." Whatever it is. To be desired. Wanted. Appreciated. To be the object of your unbridled lust. I tell her,
"Put my pussy on the phone." She does. If she's at work, she goes to the restroom. I tell her, "Daddy wants to talk to it. Put my shit on the phone, immediately. Daddy wants to jerk his thick, long chocolate Beast to your pictures and videos."

She doesn't care for titles or others. She just wants to be called "mine." Doesn't beg for love. But if you love, it's a bonus for her. She yearns for my approval. Prioritizes serving me over completion of any other tasks. Her only job is to please me, and that is it. My job is to make sure she focuses on nothing but. She doesn't want money.

Doesn't strive to make me angry, but proud. She doesn't care for what a Dominant can provide, she just appreciates whatever I can provide. Men need women, or a woman, that is truly his. That's at his feet. Anything less is non-fulfillment for him. If a man feels you can't trust him, he will never give you his respect. His love. If a woman feels she can't trust you, her attraction for you diminishes.

Even if you were still engaged in physical activities, the connection is not there. It now becomes just a physical game. We connect because we are both fucked up. We connect because we both are not ordinary. Tortured souls find comfort in how our demons play well with each other. Submission is to be of use. Not used. Weak men will never understand this. Weak women will never be able to grasp this concept. To have love for women and never enjoying them is like, loving vodka and never tasting it. Or cannabis and never smoking it. It's like having a talent, and you're never able to use it. In most cases where you see, "the bottom", the person who may enjoy the pain aspect of the lifestyle, wishes to be at the receiving end of the paddle. Whip. Flogger. The bottom maintains the control. Act of bottom is not always sexual, but in most cases it is. It's more of a mutual partnership. Some just love being spanked, or Dominated. Will tell you, they do not have a single submissive bone in their body. They are in it for the sexual pleasure and the pain. The bottom is more of an act, rather than a state of mind. Some women search the world, do anything, manipulate, beg for love. They yearn for their significant other to say the words, 'I love you.' As though it is to be reciprocated. Then there is a separate portion of women that just want to be called, "mine", that just want to be called "yours." That's good enough for them. The love is a bonus. Yeah she's your girl, but do you claim her? She's your wife, but do you own her? Is she with you, or is she yours? Does she belong to you? I'm not going to preach to you and tell you I'm this Prince Charming, because I'm not. Wouldn't kiss you awake but more like fuck You savagely to sleep. (You can't have a nice asshole. That's a perfect world).

I'm not even marriage material, but with me you would get nonstop thrill. Like an action movie. Phenomenal, and you will love me. It's inevitable. If you show me things of you, then you will receive my love back. I induce strong emotions. And my lifestyle is not associated with inadequate development. I will eradicate those fears. Gradually dismantle that wall and guard you work so hard to keep up. There's nothing more intimate than ownership. Love is a verb at the end of the day. Not some cliche greeting like, "how are you?"

We really don't care how you are, it's just a pleasant greeting, or a good start of conversation. But it's like a rhetorical question. Some men are too wrapped up in their work, games, toys that they forget they have a woman. A woman always feels like she's not desired, loved, appreciated enough. You have women that say they don't make love. They don't love. First of all, are you fucking him or he's fucking you? You are what you get. You get used to whatever he gives you, or doesn't give you. Y'all women are into mediocrity. Therefore y'all give mediocre. (I don't want mediocre. I want all of you. Mind. Body. Soul. Drown in me. Why? Because I know what I bring to the table. I don't desire it. I don't crave it. I fucking demand it). This is why there's so many unhappily married women out there. Most women do not feel passionately desired enough. Wanted. They don't care about anything else, but feeling wanted. Needed. Used. Dominated. She should be the object of your unbridled lust. She wants to be CONQUERED. So when we actually do engage physically, our souls will entwine and I will leave a mark for reassurance. I will leave a mark on your flesh, and your mind so you never forget where you belong. I will leave such an imprint in your heart, that anything outside of me, or anyone will need to know me in order to understand you. MINE. GIVE ME YOUR ALL. ALL OF YOU, and I promise to let you scream as loud as you want. Always.

It doesn't matter if she was thirty, thirty five, or forty, she would still address me as, 'Daddy.' The world may view her as a strong, self-sufficient woman, but she will always be my little girl. She will always kneel to me. She is Man handled. Her face in the mattress. Her ass up. "Hold on, because I'm going to take you for a rough, bumpy ride." If she's such a savage, why does she cry when I eat her kitty? If she's such a bitch, then I'm animal cruelty. She cries, whines, moans, and supplicates to me to allow her to climax. She's a savage, but when I'm in deep, all she does is moan, and her hand comes out like she's begging for less, because I'm too much to handle. She is not a savage to me. However, to others she is indeed, but she's my baby girl. I'm her Daddy Dom. A Queen only a King can tame. A body only a Beast can satisfy. A mind only a Master can penetrate. Pain only a Sadist can obtain. She loves to hurt for me. She loves giving me her suffering. She feeds my animal. As he is twisted like a Rubik's cube. I feed her masochist. This love of ours is not normal. It's dangerous. It's deviant. It's special. It's potent. It's sadistic. It's pleasurable. It's phenomenal. It's painful. It's tender. Sweet. Mean. Round for round. Pound for pound. Hours. It's Thug passion. It's Gangsta Loving. It's aggressive. It's Dominant. It's submissive. It's intense. It's bondage. It's Discipline. It's Dominance. It's submission. It's sadism. It's masochism. It's limits that are pushed. At the end of the day, her mannerisms don't mean a thing, when I'm tearing her ass up, and working her like a shift. She gives me all of her earth-shattering orgasms. They all belong to me. Every last one. Her wetness. Her cries. Her tears. Her joys. Her sadness. Her anger. Her pain. Her bruises. Her thoughts. Her words. Her arousal. Her flesh. Her soul. Her surrender. My control.

There's a few things you don't do in life; tug on Superman's cape, piss in the wind, and bite the hand that feeds you. I don't trust. But she was the type of woman you could confide in. Loyalty is everything to me. I deserve it. I fucking demand it. She's the epitome of a good girl. Trusting. Loyal. Honest. Polite. Proper. The type to lie to the judge for you, and say, "your honor, he was beside me all night, I promise." That type of loyalty in good terms and bad. Type of loyalty and trust, you can't buy. The type of trust where she would follow me anywhere blind folded, without question. Where we could walk through fire, and she knows I would shield her, as we both come out safe. Untouched. The type of trust where she sucks my thick ass long cock while I drive us on the highway.

If I could trust her, I would love her. If she could trust me. If she could love this maniac. This lunatic. She deserved everything. I exposed her to dominance and real, now she hates lames. She used to run from me, now she loves adventure and pain. I got her wrapped around my finger. I have my own ringer. In her cell it says "Daddy", she calls her father different. Because I stroke so good, like tiger woods. Then I growl in her ear like a tiger would. I put her in her place, when she gets out of pocket. There's no right way, but our way. The Bdsm way. She is not planned. We are that, I want you now, strip down way. That fingering you in the driveway, because I can't wait to get inside. That playing with you under the table at a restaurant.

She lives by rules, dominance, guidance, protection. Love. Discipline. When we are serious, we are serious. When we laugh, we laugh. When we play, then we play. Ever since I ran up in her; mind, body and soul she hadn't been the same. I taught her how to speak to me while she takes pipe.

"Yes Daddy, Yes Master, Yes King." Speak to me while she mouths me down. "Please, may I, thank you." My gift of Dominance. My gift of Discipline. I'm far from sweet, I turn good girls. Laid back women. Shy girls into freaks. Into nymphomaniacs, into sexually crazed, pain whores. Into nastier women than they already are. Into chocoholics. Bigdickoholics. You find a release and escape from submission. Adore my sadism. Leaving my marks, I'm super territorial. That moment the following day you witness in the mirror, what I've done to your flesh. Just to send me the photo, and I say, "mine." As you reply, "yours." My love is the most powerful thing in this earth. It can give you powers beyond your wildest dreams. Make you think things, do things, say things you've never said, done, experienced before. My love doesn't exist without pain. It's potent like cocaine. Not everyone is deserving of this prestigious aspect. She does what I want. When she's a good girl, I give her what she needs. I love her like, pussy, money, weed. We were missionary.

I told her not to touch me. I'm going to work you like a shift. Just lay there, and don't move. I commanded her to orgasm, "give me my orgasm. Give me my juices. The juices that belong to me. Let go and let it drip. All your juices belong to me. I want them now!"

She did as I commanded. Bullied. Pushed. Pulled. Grabbed. Slapped. Choked. Handled. With fucking authority. My massive chocolate beast was wrestling with her pussy. Her pussy lips had my chocolate cock in a firm chokehold. I had to superman punch, and spear her kitty with my beast, just so she would let go. She dripped. She released. All over the sheets. My menacing stare demanded respect, obedience and demanded it immediately. She soaked the spot beneath her. Dripping down her crack, onto the bed sheet. She couldn't help but squirt. I enjoyed making her hurt. She couldn't help but grab and claw my muscular tattooed back.

"What did I tell you?" She gasped, "sorry daddy, it was a reflex." My strong fingers whip across her mouth. **Slap**, the stinging of her cheek. Her chin. Repeatedly, then my hand grasped her throat, as my strong fingers squeeze the flesh around it, her mouth wide open. Her eyes pop in deeper love than ever before. I said sharply, "worthless. Bitch. Whore. Mine. My filthy fuck toy."

I turned her around, I didn't command. I just bullied her like a rag doll. Put her on all fours. "Arch your back. Don't lose that arch. Don't move, unless I move you, or say otherwise. I thrusted my dominant, long, chocolate, muscular beast inside her. Back and forth between her begging, submissive lips. All she could say was, "please, thank you. Daddy. Fuck. Oh shit. Fuck. And more fuck." I could see she did, I didn't give a fuck. I spoke in her ear, soft whisper, "you have a filthy mouth. Bad girl. I spanked her ass so hard with my massive chocolate man hands. Over and over. Right cheek, then the left. Equal spanks, for there's no jealousy. My big red visible hand print on her ass cheek. She said...

"I'm your worthless slut. I'm your bitch. I'm your whore. I'm your filthy fuck toy." Tonight not a kind word. Not a soft sweet kiss. No beauty in this beast that she seeks. This will stay with her. It will soak into her skin. I was fucking her so intensely, she would feel me in her dreams. She would feel it every time she's at work, and she thinks about it. It will have her silently smoldering with delicious remembrance for hours. She will crave this savagery for days after. She will ache; mind, body and soul when she does not receive this. The irony, that when I'm not choking her and throttling her, she will feel like she's suffocating. When I'm not whipping and beating her ass, she will feel like she's in pain. Everything will remind her of me. A song. A word. A desire. A chocolate bar. Whenever she would see rope. Hand cuffs. Then and only then she would know, what I already knew, which is she is mine. When I can invade her every thought. Through repetition and it grows and grows in her mind, like a muscle. When the inevitability becomes the reality. When the pleasure becomes the pain. The pain becomes a craving. That little things like romantic dinners for you aren't a major thing. That she is just happy to eat whatever I bring. When pleasing me becomes an addiction because it pleases her as well. This is when, and truly then, she will know where she belongs. I won't ever need to remind her.

Every woman wants to serve, worship, cater to, please a King. But not every man lives up to the expectations. Not every woman is worthy to serve. Some women will never beg. Some women will never search. Some women will never grow. Some women will never cater, crawl, worship. Some women have never been humbled. That's why, some women will never be happy. Most of these women that have put their pride to the side. Not going through power struggles. The nitpicking, they believe is mundane. Have let go whatever it is for themselves, relinquished complete control, and just pleased. They have just given themselves, are the happiest women that are engaged in this lifestyle.

Some women will never receive. Why? Because they never earned. I never believe a woman saying, she's a savage. The ones that say they don't care, they care and love the hardest. The damaged, and broken women have the deepest souls. She never craved a quiet sort of mediocre love. A gentle passion. She craved to be devoured. Give her submission to a man. Where it was to be masterfully taken. A precious gift, to be cherished. Heart cared for, mind stimulated, body ravaged.

My beautiful brown eyes. My dark menacing stare, fixed on her. Her body quivered in anticipation of me, telling her what to do next. Her heart racing, yearning for my savagery. I spoke soft, but forcefully...

"Look up at me, and say to me, Daddy, I'm your slut." I then began to bind her wrists with my cuffs. "I am your creator and destroyer. I will hurt you, and heal you. Demolish and rebuild you. Teach, guide and Discipline you. I know what you need intuitively. How to calm you, and how to ignite your soul in flames. You need DOMINANCE, in the good and bad times. You need structure. You need stability, you need to be devoured. Ravaged. Desired. You need to do what pleases me. It is what pleases you. You need DISCIPLINE or you forget who you are. Who the fuck I am. What this is. Where you belong."

She said, her past made her so weak, but I make her strong. Everything was upside down. Now she's right where she belongs. I said, "give me all you have; your mind, your body, your soul, your fears, doubts, your past. We could take this dynamic further if you just listen. She said, "you're not what I'm used to. You are the only thing I am beginning to need." I said, "I will be everything and more. These feeling are too strong for you to ignore. My fat, long chocolate cock gets hard when I think of you. The pain I would give." She said, "my pussy is soaked from your power. Your mind. Your drive, your dangerous dominance. Your aggressive tone. The deep bass in your voice, is like vibrations on my clit."

I smirked, then stopped smirking. I said sharply, "Silence!!" She was quiet immediately. "Being mine, all your self-doubt, fear will be eradicated. I will show you courage you've always had. Now you become great. Now you are powerful. Now you are somebody. MINE. A savage man can always tame a savage woman. An asshole can always tame a bitch. Real Kings know how to make real Queens submit. Tap out. Now I don't mean necessarily just physically. But, emotionally, and psychologically. Once he's in her psyche, he's half way there. You know what's ironic? Most men, especially rich men, think of using money to attract women, but they hate gold diggers. Most women, not all, use their bodies to attract men, but do not want to be viewed as sex objects. Meanwhile, both genders seem to think this is some type of power. And both genders always seem to want something genuine, but do this. She was a form of divine chaos, most men couldn't understand. She needed soft words of love, and a hand to hold onto. But she wanted nothing more than her hair pulled, and a red big handprint across her ass, to remind her she was alive. I knew her. I could see right through her. I understood her. The things she didn't say. The things she wouldn't dare show. She was tantalized by my darkest desires.

"Open your mouth, wait for my thick long chocolate to touch, and slide between those begging, willing lips. Bend over, and wait for my big thick chocolate Beast to stretch you open. To work you out. Give me my pussy, and I'm not waiting for you to give it to me. I'll have you up in the middle of the night, because your body craves me. On your knees, that is the proper position to please me. Surest way to get my attention. Profound act of devotion, beginning of submission, trust, loyalty, dedication, obedience. Also, because I said so."

I caressed her ass gently, while I spoke to her forcefully. "My love doesn't exist without pain. It's potent like cocaine. My love is the way I grab your plump ass, slap your pretty little face, spank you red, yank your hair, as I anchor your head towards me, bite the meatiest parts of your delicious flesh. Accepting you beyond your limits. Your perfections and imperfections. My love. The way I hurt you. Heal you. My love. Touch you, without touching you. Communicate with your soul. My love is dangerous.

Savage. Deviant. Sadistic. Passionate. Intense. Deep. Psychotic. My love is Dominant. Addicting. My love is bondage. Discipline. Dominance. Sadism. Masochism. My love is dark. You will lose yourself in its madness. Surrender to it at will. My love is magic. It's violent. It's making you vulnerable. I will take when I want. What I want. How I want. Where I want. I will give what I want. You will crave whatever I give. Gradually dismantle you, take you to your subspace. Destroy you. Just to build you back up again. I make it my business to know what you know. Proactively engage to know about you, so if I do my job, I should know what you need before you even ask me. Listen to the things you don't say. See through the things you don't show. You will know everything I know on how to please me. Everything you need to know about yourself."

"Self-development, so you can handle another person. You should trust me. But you should also always fear me. That will always strengthen your respect for me. Your respect will always ignite your attraction. Fear and desire is when true pleasure begins."

No woman has ever loved a man, she never shed tears for. No woman has ever truly loved a man that has never taught her anything. I didn't think she loved me with all her being. So I had to test her. I mean really does she love me, or the idea of me? My bad, my faults, my chaotic lifestyle? She knew she was being tested, as she was informed by me, but how? Why? When? For what? Well that was all for me to know, and her to find out. I'm in charge. I wanted all of her. All she had. Her heart. Her soul. Dreams. Fears. Doubts. Insecurities. Her future. Her past. Her tears. Her cries. Her moans, her orgasms, her pain, her pleasures, her bruises and all I gave her. I said to her...

"Give me your demons, I'll control them. I'll lock them in a Discipline box. Where only Discipline is the key. I grant you freedom." I told her, "I know what I provide. I know what you can withstand. What I provide, you will need. Give me your pain, you have nothing to lose, and many things to gain. If you choose to walk away, my advice would be not to. Because, you would just be back here in my presence tomorrow. A week from now. A month from now, perhaps a year from now. Nothing about us is normal. You are the wrong place, and I am the wrong time. I'm more than just breathing to you. I'm intoxicating. Addicting. As powerful as chocolate. I am your favorite drug. Your guilty pleasure. Your sin. Potent like cocaine. You may search the world, but all you will witness is plain. You could meet another, get married, have children. However, whenever, wherever, you hear my voice, see my words, you would say, 'yes Daddy.' I'm the type of man, you just can't shake off."

I would never demand her body, but her fears, doubts, insecurities, her hard work, dedication, honesty, I demanded. Those things belonged to me right away. Those things I deserved. I'm not like most men, "baby, it's okay, open up, be honest when you can." I never craved this. Never wished upon this. Never asked for this, nor will wait for you to be honest, open, willing when it was convenient. I fucking demanded it. Reality is, most people want loyalty, honesty, dedication, hard work, etc. But most can't give it back. Their selfish. Love is free. To love is to give. To lust is to get. If you love, sacrifice shouldn't be difficult. Opening up and being honest shouldn't be difficult. I don't want forced love. It should be natural. Like trust. It's not coerced.

This lifestyle I lead is a life of fulfillment. Philosophy. Sacrifice. Trust. Challenge beyond the body. I'm not into mediocrity. I fuck hard. I love hard. I Dominate hard. I punish hard. I Discipline hard. Firm gaze. Soulful pools of magnetism. I expect someone to drown in me. I want the things I didn't have growing up. I want the things they said I could not obtain. I don't wish upon them. Like I stated above. I fucking demand them. Shy girl is not going to come to me, to leave the same. Bitch, will be kind. Cold hearted, turn warm. Mean, I will turn her soft. Alpha/Dominant woman, she will be submissive. Not because I say, but my Dominance inspires that.

I thought perhaps she was just in love with my gangsta. Perhaps she was just appreciative of my Dominance. Perhaps she just loved Dominant men. Control. Rules. Protection? But was it my rules? My control? My control over her? Does she crave this life? Does she yearn for what a Dominant can provide? Or what I can provide? Not any Dominant, but this Dominant man? Did she just crave Dominance and not Discipline? Pleasure and not pain? Perhaps this thick slightly downward curve long chocolate muscular dick I had? Begging to slide between her begging, sweet lips. Down her submissive throat? These tattoos and muscles? The power I had over other people? Whatever type of power I had, she was attracted to it. But was she attracted to me? Did she belong to 'Doms', known as characters, or known as men? Perhaps for the rewards? She wants to reap the benefits? If she wants this dick, she needs a membership. I could ask her questions all day. She could guess the right answers. The answers I'm seeking. But love is a verb at the end of the day. So I will test her. If she fails, she will know that I'm in and out like a bank job.

If you love doing something, never do it for free. Never give it up for free. If you are great at something, it's because you love doing that something. What I can provide, I want it all. I don't crave it. I don't wish upon it. I fucking demand it. I deserve it. Loyalty is everything to me. If you are unwilling to give all of you, I will gladly take nothing. Give nothing, and that's non-fucking negotiable. Under-fucking-stand me. I told her...

"Baby doll, we are going to do something different tonight. Arch more, hands in front."

See, pleasure was redundant, I wanted her to beg for pain. I'm going to push her body to the limit, see how much she can take.

"Now baby, you are entitled to use your safe word. When you use it, I will stop immediately. We will take a break. Now if you can't withstand anymore, we will not resume. You will put your clothes on, and I will take you home."

So how much does she love me? How deep is her love for me? How intense, violent, sadistic, aggressive, passionate is her love for me? I'm going to find out. Aggression is the name of the game. Dominant, submissive are the participants. Trust, connection is the foundation. Sharing is caring. As you give me your gift of submission, I give you my gift of Dominance. Fueling me, as you trigger my voracious appetite. I'm stronger than a lion, when hunger is the prime incentive. Talking about what you are going to do, want to do, is fine. Talking dirty, assertively, is an art. Backing it all up is a gift. Sex is natural. Enjoying it is art. Art is sex, and sex is art. Some people fuck. Some have sex. Others make love. It's all not the same shit. Some are extraordinary at it. Some are ordinary. If you're great at something, never do it for free. It should come with a price, where money can't even buy your talents. Every pleasure will be earned. Every ounce of pain will be earned. She said...

"Most men don't have this effect on me. It's something about you. I'm confident. Bold. Always in control. But when you look at me, I feel vulnerable. I'm afraid. If I tell you things I've done, how I think, you may look at me different. You may run. You won't think I'm good." I told her...

"Try me, I've done things, seen things, that would scare the average person. Give me your fears, your doubts, your insecurities and I will set you free. As you give me your gift of submission, I give you my gift of Dominance."

So assertive, as I stared at her squarely. My dark, mysterious, menacing look gave her chills. My firm grip on her flesh, made her complete. In my presence. At my feet, where she felt safest. My savage was therapeutic. My deep masculine voice was hypnotic. My gaze was hypnotizing. My energy was magnetic. My smile captured her soul. My words captured her mind. My commands she used as guidance. My Discipline as cultivation. She stared and said...

"Why put up with this?" I said, "simple, most women with the highest walls, love the deepest. You may display this cold, hard exterior to others. To the world. But I see through you. And that's what scares you. The broken or damaged, love the hardest. I want that love from you. Because that love is powerful. You will strengthen me as much as I will strengthen you. So that's why. Deep down, you yearn for this."

When I was finished, all she could do is stare, I left her speechless. Lost in my maze. My passion. My intensity. We will see one day, how deep her love is for me.

"Get on your knees. Let me teach you how I like it. I'm going to be your motivation. Pay attention. Cater to it. Worship it. I am going to slap it on your face. Yes bitch, I want you to recognize your fucking place. Feel all that thick chocolate weight. That thick vein. It's the sweetest, most juiciest lollipop in the world. I'm going to force it all the way down your throat. Stimulate your gag reflexes. So you spit on that big chocolate Dominant cock. Make eye contact bitch." I slap her. "Yes, I'm talking to you. Look at me."

Best thing about a woman giving you neck. Head. Slobber. Throat. Spit. Tears. Gags. Is a woman that loves giving you head. Neck. Slobber. Throat. Spit. Tears. Gags. She's working. She's moaning on it. I hear her slurping on it. She has two hands on it. Moving her hands like she's trying to open up a water bottle, while she slurping, because she's so thirsty for my Dominant juices. Her pussy is soaked. I reach from behind her, just to slap that ass hard. Then harder.

"Get on the bed." I spoke forcefully. Nothing like that first lick. Her facial expressions. That moan. Music to my powerful ears. I trace 8's on that clit. I vibrate more than her mechanical toy.

You're my fuck toy. I stimulate your erogenous zone. My tongue is like the magic wand. The slight curve in my thick long cock, designed to hit your g spot. Love to feel it throb on my Dominant tongue. I spread her lips with my big strong Dominant fingers. Suck it like it's a limoncillo. Put my powerful tongue in that asshole. I don't fucking play. Eat that tight, drenched pussy like it's a watermelon on a torrid summer day. Learning how to pleasure her body by the way she looks at me. Her body reacts to me. The wetness of her lustful drenched lips. Her soaked warm hole. She tastes so good. As I had her drinking plenty of water and adding fruits to her diet. Dice pineapples.

"That's it, go crazy bitch. Go insane." I wanted to pop her cherry and I wanted to be the one she blamed. 69, first one to cum has to give the other an hour massage, do chores, and sleep in the wet spot. I know I will win. Because every time I suck, lick, slurp, hum on it, she needs to stop just so she can moan. Just so she can enjoy it. I don't play fair, as I bind her hands behind her. I didn't state the rules. However, how could I lose? I make the rules. I make her cum faster than cops in white neighborhoods. That shit so sensitive. She wants to fight my face off of her. I hold her down.

"Stop fucking moving." I love her suffering. For me. Because of me. Love when she cries. Yummy. Her pussy juice, I love it. That shit just conditions my goatee. I eat that shit, like a lion devours wildebeest. I spread her lips. I place a finger in her drenched hole. I grab her ass, then I place my thumb in her butt when I eat my food slow. I'm taking her soul.

"Now turn around. I'm going to fuck my pussy, like it's never been fucked before. You nearly died with my tongue. Now I'm going to kill you with my dick. As you will be reborn. Reborn a new woman."

I could care less if you're fragile or not. I love breaking precious things. I'll fucking break you, just to heal you.

See, I can look into Fire and smile. As I see beauty. Chaos excites me. Danger is my domain. I'm right in my element. I want to inflict pain. I want to hurt you. I love to see you helpless. Love to see you vulnerable. You love when I take you. Trusting to let go. Start out making love to you slow, and gently. As I warm up your engine, then drive you fast, and hard. I'm a maniac and she is like a convertible. Drop your top. Let's go for an exhilarating ride. Pressing on her petal, I control her speed. Good girl, but in this moment it's the sadist I know she needs. Innocent, but I make her spread like a slut for me. My big muscular chocolate man hand on her fragile throat. As I squeeze the flesh around her trachea. Her dainty hand grasps my strong wrist.

"You're such a good girl." I whisper. But the bitch in her begs for the sadistic, the monster in me. My callous behavior is what she yearns for. However, grabbing her throat is a hard limit of hers. But not mine. It's not something I will toss out the window, perhaps some other hard limits of hers, but not this. Why? Because I love it. That's why. My words tickle her pineal gland, and her body automatically reacts. Why are we in this position? Because of trust. Why do I lead? Because I must. So watch how I make her transition. I talk to her while I'm inside her, speaking forceful but soft.

"I'm not what you're used to, but I'm what you will get used to. My ways, my power, my Dominance, my words, my life. As I control every part of you. Grasping your flesh. Make your drenched begging lips, swallow my long, fat chocolate beast. Taming the cold, meanest bitch in you.

Ignite your bad side, to your good girl. Control all your senses. Comfort the sad, broken soul. You yearn for my voice. You have a taste of being Dominated by me. Waiting for my every fucking command. As I ease you into it gently. Mild, then severe to the point where you will beg me for 'harder.' From now on you will only want it this way."

As I talk to her, I penetrate her mind, and she can't even think of the pain. She forgets my hand is around her throat. With my other hand, I grab her breast. Pinch her nipple. Then slap her breast. As the endorphins kick in, she feels no pain. Only pleasure. She forgets where she is. She doesn't think, she only feels. I see the shy and nervous has left her. As she moans and shakes for me. Because of me. As she forgets her name but screams mine. As she loses herself in my insanity. Head swell with power. As my grip tightens and opens her flower. Drenched as she begs me again for 'harder.' I spoke to her once again. This time sharply.

"This is where you belong. In my crazy zone. In my tenacious grip. Controlled by me, a powerful man. Dominated by me. A masterful King. A beast when I feast. A savage when I damage. You are mine to own. To brand. To mark. To devour. To command. To gush when I want."

As her breathing changes, her mouth opens from arousal. I lean in closer, to nibble on her ear lope, then back up and slap her pretty little face. My grip tightens around her throat, once again. I can see it in her eyes. Mild asphyxiation, I roar at her.

"The next breath you take belongs to me. Now breathe bitch, fucking breathe." As her pussy pops open in deeper love than ever before, her eyes roll back. Then that pussy tightens around me. "Now you take this thick long chocolate beast. Take it like the slut I want you to be. The slut I turn you into for me. By me. To finally let go to a powerful King. A King who perfectly ruins you in every way you've ever secretly desired."

She allowed me to beat on her as much as I desired. Beat up her pussy as much as I pleased. Take her when, how, wherever I wanted. A King that shows you love in forms, kind and unkind. Gentle and brutal. Feeding your flower some thick muscular chocolate power. You are appreciative to be struck. Slapped. Choked. Cuddled. Used. To be mine. By my hand. She cries out, begging to cum. As I tell her that...

"Your orgasms belong to me my whore, you will cum when I allow it. When I command it, not before. This crazy love will have you begging me for more. You may beg for it, but if I don't see it fitting, you will hold it."

Beautiful as she laid. Her pussy fit tight. That shit was like tailor-made. As you question your sanity for the love of these moments. These moments I give you. Destroyed by the extent of my sadism. Controlled and complete by my powerful hand. Slapping of flesh. Rhythmic thrusts. Sound as though it's back ground music, as her moans, whimpers, cries take over. Music to my ears. As I spoke sharply...

"Cry for me. Call for Discipline. Not God, he's busy. He can't save you now. Lose yourself in my callousness. As you question how good you are, because you love this shit. As you leave normalcy. Stray away from mediocrity. Give me all of you, and I'll allow you to scream as loud as you please. Gush as much as you please."

In that moment I feel her letting go completely. I command her now to cum.

"Go ahead baby. You've earned it." She gushes all over me. I thrust harder, then I roar in her ear, as I then release. We ride, then we die together. Then we are reborn, stronger.

There are still things you must know. A lifestyle of this magnitude. A man of my caliber. We will grow strong emotions. It is imperative that we appreciate the little things. There can be no bondage, without the bond. LOYALTY is everything to me. I don't crave it, I don't wish upon it, I deserve it. I fucking demand it. Without honesty, there's no trust. No trust, no respect. No respect, equals no attraction. No attraction, no relationship. I am perhaps cool, but I'm not friendly. I don't like friendly chicks. Who crave to please everything and everyone. Yes, submissive women are natural pleasers, this is why an Alpha sub is a prize in this lifestyle. At the end of the day, you can train any woman to be a sub. The natural subs, already know the lifestyle, so all they need training, and to learn is how to please you. The ones that's never engaged in this life, take more work. They need to be educated on the life, and how to conform to your ways.

Just because she's a submissive, doesn't mean she's easy prey. Just because she is a submissive, doesn't mean she will be your submissive. A good submissive is a reflection of a great Dominant. People can think whatever they want about me, whether I'm legitimate or not. That's irrelevant. Check my resume. My success has been people. What I do, the lifestyle I engage in is not associated with inadequate development. Titles are nothing, experience and actions hold value. Power is nothing if you have no idea how to utilize it. I'm not this domineering asshole everyone perceives me to be. I'm a fair, yet strict asshole. There's no reforming me, my subs accept me how I am, and I accept them how they are. That's trust. That's freedom. That's how you build on a real relationship. Acceptance of all their goods and bad. I'm not perfect, I'm authentic. I allow my subs to be themselves to a certain extent. I'm straight forward, and they know from jump, that I make my intensions clear. You are going to please me. I will allow you to come to me, when you're weak and are in need of my strength. Vent, curse, get it out.

I don't allow them to smoke cigs, as I don't mind trees, for that's from the earth. No loop rings on the nose, or septum piercings, you're not cattle. Hair, no crazy colors. No, you can't cut it 5 inches, I prefer it long. Nails I want to know styles and colors. Just because I am this way, doesn't mean another Dom is this way. There are Dominants, and then there are Dominants that engage in BDSM. I happen to be a Dominant that proactively engages in BDSM. In and out of the bedroom. I will not adjust or conform to your ways. I have few limits. I am a master. A King. A Dominant. Over protective Daddy Dominant. A cerebral assassin. A beast incarnate. My accomplishments are not one thing, because I'm not one thing. I'm gifted with this ability to make people in my circle great. Once you realize how powerful women are, you can get on my level. Until then, drink milk and stay strong.

As for my submissives, I elevate them. I empower them. I rebuild what weak men, or the past has destroyed. I hold them accountable for their actions. I make them earn everything they get. Hard work, dedication, Discipline, and with that, they build character.

I placed her bent over the table. Hands clasped, and rope bind her wrists. Thick long muscular chocolate beast, slamming into her yielding soft drenched prize. Tapping out and submitting to my ferocious pipe. Slobbering and drooling on my beef, like her cat was a new born baby. I don't give her rough sex, I give her rough dick. It's vicious and mean. It's malicious, it's not fair. It doesn't care. It leaves its victim sore and begging for more. Gasping for air. It's a certified killa. Like medicine, it puts that cat to rest. It makes that kitty feel alive again. Sounds as though kids were smacking water. Stirring of macaroni and cheese. Her sweet juices are dripping, they are streaming down her inner thighs. It's throbbing. Blood rushing from her head, heading downward. Waiting for my next thrust. My big powerful hand, my next command. And I gaze while I thrust, she says...

"Oh, you're so deep."

I reply sharply. "You're going to take all of me. Shut up and enjoy it like a good girl. The only thing I want coming out of that pretty little mouth is, "Daddy, can I gush now!? Other than that, shut the fuck up!"

I love watching her beg, as I thrust into her yielding pool of desires. Love watching her surrender, as she opens wider for me, and embraces my girth. She waits for me to give her what she deserves. What she needs, not what she wants. And when I whip my big muscular hand on her soft ass. Firm hand kissing her flesh, loud moans and relief escape her soul. And her new journey begins. A slap in her face. A stone grip around her jaw and throat. Big, thick chocolate beast slamming into her, and her breast bouncing in rhythm. Hard and big dick, to remind her I'm real. To make her feel alive again. My strong big fingers curl inward and grasp a fist full of her hair, anchoring her head towards me. And another hard slap against her soft round ass. That opens her up even more and creates more wetness. "I see a monsoon is due, as I witness a raging river of you." My deep, menacing tone forcefully whispers in her ear, as I bring my lips closer to her earlobe, and her head is tugged towards me.

"I'd tell you, be careful what you wished for, but it's too late. You wanted this. You wanted the worst. You've earned the worst, now fucking beg my whore. Fucking beg!!"

She begs, and now look at the results. She's creaming all over me. For some people it is a need. Whether it's a man or woman. Some women need that Discipline in their lives. Some men need submission in their lives. There's two types of strengths of people in the world, those that have the strength to control, and those that have the strength to yield. When I'm not in control, I'm off balance and no one around me is Happy. And I know it's a bad habit. Trust me, when I'm pleased, the world is a safer and happier place. I have a bad temper (it's in my bloodline) but, the great thing about it is, I've mastered control a long time ago. Therefore, it's not out of control. I tame the beast very well. I myself will admit, I have high Dominance. Directness. Assertiveness. Control. I respond to pressure with Control. I won't even lie. I will become assertive and more aggressive expecting an immediate response to my instructions. I am motivated by achievement and control. I want to feel that I am driving the situation. I will be more respective that way. I reply better to suggestions, rather than orders. When negotiating with me use the power strategy, I will be more receptive to suggestions and hints rather than your attempts to indirectly control me, and directly control my decision making.

The beast incarnate. The cerebral assassin. The exception and not the rules. The disruptor of the status quo. The conqueror. The epitome of power. The embodiment of authority. It's like when I'm at work, and I'm in the office, I'm trying to close that deal with a client. I'm super aggressive. When I have a meeting in the boardroom, I'm assertive and clear with what the expectations need to be. Some people fold under pressure. They get stressed from all the responsibility. People coming to them for everything. I thrive off of it. Stressful situations are where I constantly excel in.

If you only use your eyes, you will never see her. Too many servants out here. Too many mortals out here. Not enough Gods, Goddesses, Kings and Queens. Is social media dumbing you down? Or attempting to suppress your spiritual elevation? Take notes.... and then put on some Marvin Gaye, "sexual healing." If they are not feeding your mind, how are they touching your soul? A woman will always choose, and love a man who taught her something, over a man that bought her something. It doesn't matter how attractive a person's potential may appear. You must embrace and be associated or date their reality.

Sexual tension will have you fucked up and delusional. Have you seeing connections and potential in people you should have nothing to do with. When a man can touch a woman's mind before her body. When a woman can touch a man's soul, and bring him peace, the sex for both parties is so intense and passionate. They say, 'the mouth is made for a form of communication'. Therefore, nothing is more articulate to me than a kiss (passionate, aggressive, nasty, tongue, biting of her lower lip, grasping her hair or throat while you do it)

Women love men whom are protective and controlling. Oh, and don't forget Dominant. That's why they go crazy for an intellectual gangsta. Women love to learn, so they can utilize what they've learned today, for use of their growth tomorrow. When a man is intimidated by a strong intellectual woman it is because, he witnessed the Queen in her but not the King in himself. When a man is insecure pertaining to his woman, it's because he knows he doesn't deserve her. Just because everyone is interested in you, or him/her doesn't mean everyone is eligible. When the chemistry is so powerful, the bodies ache for romantic, passion and animal.

Give her mindgasms, by going down on her thoughts. Eclectic messages seep out of your mouth, from your pituitary gland into her pineal gland. Then into her female estrogen. Oxytocin and serotonin dripping from her brain. Now she's feeling electric. Wet between her legs from this Hennessey Thug Seduction. Her breasts she's touching. Aching for your substance. A person's energy tells you about them, prior to their words. I do not chase. I do not choose. I attract souls. And when those souls match mine, I embrace them. The more adequate training a woman obtains, the more efficient guidance and teachings you provide, the better she will be. Enhancing both party's growth, development and spirits.

However, men must know how to lead. They're watching you men. Everything you do, say and don't say. Your habits and idiosyncrasies. And they emulate them back subconsciously, like a little baby girl. The way she speaks, walks, her attitudes and habits, display her choices of men. Energy is contagious, not everyone deserves your greatness. The brains, the brawns, the success, really does not mean a thing when I'm tearing that ass up, working her like a shift. Giving her orgasms as if they were gifts. However, they truly are gifts, and she will ask before she releases.

"You are my fuck toy. My whore. My good girl, my whatever I want you to be."

One thing about women, they dislike being treated better than they treat themselves. Hence, one of the reasons why nice guys finish last. She is a fox to plenty of hound dogs on the hunt. She is the kush to more kush rolling the blunt. She is here because she does not crave mediocrity. She's yelling out, "harder," my reply, "shut the fuck up. I'll do as I please and go at how I want. I do not move on your demands. Unless you're using your safe word, remain quiet and speak when you're spoken to." Her reply, "yes Daddy."

Then I shove her face in the mattress. In this moment, I don't give a fuck for her good girl personality. I am bringing out the whore that the world does not see. She gives me that face, she does not show anyone. That face while I'm pounding out the demons that she keeps inside.

The slut she craves to become. The whore she is trying to suppress. The bitch she so secretly yearned to be fucked like. When I start, I warm up the engine before I drive the vehicle. We ride smooth. Then we ride hard. We start making love. Then speed it up. It gets rougher and rougher. Brutal. What a crime scene, as I am the serial killer to her kitty. I am a calm man, to only be interrupted by misbehavior, or when we engage in physical activity. I will at this moment leave my timbs on. I want to inflict pain. Suffering. Placing the bottom of the boot on the back of your head, while I dig out her stress with my massive chocolate beast. Treat her bad. Rough and disrespectful in bed, but good outside of it. No love here at this moment. I want to Dominate every inch. The beast is set on destruction. "You are worthless," I say sharply with a vicious slap on her ass. She is my whore. Not a tender kiss, but a rough kiss. Not a tender touch, but a ferocious slap on your face. On your plump, delicious ass.

My hunger for her increases. Her moans trigger my voracious appetite. I roar like a lion at her, forcefully.

"You will feel every impactful spank. Touch and thrust. No beauty in this beast that you seek tonight. Not a sweet word to you. Not a calm voice. More like a menacing tone and stare, followed by words spoken sharply."

I fucked her viciously. Savagely. Aggressively. I pounded her into a dripping mess, and then I make love to her passionately prior to when I slip out of her. It will feel as if I am still inside her. Once I have subjected her to this type of madness. She will not only beg for more, but always crave this Hennessy thug Discipline passion gangsta loving. If she can walk to the bathroom easily at first, I am not finished with her then. For her to subject herself to this type of madness, makes her insane. But, I love it. Then I cuddle her tenderly, and make sure she's safe.......

Chapter 11: My World

I called her in the morning around 9:15 AM. She was at work and I knew this because she gave me her schedule every week, so I can plan accordingly for when I would want her again or even just to make herself available for me for WHENEVER I needed her. So I knew she was at work, but I wanted to leave her a message anyway.

Text message reads 'hope you're having a great day at work. I know it will be an amazing day for you, only positive vibes and good energy. Come by to see me later. Speak to you soon.'

I didn't badger her because of my rules. She was off limits when she was at work or with family. Those were the only excuses I would accept if I was unable to have her or get in touch with her when I wanted to. Plus, I had work to do myself. But just then she calls me back. I let it ring and answer on the third trill. I spoke clearly, "Hello." She was panting.

"Sorry I missed your call, Daddy. You never really call when I'm at work." I asked curiously, "why the fuck are you out of breath right now?" I paused to hear her reply. "I rushed to call you back. I'm in the restroom right now."

I smiled. "Oh, my fault. Are you on the toilet talking to me now or staring at yourself in the mirror talking to me? Better yet, let me answer that. You're probably staring at yourself while you talk to me now." She laughed. "Man, you know me so well." "Listen, go back to work babygirl, I'll speak to you later. Text me as soon as you're finished there and headed home, on your way to me. Understand?" "Yes Daddy."

She shows up at my place. I gave her 8 PM sharp and as usual, she's on time. She's always on time when she's on MY time. It was 7:59 when she arrived. I had two dishes waiting for us. Dishes I cooked up. Diri and Sois, arroz con pollo, zaboka and platanos. Some well-known Caribbean dishes for the both of us to feast on.

"So, I wanted you here as something different today. I like to switch things up with us. I want us to explore so many different adventures and new things."

After we ate, it was time to play.

"You haven't seen all of my toys and I want you to see them and get familiar with most of them tonight. It's 'play time' and I want to welcome you into my world properly." I grab her, and I toss her onto my bed. She sees some of the things I haven't shown her yet. "This is like the jungle and I am the most fearsome, most Dominant predator here. You have been cordially invited to the jungle where you will be preyed upon, conquered, Dominated and devoured completely." I tied her up and whipped her entire body. "The only thing you can trust are my words. The only person you can trust is me. If you ever care to believe the darkness will make you feel better, it won't. Darkness is not your ally, these shadows, they belong to me. Your doubts and fears are mine. Your insecurities belong to me. Your body will betray you. Even if you wanted to attempt to fight me, which you wouldn't, your body would always submit to me. Stay just like that and take whatever punishment is coming like the worthless slut you so yearn to be for me. Sometimes I want to use restraints, sometimes I want to use my paddle to mark your ass, so you never forget where you belong. Mark you for reassurance. Mark you because you are mine. But sometimes I rather use my physical strength so you can feel my intensity. So you can feel my power, my passion. I keep you warm like wool and change your body temperature. I attack you like a wolf, you are the object of my unbridled lust. I'm set on destruction, I want to devour every inch of you."

She was loving every minute of this Discipline thug passion. This fucking therapy. I can tell by the change in her breathing and I can see it in her eyes, in her face. I said...

"I don't give a fuck which face you're displaying to the world. The sweet and innocent, the shy and quiet, the laid back or the mean bitch. I don't care. See, I know your true face. I know the face you create when I'm thrusting this big fat, long fucking muscular, chocolate dick inside that begging wet pussy. Captivated, staring into my beautiful brown eyes. The face you make when you're horny and the face you make when you finally cum for me. I know the face you make when you're on your knees before me. I know the face you make when you finally submit to me, absolutely and completely."

Play time was over and cut short. I needed to go grocery shopping. She actually wanted to do it for me, but I was pressed for time. So instead of writing a list of things I needed and giving it to her, I just went myself.

"Let's go, you can come with me." We came back after getting everything I needed. "So, you're off this weekend as am I. We'll be going to a club." She's so happy she starts clapping and asks where. I smile, "Don't worry about it nosey, I'll let you know what time I want you dressed, how I want your hair styled and what color to paint your nails. As far as the destination, you don't need to know. You're going to be with me. I'll be picking you up and you'll be riding with me."

The weekend came and prior to that, we hadn't seen each other for a few days. We both work busy schedules so we constantly keep in contact, whether it be via text messages, emails, phone calls or facetime (visual communication). That Saturday morning I texted her, 'Good morning my Precious, I hope you slept well because tonight we will be dancing the night away. We're going to a nice club out in the city. Get your hair and nails done. I want blue for your nails, Royal blue to be more specific, and plain, no special designs. Not French manicure just plain royal blue.' My instructions followed... 'A black dress and stilettos are fine. Wear your hair straight not curly. I want you dressed like you fucking own this goddamn club, not dressed like you're trying to get in it.'

She text back immediately, 'Yes Sir, yes Daddy.'

I had plans on wearing a nice tailored black suit with a blue dress shirt and a royal blue tie. I wanted us to match. When people see us, they'll know we were together. 'Oh yeah, wear that sexy diamond necklace I bought you last month as well.' She text back, 'yes Daddy.' I follow the text with, 'Be ready by ten pm sharp. Not 10:01, not 10:02 because you know I'll be at your house by 9:58 pm.

Don't keep Daddy waiting.' She answers back immediately, 'yes Sir, yes Daddy.'

I finished the conversation with a, 'Have a nice day. Great vibes and positive energy only for you and I'll see you later tonight.' I'm sure she was flustered with all she had to do to get ready for tonight. I was pretty understanding. I hit her up early in the morning for an adventure with me later that night. I know how long some women can take to look good for us men, and she would never want to disappoint me with lateness, therefore she put a little pep in her fucking step.
I was thinking of taking her to the spot where we met the second time. Where she was so intoxicated her friends left her with me and I took her home. I think about that night often, I mean, she let me take her home. I could've been a fucking serial killer or even a rapist. What the fuck was she thinking? I learned plenty of shit about her that night. One thing we had in common was music and what it did to our bodies. We both love to just dance and have fun. But, no, I wasn't going to take her to the same place. I had a different place in mind for tonight. She doesn't need to know where we're going, she just needs to get her ass ready when I say so.

All day long, she was taking pictures of her nails, how the color looked. She was asking for my input on the dress. She had many to choose from and needed help. I picked the one I wanted her to wear from the selection she had sent me. Seven pm came, she texts me, 'Just got home, I'm going to get ready.' It was 9: 58 when I arrived. I knocked on her door and waited. She answered fully dressed and ready to go.

"You're so beautiful. The stars in the sky would be jealous of the way you shine." I took her by the hand but not before she said, "Thank you, Daddy."

We shut the door and locked it. I held her hand, clasping and interlocking our fingers together as we walked to my car. I held the door open for her as she got in then walked around to get in my side. I placed the key in the ignition and started up my vehicle. I didn't put any music on and I normally do, but this time we had some time to actually speak and I wanted to take advantage of this time we were granted.

"Tell me somethings about yourself. Tell me about your past. Tell me things about your future goals. Tell me the things you fear, doubt and care about. What are some things you can do today that you didn't have the ability to do in the past." I asked. She was quiet at first.

"That's a lot of questions but I will try to answer all of them." she finally answered. I smirked, "Yeah you'll answer all of them. Please by all means, take your time. We have a pretty long drive."

She took a deep breath then began to answer everything I wanted to know.

"My fear is I will not be able to help someone in need when they are in need. Something I can do today that I couldn't do in the past is save lives, change lives and give life. I've always wanted to be able to help people, create a change in their lives for the better. I've wanted to be influential and I've wanted to give and create a huge impact in people's heart, minds and spirits. When I found you, you did all that for me."

I grin at her. "Cut the bullshit and fairytale answers here. You know I stress you out. I'm like a job, you're constantly on call with me. Any given time, day, place, etc." She smiled.

"You keep me on my toes, you keep me grounded and I need that type of Discipline in my life. Your type of Discipline, and I absolutely love doing things for you, my King."

We finally arrive to the venue. Valet took the car and we walk in. Her eyes light up. "Wow, this is really nice."

She said, staring around. It was a nice hot summer night. It was a nice inside and outside affair there. Everyone was staring at us. We were the main attraction tonight.

We walk to the bar and after several minutes women crowd around. Then men.

"Daddy, where did all these people come from?" I laugh. "Our powerful energy and aura is attracting them." She was the prettiest woman there. There must have been 200 women from my estimation after scoping out the place. We had the club going crazy. All these women in here but my eyes were on a Goddess. We walked around, it was a nice scenery. I said abruptly, "I need to go to the damn bathroom, I'll be back." I left her by the bar.

"Okay Daddy, I'll wait for you here until you get back."

I didn't walk up to her right away after using the restroom. Yes, I knew throwing a banana in a monkey's cage could be dangerous, but I was going to see what would happen or what wouldn't. Guys were salivating, I could feel the energy. Women were envious. I kept my distance and watched her from afar like I was stalking her, but not really. I witnessed men walk up to her and thought to myself, bingo, let's see what transpires here.

They were talking for a good thirty seconds. I walk up to her and immediately the men scatter. I kiss her on her lips and grab her ass cheek firmly. I then whisper in her ear...

"What was all that about? The man that was standing here with you?" She answers, "Nothing Daddy, he was just saying I was beautiful and I said thank you, but I'm not interested in conversation or anything else. I belong to someone." I stared at her firmly, then replied, "Good girl." I hugged her once again.

"But, there is no reason for you to even thank him." Her lips parted, and her mouth opened wide. "Oh, I'm sorry. Did I make a mistake Daddy? It won't happen again." I just smiled. I wasn't going to let no man or woman see her or I sweat. I wanted us to enjoy the night. I wasn't about to create a scene. She was so happy, and we were having a good time. She was looking real sexy too. I'll address this shit later, right now we owned the fucking night. So tonight, we dance the night away. Tomorrow, we train her on a little bit of "Discipline etiquette."

She spent the night at my place and we woke up together. So, we're laying in bed and it's now daylight.

"Good morning sleepy head." I say. I then stroke her hair with my fingers. "I want to address what happened last night. I wasn't pleased, however, I wasn't going to make a damn scene. I get that what you do on a daily basis is to be friendly, and you're constantly assisting people, but that's your time. You can do that on YOUR time not mine."

She cut me off. "I'm sorry Daddy, I know, and it won't happen again. Now I know..."

I put my index finger up facing her.

"I'm not done and don't cut me off again. When I'm finished talking you will be permitted to speak but right now you will fucking listen. I get that you're friendly but honestly, you're too damn friendly. Men are men. The moment you open your mouth to them about anything, they think it's a fucking invitation. From now on I don't give a fuck if men say you're beautiful or give you a million compliments, you do not and will not say shit to them. So, to further assist you with this, I have a short task for you today. It's a learning process and I want you to practice this thing I call 'sweet silence'."

I believe she talks too damn much and way more than she actually needs to, to others. I will temporarily take away her voice.

"For you to appreciate your privileges, I'll have to take them away. It can be for a short time or a long time, it all depends on you."

She was frantic, tantalized with what was to come. I wanted her to be better, to do better, to strive for greatness. For herself and for me. I grab a small sized tangerine. I say...

"I want you to go to the grocery store for me. I'll give you money and a list." She said, "No Daddy, it's okay, I have money. I'll get whatever you need." I then continue with my instructions. "You will go to the store for me wearing your sexiest outfit. Short skirt, whatever. Cleavage, the whole fucking nine yards." She gasps. "Really Daddy? You sure?" I replied. "Yes. Wear your hair down, no ponytail. Yeah, no handles."

She wore the sexiest outfit I've ever seen with these insane 'fuck me heels.' I nod my head in approval.

"Now open your mouth." She looked at me like I was crazy but did as I instructed. I placed the tangerine in her mouth.

"Do not damage it. Do not chew it or swallow it. If you do, I'm going to punish you severely. You will never know how or when I will punish or if it's a onetime punishment or a lifetime punishment, so act accordingly. Understand? Facetime me as soon as you get there. Here is a list of things I need for you to get for me." I handed her a list of mundane items I wanted. I really didn't care for the stuff, it was about the learning process. She doesn't know what is going on nor what she's in for, but I do. I have a pretty good idea.

The fruit was small enough to comfortably close her mouth and smile without the fruit ever being noticed. I wanted her in a crowded place where she can interact with others. Now she doesn't know why she's doing this but I'm teaching her the 'sweet silence'. This will teach her never to forget that I, her Master, her Dominant, her Daddy, her King is the first and last person she talks to. Every day and every night, while she serves under my guidance and my command, she is to answer the damned vanilla (ordinary) world with nods, gesticulations and hand movements.

"So when you come back to me, you are only allowed to let the fruit out when I open my palm in front of you. Do you understand me?" She replied with a nod and a 'yes Sir'. I then slapped her ass hard and said, "Good girl, now go get me what I want... you go girl!"

As I cheer her on. Before she walks out, I grab her ass and say, "Hold on. I actually want you to wear some jewelry that I got for you." She smiled from ear to ear and squealed, "Awww Daddy, thank you" until she saw me pull out my stainless-steel butt plug. Her smile turned into a flat stare real quick. I leer at her and say...

"I want you to wear this the whole time. DO NOT allow it to slip out of your asshole." She couldn't say anything but, "Yes Daddy. Anything for you." I smirk as she walks out. This was going to be fun, fun for me actually. I know what you are thinking...'you're throwing her in as bait.' Hook, line and sinker. A banana in the damn monkey cage filled with hungry monkeys, but fuck all that. All that is irrelevant. It's about how she deals with the pressure and challenge.

She arrives at the store and just as I expected, men approached her left and right. "Hey what's up ma, how you doing there Miss?" "Can I talk to you for a minute? Can I get your number? Oh my god, you're so damn pretty baby!" It was hilarious. They were going crazy for her, calling her pet names and asking for her number. Some men were so pissed she wouldn't even look at them or speak to them. She would just nod, and they gave her mean looks and called her nasty names while they were walking away. I enjoyed it. I was chuckling while I watched. Women were staring at her as well, giving her strange looks.

See, it's not about how the world views her that counts, it's about how I view her that matters. She's a different woman now. She's mine. She's in Discipline's world, therefore, she is to conduct herself differently than the average woman. She was paying for the stuff I wanted, and the cashier asked, "will that be all ma'am?" She nodded yes, I mean what else could she do? She smiled and took the bags and headed back. She came straight to where I was, and I opened my hand. She dropped the tangerine in my big palm. I asked her...

"So, how did that feel to you, exactly?" She replied, "That was so mean Daddy. It was so embarrassing for me." I chuckled, "You need to learn your damn lesson. Listen, I know you're friendly and you don't have to be an asshole like myself, but you should know what the correct and proper behavior is. What pleases me and what displeases me. You should not care how the world views you. You're not A whore, you're MY whore. You're

Daddy's slut and that's a big difference. In public, you are fully aware on how to conduct yourself. I don't need to elaborate further on this do I? You know what I like and now you know how I want you to interact with others as well. It's a learning process and now let's move forward. Come on baby girl, let's eat this delicious fruit you had in your pretty mouth, then I'm going to eat YOU, savagely. You earned it. You're lucky you didn't damage the fruit. The punishment I had for you would have made your head spin. By the way, turn around. You can take out the butt plug I had you keep in there as well."

She gave me what was mine and she learned her lesson. She never let it happen again after that humiliating experience.

Chapter 12: Strip Or I Will Rip Them Off You

It was a long work day for myself and Precious, but I was not going to allow that to fuck up my energy. Her and I had plans to see each other later, and like I said nothing, and no one would come in the way of this. It was about four- thirty in the afternoon and we had a conference call with the vice president. The call had about hundreds of other general managers from different states on the call as well. I was dreading this thing, these calls are so boring, same as the boring board meetings I am in charge of, and the fucking other meetings. Like I cannot believe how many people fucking need motivation, to fucking do their job.

Waking up out of bed, and the fact that you are making money, should be the damn motivation people need. It's so difficult to find self-motivated individuals. Too many people love being held, they love for others to hold their hand through everything. And I hated being a baby sitter. But I was too damn good at it, I could sell anything, talk my way in and out of everything, and talk anyone in and out of anything. I was the best closer in the fucking company. Rising up the ladders so quickly, I gained some silent jealous enemies. But my secretary was always by my side. Maria was her name, she was always trying to do extra for me, like I was never the type of boss that loved people to kiss my ass, I hated fake personalities. What do I look like? Like I was going to treat you or anyone different because you kiss my ass? You work hard, I reward you, that means, you get what you earned and deserved.

But Maria, was not like that at all, but she loved to do extra for me, she was foreign, and she would tell me constantly, that's how she was raised. Just to provide and always give. She would always greet me at the door, with a mug of coffee in the morning for me. What type of man do I look like? Some fat slop, whom did not know or was insufficient to not get his own coffee? First, let's get it straight. I was not a fat slob, and second, I could get my own coffee. She and I bumped heads because of that. I never met a woman whom was mad because a man would not allow her to get something for him or do something for me.

Well, Precious is like that. Maria was just my secretary, nothing more, and nothing less. I never shit where I ate, it was always and will always be bad for business, why? Women are emotional, no matter what they do not tell you, or no matter what they tell you. Maria was tall, respectful, old fashion, conservative, and had pretty caramel skin. She had a prefect smile, that was so contagious. Anyone whom was upset or angry, she could smile, and she could make them smile as well, I bet. But a woman like that whom was stressed out constantly, I mean I never gave her difficult work, and if she did not love her job, she would not still be here. Perhaps, it was dick she was missing in her life, I mean normally when relationships are sour at home, women are just not functioning properly at work. Or they are in terrible moods, which cause them to not function properly at work. I then asked her...

"Maria, can I ask you a personal question?" She looked at me and said, "yes sir." I then continued, "well, do you get out much? Its Friday night, I don't need you for the rest of the day, why don't you go have fun? Get out, enjoy yourself?"

She replied, "listen, I don't have a man, I don't have kids, all my friends want to go to the clubs every weekend, and I'm sick of that scene, all the time. Once in a while is fine, but all the time, is boring. I'm a boring person, is that what you want to hear?" I smirked at her. "Maria, be careful, that great personality of yours allows us to get along. Perhaps you must go out, meet someone, that is the only way to meet people. Become an extrovert, you love being an introvert, but sometimes you must push yourself to be an extrovert."

She shook her head. "No, I'm fine, I have my toys." I laughed, then she laughed back with me. I liked Maria, as far as a person, she was real. I didn't want to be here anymore for this drag of a fucking meeting.

"Listen Maria, take all my calls coming in, I'm leaving for the day, but if anyone asks, I'm in the bathroom or something." She replied, "boss, you are heading out early, don't worry I got you." I smirked. "Yes, Precious and I have some plans." Maria looks at me with her eye brow raised, "uh huh, hmmm." I smiled at her. "Don't do that Maria." She started laughing.

So I met up with Precious, she was going to spend the night with me, and before I went to bed I was downstairs in the basement where I kept all my fun things and boy toys. I was shooting pool and she abruptly came down. I guess she was looking for me.

"Daddy, what are you doing? You're not coming to bed yet?" I didn't reply. "So, you play pool huh? I had no idea." I then asked her, "What do you know about pool? It's famous in Europe and Australia having six receptacles, called pockets, along the rails, into which the balls are deposited as the main goal of play. There's hundreds of pool games. Eight ball, nine ball, Straight pool, one-pocket and bank pool, just to name a few. You see this pole? It's called a 'cue stick'."

I started stroking it attempting to hit the ball. "The goal of Eight ball, which is played with a full rack of fifteen balls and a cue ball (which is the white one) is to claim a suit. Commonly stripes or solids in the US, and red or yellow in the UK. Pocket all of them, then legally pocket the eight ball, while denying one's opponents opportunity to do the same with their suit, and without sinking the eight ball early by accident. I'm telling you the rules to be fair, if one day you choose to play me, I want to beat you fair and square." She laughs. "Ha, ha, ha. How do you know I don't already know how to play pool? Perhaps I will beat you, Daddy. Ever think about that?"

"Let's up the stakes a bit. Every ball I get in the hole, you will fucking strip for me. Every one that you hit, I'll strip for you. The one that has most of their clothes on has control and gets control. You have the power to decide the next move, and we do whatever the other wants, this is a great opportunity for you, to gain some great access."

She loved that idea. "Oh yes Daddy, this will be fun. I love it."

See, I told you she loved that idea. Honestly, I had no intentions on losing. Not this game nor the contest. I gave her one of my nicer cue sticks and spanked her on the ass. "Ladies first, do your worst!" She turned her head to me and shouted. "Hey!" I gave her one of my most wicked smiles, one I knew would make her melt. "Go ahead, hit that cue ball. Let's see which one goes in the hole, stripes or solids, that's the suit you will be choosing."

She leans forward against the table to get a better aim. She's cheating! How will I be able to concentrate with that pretty round ass staring right at me? Now, I'm not playing to just Dominate this game. No, I'm playing to win, by any means. She broke, damn, this woman has stroke. None of the balls go in though. "Oh well, my turn." I say. She moves closer to me. "No, no, no. Stay over there!" I laughed. I aim my cue stick at the cue ball and it meets with a solid six and that six ball goes in the corner pocket.

"Well, I guess I'm solids and you're stripes." I smirk at her. My next move, the cue ball grazes a solid red three and that shit didn't go too far where I wanted. Maybe I missed on purpose, to see what she has. "My turn!" Precious shouted out to me.

"Don't get loud in here. Just because we are engaging in this little vanilla (ordinary) game doesn't mean you get to forget my rules." "I'm sorry Daddy." She apologized immediately and then lowers her voice. "My turn." She whispers. I smile at her. The cue ball hits a striped fourteen then she gets a striped red eleven. Whoa, she was on a roll. Is she hustling a hustler? Is she hustling me? Perhaps she's better than she's leading on? She finally hit a ball that goes nowhere. I hit three solid balls in the pocket in a fucking row. There were nine balls that remained. Four solids and Five stripes. She took off as little as possible. I couldn't take much more off, shit I was already in a tank top when she came downstairs. I mean, she was down to her bra and lace panties already. She took them off slowly and seductively. I fucking took my eyes off the ball for a second to stare, and the cue ball just grazed a solid five that went absolutely nowhere. "Fuck." I said sharply. She hit one in the pocket after another. It was down to five balls. I had three solids and she had two stripes. Even if she gets all her balls in, she would still have to get my "balls" in AND pocket the eight ball. She pocketed all her balls but couldn't hit the eight. I grabbed her and ripped what little that was left clothing her.

"Hey Daddy, you're cheating," she murmurs as my strong, muscular, chocolate man hand goes around her

throat prior to my lips pressing against hers. I tell her,
"you were gonna lose anyways."

I kiss her on her neck, sending chills down her spine,
right before I grab a breast. She gasps. "I didn't want to
win anyways. You always win, my King." Her words were
broken up from the fervor. She couldn't speak, only feel.
I pick her up and lay her down on the pool table as I begin
to devour her pussy like it was my last meal. Tasting her
and enjoying the delicious elixir that came from the
heavens. I'm going to fuck her so deep and so aggressive
like I found magic in between her fucking thighs. I place
my large tip in position to hit her triangular image. I aim
on 'cue'. I then control where my balls go. Balls deep in
her hole, I 'stroke' and take my time to shoot. I'm going
to hit it hard and accurate. Back shots, no look shots,
missionary shots, hard, slow shots. Thumb down, my pool
stick sliding back and forth to hit her cue likes its double
penetration. My aim is on point. I'm an expert in finding
the hole whether it's in the light or dark. I am in complete
control of this game. Dick game is potent. I want to milk
her and there's no expiration date. I'm in complete and
'solid' control. Mind, body and intertwining of our souls.
The way she moans, I see her true 'stripes'. No fear, no
thoughts, just senses igniting. I rerack and I aim to break.
She's so fragile, so 'precious'. I want to ravage, devour,
slaughter, annihilate and conquer her. What choice does

she have but to just lay there and allow me to take and Dominate? Losing herself in my insanity, I witness her go crazy. She can't ever beat me, that's why she'd rather just join me. I'm going to get in that ass like a wedgie, yes bitch, I'm so nasty. So nasty, I pinned her legs back almost to the point where they were touching her chest. I held her legs in that position with my massive hands. My firm hand placed on the back of her thighs. I dove in head first into her pool of lust. Her lips were soaked before I could place my own lips on them. I ran my muscular tongue from her crack to her pussy.

I stare at her while I do this and her back attempts to arch off the sofa I had thrown her on, before I started to take and claim her over and over again. Her moans were sweet music to my ears. I tasted her and enjoyed the delicious nectar that was heaven sent, devouring her as if she was my last fucking meal. I needed her. I need her, not today, not tonight, I need her right now. I touch her everywhere, mind, body and soul. I taste her everywhere, then I fuck her like I found magic between her legs. I've ruined her. I own that pussy even when we are not engaged in physical activity. It's impossible to find someone to replace what I have already exposed her to. She is in constant need of my power, my strength, my muscle, my love, my pain, my pleasure, and my Dominance inside her. My touch enhancing oxytocin, increasing the serotonin and dopamine in her brain. The way my gaze just pierces through her soul when I stare into her fucking eyes. I inspired, sublimated and stimulated her self-esteem.

Slurping on her pussy while my arms and hands are wrapped tightly around her thighs, I take my huge chocolate cock and rub it against her smooth skin. Thrusting my big dick inside her dripping pussy walls, stretching her insides to accept my size. Big dick throbbing inside her, her clit vibrating and her pussy begging to release as I mold myself deeper and deeper inside her. She will feel hollow when I, yes I, am not around. She needs her pussy beat up. The best stress reliever, fuck Tylenol. I own what I own and when I take, I take completely. She's drunk off my love, this Henny thug passion. Back shots.

"Take all of me." I whisper softly. Then I begin to thrust roughly again. I pause abruptly. "let's take this upstairs. Leave your clothes down here, don't worry about them."

I take her hand and lead her into the master bathroom. I start the water running and we step in to shower. Water running down our bodies, I pin both her wrists to the wall, touching her, kissing her. I turn her around, yanking her head back towards me from the fist full of hair I had in between my fingers. I curled them inward and the lips on her face parted prior to the lips on her pussy. I shoved my big dick inside, sliding into those begging lips, into those craving walls of hers. Those walls that wrapped around my fat long chocolate dick so perfectly. Those walls where I could stare squarely at her and they perform miracles. Those same walls that as I thrust so deeply in them, blessing her cervix, has her pussy screaming, "Daddy!!!" Such wetness, it sounds as though children were smacking water, as though I was stirring mac and cheese, however, I told her to cum for me, and that's exactly what she did, and we came together.

We had a great shower and I said to her, "we have a lot of sex but I can't get you used to all this great sex because then you'll become dependent on it. You're becoming a bigdickaholic, you're adDickted. You will lose sight of what this is, forget who you are, who the fuck I am and who you are to me. It can change your behavior, your emotions and the way you normally rationalize things. Don't change!"

It was more like an order actually. "Don't ever lose focus on what your job entails, which is to make sure you focus on nothing but." She didn't spend the night. I had to be at work in the morning bright and early as did she. Let's be realistic, if we were together every night, it would make it difficult for us to get to work on time. I kissed her goodnight and she said, "I love you, Daddy." I told her, "get home and drive safe. Text me as soon as you get there." "Yes Daddy." She did what she was told. She hated getting in trouble with me. Once she arrived to her place, she did just as I instructed her which was to text me. 'Hi Daddy, I'm home safe and sound. I'm getting right to bed, and I will be wishing you a goodnight, better dreams and seeing you very soon.' I smirk and text back, 'goodnight, sweet, nasty, dirty, sexy dreams.'

Before she turned in, she noticed one of her pictures on her nightstand was moved. She has a very good memory, I could say like an elephant and has OCD. She's extremely organized and places things in specific spots where she will always remember where they are.

"Hmmm, that picture wasn't there last time I left from here. Maybe it's just been a long day and I'm just bugging." She let out a long, tired breath and then turned in for the night.
The next day she texts me.

'Good morning Daddy, I hope you have a really good day your highness.' I text her back. 'So, how did you sleep?' 'Not too well,' she replies. I text her swiftly, 'We will speak on that later, on why you didn't get your rest.' She was tossing and turning all night. I mean, she felt as if

there were a presence in the room with her. Her energy
was so off, and she could not put two and two together. I
was trying to work, I wasn't tied up at work because I'm
the one who does all the tying, but it was busy. I was
stuck closing deals left and right, so I couldn't give her all
my attention, but I was determined to find out why she
was unable to sleep properly last night. I text her. 'Let's
meet up tonight. We can have dinner and walk in the
park. It's gonna be really warm tonight. Wear my favorite
sundress!' She texts me back the first opportunity she
got. 'Yes Daddy.'

She gets out of work and texts me to let me know she's
heading home. She places her phone in her purse and she
thought she saw someone that looked familiar. He kept
staring at her from a distance, but he was too far for her
to make out his face clearly. When she reached for her
phone frantically and looked down, the man was gone.
She shrugged it off.

Later that night we met up, and we indulged in some
good food and some red wine and a nice walk in the park.
I saw a park bench. "Let's sit right here. We have plenty
to discuss." She sighed. "We don't have plenty to discuss,
I'm probably just imagining things or just off balance." I
was quiet and had my thumb and index finger on my chin.
"Hmmm, think about it Precious, you're not just about to

be off balance for no reason. See, it's the dick game. That shit got you all fucked up." She laughed. "No Daddy, I mean it is extremely good but that's not it."

She was so adamant about that it was something else. "You know what? When I take you home today I will scope out your place and make sure everything is up to standards." I didn't just drop her off, I went inside just to make sure nothing was out of the ordinary. Everything was fine. I kissed her goodnight and wished her a better night and a restful sleep. The next day she let me know she did in fact sleep well.

"Daddy's magic touch," she said. "Always making sure I'm safe, perhaps that's what I needed," she added.

She went to work and received some flowers. Roses. Red roses. One of the nurses brought it to her. "Hey, you have a delivery. There's no note in it either." She took the roses and said, "no note? You're so nosey, huh?" They both laugh. Precious insisted that they were from me. "They're probably from Daddy, but the crazy thing is Daddy doesn't do roses."

She said to one of the nurses. The nurse shrugged her shoulders and left the office. Precious didn't wait, she texted me right away, 'Thanks Daddy.' I replied. 'The fuck

are you thanking me for baby girl?' She replied two
minutes later. Pondering to herself, he's fucking with me.
He's trying to get me to say it to him. 'The roses you sent
me this morning to my job.' First thing I reply is, 'what
fucking man is fucking sending you damn roses because
you know it's not me. I do rope, not roses. I'm not that
sweet or nice!' She answers. 'Wait a minute, you didn't
send those? I kinda figured you didn't but then I thought
you were trying to surprise me. You tend to do that
often.' 'Yes but I have never been out of character at all.'
She agreed. I jump right back into my unanswered
question. 'So who the fuck is sending you roses?' She
replied. 'There's no note. I have no idea, and this is
getting really strange.' She looks outside her window and
a man is standing outside, staring at her. She looked away
for a split second and when she looked again, the man
was gone. She leaves her office.

"Listen, any calls for me today just take a message. I
have a family emergency." She called me immediately.
"Daddy, something weird is going on and I need you!"
She left me a voicemail. Once I finally heard it, I called her
back.

"What the fuck is going on?" I demanded an answer.
"And where are you?" She was taking in deep breaths.
"I'm in the parking lot in my car. I was waiting for you to

call back." "You were waiting for my call? You called thirty minutes ago!" She said, "yeah, and I'm the one who can't be on the phone with the type of job I have. Things are weird, first the picture then the roses..." I cut her off before she could forget or finish her sentence, she was so anxious, and she sounded as if she was shaking. "I'm coming to you." She cut me off. "No Daddy, I'll be fine." I was annoyed, "the fuck you will, I'm coming. You should've never told me this shit, then I wouldn't be coming, but I'm already on my way."

So I get there and walk up to her car. I get in with her and she's shaking like I've never seen her shake before, well she's shaken when I've fucked the soul outta her, but nothing like this. All I could do was hold her and ask, "tell me what's actually going on here?" I asked softly but sternly.

"I get these roses at work and then all of a sudden I see a man standing outside my window, but he was too far for me to see him clearly. I look away for like a second and then when I look back, he's gone!" I shook my head. "Are you sure? I mean it could've been the mailman or someone else."

No one is that fast, what's going on here? "I'm taking you home." I drove my car and she drove hers, but I told her to come to my place. "Leave your car at my place today and tonight. I'll bring you home." We arrived to her place, I say around 7:30pm. The window was open and there was a calm, cool breeze. We walk in and she noticed several things are moved, and the picture that was moved the very first time, is now on the floor. She lifts it up and the glass on the frame was shattered. The picture was fine, but the glass had been shattered.

"See what I mean?!? Things are moved around, this is broken!" She points to the frame with her picture. "The window is open though, maybe the breeze knocked the picture frame over baby girl." She rushes over to the window and then says to me, "I did not leave the window open!" I raised an eyebrow. "Hmmm, interesting. Okay, I'm not leaving you alone tonight. let's go back to my place." As she starts to attempt to put things back together. "Listen, I need to tell you something. I'm not saying it's so, but I should still tell you. I used to date this man and he was insane, like a psycho. Insecure, extremely jealous, a user and an abuser. He took six years of my life." I said to her, "guess you turn them crazy, huh?" I started laughing. "It's not funny Daddy!" I cuddled her closer. "Look, I've had women who were insane as well, not a big deal."

She cut me off. "This person whom I speak to you about was on a different level of crazy. He went to jail and I'm starting to think he's probably stalking me now." I scoffed. "No, can't be. Like you said, you 'think' he's out but you're not for certain."

She looks me in my eyes. "But what about all this?" As she gestures towards the broken picture frame, "and the flowers and all that?" I answered, "just means you might have a secret admirer. Could be anyone, like I said, the mailman, UPS guy, someone in the kitchen. Shit it can even be a woman. You are desired by both genders." She said to me, "no, I feel that it's him. My window was shut and locked. It's summer Daddy, I have the air condition on. None of the windows are opened." While she was talking I started rolling the blunt. I had the kush inside it.

"You're going to smoke some of this medicine here. This is some 'Discipline therapy'. You need to calm your nerves, and this is going to help with that. She took some pulls, yes, she was calm and lit. I took some strong pulls after her. "Listen, I'm going to think on this tomorrow, but I don't want you going in to work, so you won't. I won't go to work either. I have a pretty good plan and the plan is to bait out whomever you think is playing these games with you. We are going to play it better than them. In the meantime, get some rest. We will discuss more tomorrow. You have not had a goodnight's rest in a couple days. Tomorrow we plan, tomorrow we strategize, tomorrow we execute, and we get to the fucking bottom of this shit." She laid her head on my strong muscular chest, "goodnight Daddy."

The next day we both wake up, but I was up earlier than her making phone calls and planning. She got out of bed.

"Who was that, on the..." I stare at her. "Don't ever question me or interrupt me while I'm on the phone. If I want to tell you, you'll be alerted but other than that, when I'm on the phone...It's none of your business. In this case, it happens to actually be your business because it concerns you. I've made a couple of phone calls. I have my guys working on your place right now." She looked confused. "Working on my place? What do you mean by that?" I replied, "we will be placing security cameras in your place." She put her hands on her face. "No Daddy, it's not that serious." I took her hands, "yes, it is. Your safety is always priority." She smiles that beautiful smile. "Yeah, I bet you're loving this. Now you can check up on me with a click of a button." I laughed, "well, this is going to be for you. You can actually watch it on your smartphone. You will be watching and keeping me updated." She was surprised I was entrusting her with that type of empowerment.

"Listen, you're the one that knows how your place is set up, how you keep things and when things are switched around or moved from its place. You're going there as bait but don't worry, I'll be close by. Go there and plant your seeds. Move shit around, shut and lock them. Look, if you are wrong, you can see for yourself that you are wrong. If you're right, we will need to move forward accordingly, but we'll get there, if and when we do. As for now, go plant your seed. I'll be following you, watching your back to see if there is any weird going on. Keep me updated."

She nodded her head. "Yes Daddy." She said with a smile on her face and ready to do the damn thing. We each take our cars and I follow her from a distance. I remain parked outside, not by her place but a few houses over, so it doesn't look suspect at all. But I'm keeping an eye out just in case I see anything or anyone strange around or attempting to follow her. She arrives and goes inside. She does exactly as I've instructed her to do. She moved things around, locked windows etc. I then text her. 'When you leave your place, slam the door really firm.' She did as I said, no questions asked. Normally if someone is tailing you and you shut the door like I said to do, it's a statement, a nonverbal statement saying, 'I'm leaving and not coming back for some time.' She jumped into her car and drove off. I began to follow right after her. We got back to my place, where she would be staying for the time being.

She opened her phone to watch the security cameras I had set up at her place. Inside and out. She didn't witness any strange activity of people yet. She was watching that thing for thirty minutes to an hour. I was exhausted.

"I'm going to bed. Make sure you turn off my lights when your done finding nothing, because you were so paranoid." She pouted her lips at me. "Hey, I was not paranoid. I know something is off and I will get to the bottom of it." She was so damn determined. She was starting to get a little restless and wanted to doze off. Her eyes kept blinking. As soon as she was gonna shut them and shut the lights, she saw a body on her phone. The body of the person was moving in HER place. I guess you find shit when you're not looking for shit. She was on that phone watching forever and now that she was ready to turn in, she sees activity. She sees a person dressed in all black and a ski mask going through her stuff. She begins to wonder, 'How did he or she get in? Through my door, did they pick the lock? Through a window?' The man was going through her belongings, looking underneath her bed. What were they looking for? They're not there to take anything. Are they looking for someone? She pondered all these random thoughts that came to her mind while watching this person on the cameras through her smartphone. She wanted to alert me badly, however, it was a difficult decision for her to make at the moment. I was sleeping so peacefully, and she didn't want to be the one to disturb me so therefore, she did not wake me up. She let it go and went to bed.

The next morning, she woke up before me, sucked my dick and gave me a nice massage. "So, before I went to sleep last night, I was right all along. There is someone stalking me."

I cut her off. "Oh hell no! No one is allowed to stalk you but me! We are going to handle that shit real quick." She wasn't amused. "Uhh, I just said someone is stalking me! You must not have heard me, this is serious, and I can't even show you because you were sleeping, and I didn't want to wake you up." I told her to stop massaging me. "You can take a break, where is your phone Precious?"

She goes over to the nightstand where she left it and grabs it. She then hands it to over to me. "Here Daddy, take it." I took the phone from her hands. "There's playback on the security cameras babygirl." She was surprised, "really?" I smirk. "Yeah, I got your ass some top of the line shit." So then I demonstrated to her how to play back the footage. "You see, you play it back just like this. Go to the date, time, speed, slow motion, etc." Her mouth was opened in shock. "Oh, very nice to know!" I was looking at the video closely. "So Daddy, what are you thinking here?" I was quiet and just watching the damn security camera footage playback. I grab her by her damn throat with my massive, chocolate man hand.

"Are you fucking lying to me?" She was confused and trying to catch her breath. "Daddy, wait, what? What's going on here? Lying about what, I would never lie to you?" I then began to explain. "lying about not knowing who this guy is. Clearly, it's a guy, broad shoulders, body type. It's a man, unless it's a tranny, but this is a man and you know him. So no more lies."

I growled into her face. One hand remained on her throat the other with her phone. "I don't get it. I don't know this person you assume, and think is a man. And I'm not lying or playing games here." My grip got tighter but it was turning her on, therefore I let go.

"I don't think it's a man, I know, that's one. Secondly, he knows you and vice versa. If this was a random hit, why didn't they take shit? If I was going in your place, you have so many nice and fancy things. Why would I not take anything? Exactly." She then nodded her head, "Oh, that makes sense." My eyebrow rose up and I placed my index and thumb on my chin indicating I had a brilliant idea.

"I got it, we are going to set him up and you, you're gonna be the fucking bait!" She said loudly, "wait! What? I can't, I'm scared!" I nodded my head, "good, see pressure will make you perform better. Plus, I will be right behind or aside from you when you go in. You need to trust me. I got you. I have a plan, we need to figure out a way to bring cheese out, so we can catch the rat. Spread seeds out, to catch the bird. Draw out honey, so we can get the bee. You're that bait. We're going to use you because apparently this guy is not interested in anything else in your place but you. So once we bring him out, I'll take care of the rest. I will find out why he's here and what he wants. I'm bringing my pistol with me."

I had a suit on and I place my desert eagle magnum .44 in my back, between my pants. I tightened my belt to hold the pistol against my back. It was secure, and I had the safety on it.

"So here is the plan...you are going to waste time pretending you're doing shit. That will give him enough time to actually keep tabs on you. Apparently, he's following you, watching when you go into your place and out of it, so I assume he's probably seen me, therefore, if

I'm there, he's not going to ever come out." She nodded her head. "Yes Daddy, you are correct, good thinking." I then continue with what I wanted her to do. "So once you leave, that's when he's going to go into your house and plant whatever seeds he has so you know something is off. Eventually this guy is going to pop up on you, but he's either leaving clues or working you up to that point. But we'll catch him before he can reach that level." She went about doing what I told her to exactly how I told her to. She went in her place and fidgeted around for a fucking long time, then walks out of the house. She goes into her car and drives off. We meet up and I tell her to leave her car where we met up. Scratch that, we left it at my place.

We watch the phone and, bingo, he's at it again. As we're watching the security footage, I open my glove compartment and pull out a Smith and Wesson. I put the safety on.

"Here, take this with you. The safety is on, this is how you take it off." She shook her head, "I can't take this!" "You don't have to do shit, just hold it as a deterrent or what not. You're not going to pull the damn trigger, relax. It's for protection. Now the safety on my gun will be off. If shit goes down, I'm fucking shooting first and asking questions later, I don't give a fuck. Your safety is my number one priority. Let's fucking go!"

I pull off, speeding in my vehicle. We get to her place and I'm telling her to grab the pistol I gave her. She does just as I say. "Walk in there and pull the gun on the person and calmly ask him what they are doing there and what exactly do they want."

She walks in on him going through her drawers and closet. "Hold it right there. What are you doing here and what do you want?" He had no time to escape prior to our arrival. I parked a few houses away, so you wouldn't hear the car and we snuck in quietly. The element of surprise was totally on our side. He was dressed in all black from head to toe. He then answered her questions.

"I'm here to take back what is mine." His voice seemed very familiar to her. He rushes at her and they struggle, and all of a sudden he ends up with her gun, well actually my gun. The one I gave to her. I walk in and automatically panic. I think fast and act fast.

"Listen, whatever you want doesn't have to be with her. Take me." He had the pistol pointed at Precious, but when I spoke he turned and pointed it at me. Precious and I both had our hands on the back of our heads. Raising my arms made my suit jacket lift up a little and you could see the desert eagle I had tucked in the back of my waistband. I moved forward so Precious could see my back, but she didn't look at the gun. The trespasser then says to me sharply.

"This has nothing to do with you!" "Well actually, this has everything to do with me. This is my woman, and this is her place." He growled, "SHUT UP! I'm the one with the gun! Now be quiet!!" I remained quiet and he's going on about why he's here and what he actually wants. Precious slowly grabs my pistol out from my back and at that moment I knew I had to think quickly. I said, "Look, I know you said for me to be quiet, but I have one question. Why is the safety on your gun?" He stares at it, taking the safety off and I yell at Precious. "NOW!!" He pulls the trigger and it shoots out...nothing. Really, nothing? Yeah, there's no bullets in the clip. Precious shot him once in the fucking chest and he falls to the ground. She shoots him again and again and again. Four shots. I never gave her a loaded gun. I didn't trust her to pull the trigger, but she did. She pulled the trigger when she thought I was in danger.

She was still and didn't move, the gun still in her hand. She pulls off his ski mask and it's no other than her ex that she told me about. The one that was in jail.

"It's him." Her eyes open wide and her mouth remained wide open. "My ex I told you about." I stare at her. She was shaking, the gun still in her hand. I slowly touch her hand and reach for the pistol. "Precious, let go of the gun. Give it to me, slowly." She finally let it go. She was shaking like a leaf. "I couldn't let him kill you! I did the right thing, right Daddy? I couldn't let him kill you."

She kept repeating that over and over again. "I'm going to protect you, I grabbed her, so she could feel me and stop talking. "Listen carefully and do exactly as I fucking say. Just in case someone followed him or knows where he's going or even knows that he left, you don't know shit. Understand? Take your clothes off." She questions me. "What?" She must still be in shock, she NEVER questions me. I say to her, "Strip, or I will rip them off you." She took off her clothes and I took my suit off and gave it to her. "Here, cover yourself with this. Take my keys. Drive to my place. If you get stopped by police or anyone, you're getting off work and you're tired, exhausted and you're just trying to make it home. Wait for me there, DO NOT answer any strange numbers or calls, matter of fact, do not answer ANYONE'S call unless it's mine. Do you understand me?" She nods her head. "You want me to lie Daddy?" I nodded, "Yes, I want you to lie to protect yourself so I can protect you. Now go.

GO, GO, GO NOW!!" I reiterated. She turns to leave and I stop her. "When you walk out of here, do not run. You do not want to draw attention to yourself, at all."

Good thing is, I had a silencer on my desert eagle so you could hardly hear it when it let off. I made some phone calls and I had a guy come immediately to get rid of the body and have her place cleaned thoroughly. I got dropped off at my place. I walk up to her, she's on the bed still wearing my suit and shaking.

"Take the suit off now!" She did just that. "Everything is taken care of just a few more things I have to take care of. I have to burn this suit..." She cut me off. "Daddy, that's one of your favorite suits." I became angry. "So, who cares? I'll get a new one, I need to burn this one just as I burned the clothes you took off and gave to me. Take off the rest of your clothes, bra, panties, etc. I'm burning all of them. You were in a struggle and his DNA is probably all over you. You have to go shower. I want you to shower three times. Soap yourself up over and over again. Wash your hands over and over. Take a toothbrush and clean under your fingernails with alcohol. Do it and do it again, repeatedly. Shampoo your hair like three time. Don't come out until you feel you've rinsed every last stain off of you."

She finally comes out from showering and I cuddle her in bed. I wasn't leaving her side tonight. "Daddy, I need to ask... you know what, forget it." I stroked her hair gently. "No need to ask. It's taken care of. It's not like I'm keeping a secret from you or lying. It's just the less you know, the less you can say in court if that was ever the case but it won't be." She cuddled closer to me, laying her head on my muscular chest. "Daddy, I'll do anything for you, even lie in front of anyone for you."

Damn, this woman was way too good for me. How do I deserve this type of goodness in my life? She was too good to me. "Tomorrow you will go to work. I was going to say take the day off, but you should go in. Don't talk to anyone. Smile and if there are any conversations that will emerge, cut it short. Make it your business to show you are there to work, not socialize...Anyone asks where you were yesterday, you were not home. You were with me and you spent the night. I don't want you going back to your place until I know my people had your place cleaned, wiped down and I know it's safe for you to go back there. Make sure your stories remain consistent and if you tell one soul something, make sure every soul you tell has the same exact story you told the one prior to them. Sleep well, sleep tight. Daddy has everything under control." She didn't ask, she just obeyed. She saved my life, I'm going to save her.

I had her go to her place with supervision from security that I am close with to go get some clothes, at least some of it for the time being. She was going to stay with me until the place was properly cleaned and lay low until all the craziness was done. "Daddy, I believe this is OD (overdoing it). There's no need to do all of this." I cut her off. "First, I do what I want. Second, when it comes to your health and your safety, I take that shit serious. Shut up and let me do what I do.

Chapter 13: She Finds Peace In My Chaos

She was compliant. "Yes Daddy. Thank you, my King." Loyalty is everything to me. I don't ask or beg for this, I fucking demand it. I deserve it. I will give what is given to me. I will protect her if it's my last breath. I don't give a fuck what she says or does, she's not my boss and I do not answer to her. When she came to me, beautiful and strong, I made her weak. When she came to me weak, helpless and uncertain, I made her strong. Love is free, if you treat it wrong, somehow you always pay the damn price. Trust is expensive, not everyone can afford it. Devotion isn't taken, nor is submission. Understanding isn't forced. In the end when her mind has traveled to places it's never been. When her soul is obtained by me at the point of no actual return, when she feels nothing of her former self, when her body is begging to be held, when her pussy is throbbing and begging to be fucked and filled by me, I take and she gives because she ultimately feels complete and happy when I am happy. However, in this moment, this has nothing to do with me and all to do with her and what she needs. Quite frankly, I had one hell of a crazy lifestyle but 'She finds peace in my chaos.'

I grabbed her by her throat with my immensely huge, muscular hand. I squeezed the flesh around it. I then began to ask her a question I already knew the answer to. "What would you do for me? What would you give me?" She released a gasp of air prior to her reply.

"I would do ANYTHING for you." She then answered my second question without taking a pause. "I would give you my life." Shit, that's intense right? Not really, you see, a regular man would never understand. A weak man is not built, nor will he ever be built to love a very strong woman. Man, she made my dick so fucking hard. My hand still remained around her throat.

"How much do you crave to have me inside you right now?" I asked her while I kept a firm hold on her neck. "How much do you crave my big, thick, chocolate cock inside you right now?" I believe she needed a big release and so do I. I brought out the toys. "Stay right there." I commanded her. I brought out the rope and tied loops from her wrists anchoring her hands close to the bed posts, however, instead of having her on her back, I told her to get on her knees. She was in the doggy position on the bed. Each wrist was bound to rope and connected to each bedpost. I brought out my thick paddle and began spanking her.

"Do you remember what your safe word is?" Band aid was always her safe word. She answers me. "I have no desire to use my safe word Master. Do as you wish with me. Take me for your pleasure and your pleasure only." I spanked her again, this time more savagely, more viciously and with less remorse. I spanked her again and again and again. Every spank left her with a release and a huge gasp of air. The redder her ass got, the harder my big dick became. I untied one side and retied with the other side. Now I had her on her back staring at the ceiling. I held her ankles with my massive chocolate man hands. I knew what type of trouble I was going to cause her body and I wanted no sudden movements and no running. I didn't need to tell her this, she had no desire to run from me, and honestly, she has been properly trained, to the point where rope was no longer needed or necessary. However, rope was something that I thought was always fun and she loved to be overwhelmed. To feel helpless and feel scared. I tantalized her with my darkest desires. I took the flogger. I ran it down her neck, then her luscious breasts. She was going to just lay there, and I was going to do whatever the fuck I wanted.

The flogger went from her neck to her breasts to her clit. I placed the blindfold on her, over those pretty eyes. I pressed my full lips upon hers and I pressed against them firmly. I bit her bottom lip and tugged it aggressively towards me. I then placed my tongue inside her mouth and my tongue explored the depths of it. My tongue

Dominated her mouth and her tongue as well. I ran my strong, muscular fingers up and down her body, tracing every curve with my hands. I attacked her nipples, pinching them. I slapped the right breast ferociously (her left, my right). I then slapped the left breast (her right, my left). I mean, I couldn't just do one, the other would get jealous. I placed her breast inside my wanting mouth and began to tug roughly on her nipple. She let out a pleasured moan. I tugged then released, tugged on the nipple once again, then released. I loved teasing her. She was biting her bottom lip, her eyes rolling in the back of her head. I created a circular motion with my tongue around her stiff, erect nipples as I sucked on them hungrily. Clockwise then counterclockwise. Her breathing began to change as her lips parted. No sound came out of her mouth except, "Oh fuck Daddy."

I slowly ran my tongue down to her navel and even further down as it finds her clit. I flick my tongue up and down on it. Her submissive, drenched and begging pussy lips part. My tongue splits her wide open slowly, building her up before I devour her completely and take her soul. My tongue deep inside her drenched hole, movements like the ocean waves, side to side. I control the ride, her back attempts to lift up off the mattress just so she could arch her back. I sense it but she remembers, she's to make no sudden movements. She's flooded, her moans and cries are loud. Her legs begin to tremble and I make it worse as I start to speed it up. Her breathing is labored, and she realizes an orgasm is much closer than she anticipated. She's begging, "please, please, please." I wanted her to say it. "Please what?" The last gasp of air and then, "Daddy may I cum, please??" There she goes. "Go ahead and cum for me, cum and drip all over the sheets!" And that she did, right on command. That she fucking did.

My callousness calms her soul, my ruthless aggression moves her body. My Dominance places her mental at ease.

"Precious, these powerful hands will always hurt you, always heal you. Always guide you and Discipline you. Always punish, slap, spank, control, manhandle you. Always change you but ultimately protect you. When there is a hint of fear and desire, that is when true pleasure begins." She asked if she can ask me a question. I raise an eyebrow.

"Indeed, you may." She says, "would you rather be feared or loved?" I smirk. "Well which one? You asked two questions. Two of the same actually but worded them differently." She lets out a sigh. "Man Daddy, do you have to be so difficult?" I then smirk at her once again. "Well, difficult is my cup of tea." She shook her head. "Okay, so which would you rather have? Loved or feared?"

I placed my hand under my chin as my thumb and index finger hug my jaw. "I would rather be feared!!" I said sharply. "To be honest with you Precious, I wish I can have both, but fear, well it lasts longer, and I'll elaborate.... Fear lasts longer than love and respect sometimes. For example, you love me, but allow me to piss you off to your core, how do your friends who've never met me think of me? How much respect or love do your friends, family, coworkers, even you yourself have for me then?" I asked her a rhetorical question. Then I asked her another.... "Would you forget who you are? To my face, behind my back? Fear is when your friends remain close to you because of the power you have over other people. They kind of feel empowered themselves. The power you have, whether it's other women, money, the way people bow to your will physically or emotionally. When you snap a wack joke but people laugh, when you, yourself know you're not that funny.

She gazed. "Am I going to get in trouble for asking this?" I laughed. "No." I laugh again, she had fear in her eyes. My point exactly. "Chill babygirl, we are engaging in vanilla (regular) conversation." She was relieved. I then continued, "but don't ever interrupt me again." She apologizes. "I'm sorry my King." I then continue.

"When someone speaks behind your back but shake your hand or remain silent when you walk past, that is fear. All that is associated with fear. Love is fucking great, I swear you this, but fear lasts longer. Fear keeps things in line, it is a constant reminder that nothing and no one will be left unhandled. You may have a boss you're cool with, however, there is still a level of fear there. You may kiss his ass more because he is your boss. Not you Precious, we're speaking hypothetical here." She nodded her head.

"So fear lasts longer. I fear you Daddy, but I love you as well, so you do have both." I smiled to myself, I mean she's right. I do have both. "But it's that fear in the back of your mind that allows you to never really lose control." She then said, "but the love I have for you is to never care to have control, so therefore, do I really have fear if my love outweighs that?"

I did not answer her question, as a matter of fact I did what I do best and that's change the subject.

"How are you fucking flipping the question you asked ME to answer?" She began to laugh, and I shook my head. She paused then said, "I'm not getting in trouble for that am I?" She asked this twice, as if she loved and wanted to be punished. She hates to be punished so she does what she needs to do all the time, so she won't be. Shit, I don't care how much Precious says she loves me, the level of fear definitely outweighs the love.

I didn't answer her question. I let her think about that one, but no, I wasn't going to punish her. I told her prior to me grabbing that ass firmly. "Be less afraid of the monsters you run from and more afraid of the ones you run to." Shit got real serious. "I am the worst, most dangerous but precious thing to ever have. You will always fear me because you respect the way I Dominate, the way I handle you. You respect my character, my principles. I want you to always be safe but never comfortable. I will always overwhelm you, leave you helpless. The helplessness turns you on, the fear in your eyes trigger my voracious appetite and gets my big, fat, long, chocolate dick rock fucking hard." I was horny just speaking to her about all that. I ripped her clothes off and took her over and over and over once again, shoving my massive cock between those drenched pussy lips. Roughly Dominating her submissive hole. Her wall close in around me and I say in her ear...

"No, no, no open that pussy up for Daddy. Let go of that dick and you will not clench until I say so, because I say so." She opened up that pussy so quickly, she was so wet. I had her wetter before but this time she was wetter than she has ever been with me. That pussy belongs to me and I will show her why....I was in and on that pussy and I showed her exactly why I owned it.

Chapter 14: Her Dominant, His Submissive

"A true sub is not created in pages of fiction, by dressing up, role playing, calling her man 'Daddy' or just after sex. She is born or is revealed by a true Dom, what was hidden within already. A true Dom isn't created or made by you or social media. You can't turn a vanilla man into a Dominant. He is fucking born baby girl."

She nodded her head at me, so attentive and she didn't take her fucking eyes off me nor did she fucking blink.

"I found you for a reason. My soul found you and when you came to me the second time unknowingly, your soul had to come back to that powerful energy it was blessed in." She knew I was on point. She could not deny that at all. I continued to guide and educate her.

"Our relationship will never change, why? Because of who I am and you've made the choice to be with me. And part of being with me is not changing me. I mean if I 'change', you wouldn't get a 'penny'. We will never link vanilla and BDSM together. It will never work. When I met you the first time, why do you think I didn't engage physically with you from the jump?" She had no clue. She shrugged her shoulders. "I told you back then, if I fucked you that you would be fucked up. If I made love to you, your soul would be forever bound to me. My words touched your pineal gland and you would follow me anywhere. If I kissed your lustful, begging lips, you would do anything, be anything that I wanted. You were a brat and what did I call you? Intellectual snob?" She smiled and nodded her head. "Yes, you called me that." I then continued. "You were that and more because your walls were crazy high, you needed Discipline, guidance and quite frankly, good dick in your life. But you never received nothing until you proved you were worth something. I would then eradicate those brat tendencies you had. I mean let's be honest, you were in control until I came along, and no other man will know you as I know you. You want to know why? Because your stubborn ass will not let them."

She smiled because she knew I was absolutely correct. I put the music on and told her, "I'm destroying you to every song so that when you hear them and I'm not around, all you do is think about me."

I took her by the hair and yanked her head back towards me. I then shoved her body onto the sofa. The music playing so loud. Face down and her ass up. I placed my hand on her head to shove her face in the soft seats, while my massive cock was inside her, fixing her organs well. I leaned in towards her earlobe and whispered forcefully in her ear.

"Stay right there and take all this dick whore...Take it like the worthless slut you want to be for me. Now scream bitch, scream! Scream for your owner whore!!" I was working her like a shift, orgasm after orgasm, like a gift. She came so many times she won't be able to feel her legs when I'm through with her. I will leave her a dripping mess. Pussy so wet as I thrust, sounds like kids smacking water. It sounds like I was stirring macaroni and cheese. Her pussy was so wet, when I'm inside her I feel as though she cleanses my sins. She blesses my soul in her pool of lust. I spread her open with my thick, monstrous cock. She creams on my dick and doesn't stop. Oxytocin and dopamine releases from her brain. Euphoric experience, her walls are no longer the same.

"Cum for me my whore, cum for me my slut. Cum for me my Queen, cum for me my bitch, cum for me my prize, cum for me my doll, cum for me my Submissive!"

I commanded it, what choice does she have? No choice but to do as I say, which was to cum. Cum for me, her beast, her Alpha, her sadist, her top, her master, her Dominant. To submit to me was in her blood. To kneel before me was in her soul. To call me Daddy and King was in her heart. There was a nerve in my heart that only responds to the nerve of her submission. There were parts of her completely untouched until I came along and left my mark on every fucking single inch of her. Her Dominant, his submissive. I have never met a bond so powerful and stronger than these two dynamics together. Not a sexual, emotional, passionate and intense connection or bond stronger than these two. She is such a savage, but to me, she is very meek. If she is a bitch, then I am an animal. She cries, moans, whines and supplicates to me, to allow her to climax. I am her Daddy, I am her Dom.

She is a Queen only a true King could handle and tame. A body only a beast can satisfy. A mind only a Master can penetrate. Pain only a sadist can give. She loves to hurt for me. She loves giving me her suffering. She requires my animal, but I warn her, he's twisted like a Rubik's cube. I feed the masochist in her. This love of ours is not normal. It's dangerous, it's deviant. It's potent, it's sadistic, it's pleasurable, it's amazing. It's painful, it's tender, it's sweet, it's mean, it's round for round, pound for pound. It's thug passion, it's gangsta loving. It's aggressive, It's Dominant and it's submissive. It's Bondage, it's Discipline. It's Sadism. It's masochism. All this fancy talk and nice things do not mean a thing when I'm tearing that ass up, working her gears like a shift. She gives me all her earth shattering orgasms and they all belong to me. Every last one of them. Her anger, her pain, her marks and bruises, her insane, her wetness, her cries, her tears, her joys, her sadness, her arousal, her thoughts, her words, her flesh, her soul, her submission, MY control.

The next day she went back to her office. There was one of the nurses that she felt close with. She was one of her friends. This woman asked her, "so, Discipline, can I call him that?" And Precious nodded her head, 'yes.' The friend then continued, "so what is your relationship with him? You always tell me everything, but I hardly know about this new guy. Damn, you changed your nail color I see, blue is not even your favorite color! Is the dick that good girl? You do things for this man, you hardly do for

others? He has a couple more subs, right?" Precious
answers, "yes, I told you that." Her friend shakes her
head.

"Yo, I could never do that! I'm greedy. I like all the
attention." Precious then said to her, "him and I spend
more time than he does with the others, and it's not
about begging for attention constantly. It's not about
being selfish and greedy. It's about doing your job. It's
about giving, it's about respect, and trust." Her friend
laughs, "so he's like your boss now? Haha, sorry, but,
what is he to you and vice versa?" Precious replies, "I am
his submissive, and he is my Dominant." Her friend just
doesn't understand it. "I would love to see how you two
act towards each other. That's crazy. This man has you
doing shit you never done. This man has so much control
over you, and it's crazy. Do you love Him?" Precious
nodded, "yes.' "I love him, more than I've ever loved any
man in my life, and I won't find another love like his, ever
again. He is my Dominant, and I am his submissive."
Precious' friend was quiet. But only for a second.

"Look, I found a Dominant months back, but he didn't
seem legit." She'd only wanted to experience the kind of
pleasure she'd read about—the kind she wanted to write
about, the kind that came from submitting yourself
completely to someone else's control. So she'd found a
willing Dominant online last year, sometime around June,
she told Precious. Had made all kinds of dark promises in
his emails—restraints and punishments, things so taboo
that she'd blushed like a middle-schooler. She'd naively

assumed that it was all part of the game, that the romance would come later. Dumb, dumb, dumb. Real life was nothing like a romance fairytale.

The smooth, unrelenting steel of the bench beneath her back. Her wrists and ankles bound with hard metal cuffs that cut off her circulation and chafed when she struggled. The gag that almost choked her. The overpowering fear, the anxiety she felt. Precious then interrupted.

"There was no consent with you two. You both just rushed into it, because, he wanted to Dominate you. And you wanted and craved to be fucking Dominated. Rushing before you trust a man you're giving control of your life, mind, body and soul can be dangerous. Safe, sane and consensual. I mean you must be willing to give to receive. But, if your heart is not into it, you won't be. Your body and mind is where your heart is."

Her friend cut her off. "Oh wow, so much I don't know, looks like your 'Dom,' is training you very well. "Look, what you need to know is, if a man is claiming he's Dominant, two things he won't do; he won't rush you into sex and he won't beg or ask you for anything. When Daddy and I met, we met at a library. I was reading my book, and he walked up to me. As confident as can be. But, I didn't look directly at him. I felt his energy. He had swag girl. He was a smooth talker as well. He approached me and said, 'hello there miss, what's that like?' And I answered him with my eyes in my book. Yes, it was disrespectful, but, he made me pay for it later on. I mean, guys come up to me all the time. They talk much, show nothing. Talk a big game, but back up shit. I had my guards up. I said, 'what's what like?' He answered, 'what's that mind like?' How many guys will see a sexy and attractive woman, but ask about their mind? It's almost too good to be true huh? I throw as much rebuttals and objections as much as I can. He ate them. I throw him so many curve balls, and he damn hit them out of the damn park. If he was a regular man, he would have just walked away. But, he took the time to get to know me. I didn't know if I would see this man again. We didn't exchange numbers."

Her friend cut her off. "Yeah, then later that week, we saw him at the club. What a damn coincidence huh?" Precious then said, "no, Daddy does not believe in coincidences. We were supposed to see each other again. He knew I was his, before I did. When two souls are meant to connect; location, timing and circumstances are irrelevant. They are a magnet for one another and despite their efforts to fight it, the universe somehow manipulates it all in their favor and in that moment when they finally give in, a new love is born. You'll never truly please a woman until you have surfaced the deepest parts of her mind. When the mind and soul connect, the body just follows. Wise souls speak in silence. Plenty of times, when souls connect you can feel it from across the room. You can tell what the other is thinking, without words exchanging. Love harder than any pain you ever felt. The key to growth is the introduction of higher dimension of consciousness into our awareness. Once someone is attracted to your mind, they find beauty in everything you do. It's not sex that provides the pleasure, it's the lover. I mean, I've changed lives of a few and enticed minds, thoughts, and existences of thousands forever. Even those that were uncertain, feared, doubted. Water your mind, to grow your soul. If I could give anyone advice, it would be to mold your spirit. Your spirit is forever, even when you die. Mold your spirit, your mind and body will follow."

Precious' friend, and nurse said, "wow, that's some deep shit." Precious said, "that's Daddy rubbing off on me. No woman will ever love a man she cannot learn from, and he's taught me a lot. When you have love and great sex, that's so powerful." She said.

I mean, women will always talk, it's how they talk behind your back. I mean, if she's not sub to your face, behind your back at all times, she is not sub. She is pretending, and she does not deserve to have one. Loyalty is everything to me. I don't ask for this. I don't beg for this. I don't crave this, I fucking demand this. I deserve this. This is automatic. I don't believe in half submission. Plenty men talk, but never back it up. Plenty of women talk, but never deliver. This isn't something you learn on the internet. In chat rooms, nor in school, and you don't get a late start. Dominance is to submission as peanut butter is to jelly. As yin is to yan. One cannot crave to be Dominated and not Disciplined. One cannot crave Discipline and not Dominance. One cannot offer their soul and not their body and mind. One cannot offer their body and not their mind and soul. One cannot offer their mind, and not their body or soul. Well, one can, but with me if one is unwilling to give me all of her, I will gladly take and provide nothing.

Cultivation of a unity of a man and woman. The biggest myth pertaining to this lifestyle is, one must be weak in order for the relationship to be successful. What they fail to realize is, they both strengthen each other. What's a Dominant without a submissive? What's a Slave without a Master? What's a Queen without a King? What's an Emperor without an Empress? What's a God without a Goddess? What's a Daddy without a Little? What's a Sadist without a Masochist? What's a kitten without an Alpha? What's a pet without a Beast? What's a DaddyDom without a BabyGirl? What's a nice body without a beautiful brain? What's a vehicle without an engine valves and pistons? What's a writer without his/her pen? What's a sculptor without clay? What's a dream without hard work, and passion? What's a plan, without action? What's a world, without people? What is sex without a little pain? What is a connection without conversation? What is balance without structure? What is structure without stability? What is order, if there's no Discipline or control? What is time, when it's really non-existent?

She's harder than Chinese algebra. She's tougher than the concrete. I have this power over her, a look, my deep voice, a touch, a gesture, could make her freeze. Quiet her busy thoughts. Smoldering desires within her soul. Inch by inch, I kissed every curve on her body. I kissed her insecurities, doubts, and fears away. There's more to pleasing a man, than what is between your legs, or mouth. One of the biggest misconceptions when it pertains to a relationship is, the man is required to do all the spoiling. What generation are we in? I know I'm young, but back in the 50's, those where the epitome of real women. They cooked, cleaned, catered, served and they knew their place. When she cooks you lunch or dinner for you to take to work. When she meets you somewhere or comes to your business, to give you food. Or when she cooks for you, and she brings you your plate, and she doesn't eat until you eat first. I mean, even the carnivorous felines in the jungle, understand this concept, as a group of lionesses do most of the hunting, and they don't even eat first. They wait for the Alpha Dominant Lions to take that first bite.

Now, back to human beings.... That's not something you teach a woman. That's not something you learn in school. One does not create a submissive, a Dominant just reveals what's already inside of her. Take her natural tendencies, and mold that into something greater. Elevate the Queen in her, she will strengthen the king in you. Plenty of women are afraid to tell her significant other their desires. Their friends their desires. Why? I'll tell you, the judgment and resentment they experience. But, just because you love this, life, that vanilla(regular) people would call, 'crazy, weird, sick, etc,' that we call normal doesn't mean they are right. Most vanilla, are stressed, paranoid and go through all this uncertainty because they

do not have that closeness with their partner. They do
end up being dishonest, distrusting, keeping secrets. What
men don't understand, when a woman can't release, it's
because she does not trust. When she can gush, hold
secrets, lie, etc it is because she does not trust. Her
desires are confined because of it. A man's desires are
confined, when he has no respect for you. Love and sex is
a powerful thing. The ones that engage in this lifestyle
24/7 are just a bunch of intense, passionate individuals.
Whom require a connection so deep it transcends the
parameters of what a basic traditional relationship has to
offer. We love hard, we fuck hard. I Discipline hard, I
punish hard. Bdsm is not associated with inadequate
development and it induces strong emotions. You are
changed mind, body and soul are changed forever. The
deepest connection possible. The strongest sexual,
emotional, psychological bond I have ever witnessed in a
Dom/sub. Master/Slave. Top/Bottom. Daddy/Little one.
DaddyDom/Baby girl. King/Queen, and I'll even throw
Sadist/Masochist in there as long as I have lived. There's
no way you could have a friends with benefits
relationship. This lifestyle and relationship is the truest
form of unity between a man and a woman. And if you
had a man or husband, coming into this relationship, this
relationship is so intense, it would cause you to resent
your man or husband subconsciously. Why? You lost
respect for him. Women only respect real men. Men
whom can Dominate them, whether that be physical,
psychological or emotional. Men only trust women that
respect them and give their all to them. We are natural

born hunters and we pride on ownership. And women thrive on being owned.

I spoke to her softly, but forceful. "I knew that once I've had my hands on you. Once I've had you. Once you've been controlled by a powerful Chocolate King. I'll have you looking at vanilla(regular, boring, ordinary) men like, 'eww.'And you will never think it's a real relationship. I knew you were mine before you did. I knew if I can touch you once, you would do anything. I knew if I could press my lips against yours once, you would be everything. A nice guy will tell you you're beautiful. You're sexy. That they want you so bad. But only a King, a Dominant, a Master will show you, and make you believe it. You will feel like a real woman. My masculinity will inspire your femininity. And I will kiss, slap, bite, spank, throttle, choke, thrust, penetrate, verbally abuse, dominate, devour, claim, hurt, punish (if need be) and ultimately love you savagely. Brutally, indecently, inhumanly, ruthlessly, viciously, wildly, ferociously, insanely, madly, maniacally, atrociously, barbarically, barbarously, brutishly, callously, demoniacally, diabolically, ferociously, fiercely, hardheartedly, heartlessly, inhumanly, meanly(I don't know if that's even a word, but it is now), mercilessly, relentlessly, remorselessly, ruthlessly, like a pit bull, monstrous, no holds barred, passionately, riotously, roughly, painfully, powerfully, immorally, maliciously, sharply, energetically, frantically, and fucking angrily. No matter how I love you, you will feel that shit in every cell in your being. Every vein and your core. You will feel it in your mind, as well as your body and soul. For as long as you live, you will never get a kind of love like this ever again."

I loved to use her, and she loved being used by me. I kissed her on her lips. Do you think kissing is overrated? An erotic kiss is always how it begins. The right type of kiss and touch, can arouse her body and render it fucking weak. It can make her drip, surrender her legs, have them spread wide open. And now her other lips are throbbing and dripping for you. Never underestimate the potential of a well-deserved kiss. She believed she was made for me. Born and brought into this world, and into this life just to love me, and be loved by me. The only things in this world that made sense to her were my presence. My touch. My words. My teachings. My understanding. She could talk to one hundred people a day, but nothing compared to the smile I put on her face, in just a second. She would always remain bound to me, bound by me. No matter what. Whether it was with my strength. My Dominance. My words. My spirit. My rope, or my invisible rope. Whether it was physical, psychological or emotional she would forever remain bound to me. The greatest gift a woman can give a man is the gift of submission, the most prestigious thing a woman can obtain from a man is the gift of Dominance. She gives me her most precious gift of all her submission, and she is granted the most prestigious gift in the fucking world...MY DOMINANCE. Her Dominant, His Submissive.

Chapter 15: My Control Becomes Her Escape, Her Desire Becomes Her Surrender

She was finally ready to leave my place and now start spending time at hers, but there was a catch. I would have her under surveillance like 24/7 for her own protection.

"Listen this is how it's going to be until I know shit is really in order and up to par." She smiled. "I love being around you, you're my escape, my stress reliever. I will always look to you for guidance, you are my teacher. You have taught me so much already and have helped me accept who I am, and the mistakes I've made prior to you. I hit the jackpot when I met you! You are definitely one in a million, with everything that you are. I am in love and I love you, how you live, what you are, the things that you do. You are just incredible, and I am so lucky to have you. I am grateful that you are in my life. I am an Alpha and always need to make all the decisions, whether that's at work, with friends, family but with you, I never need to worry about that. You do everything, and it takes a big weight off my shoulders. Everything about you is my desire. One look from you, and that is all I need to be turned on, to freeze in my tracks, no one has ever had the control you have over me, ever!" She reiterated.

"There is no need to physically touch me with your hands. You can just disarm me with poetic words, and whisper across my heated flesh. Your words resonate in my mind. You feed my soul, while making me crave more. The power you have, you are my Dominant."

She touched my heart with that, such prize from a proud and stubborn woman. Yes, she is a boss in her own right, but submissive to her King, me! No matter if she was cuffed and bound, gagged and collared. Curves that beg for freedom, that they don't want. And the eyes that roll up every time I play with her with my fingers. My little sinful prisoner. I used, 'prisoner,' but she has no desire to be released, it is ironic huh? But who is she? She is my lady, she aches to please me, she begs to serve me. She yearns to worship me. She is my slut, my baby girl, my fuck toy, my love, my property, her heart beats for me, her soul longs for my possession, she was born for me. She was made for me. She is my submissive, not your submissive, not submissive to the world, not the world's submissive, she is in my world, she is my submissive. She then continued....

"I find myself in another world, a more beautiful world when I am with you. I was in control, until you came along, now I learn that not being in control, is the sexiest thing in the world. Not being in control, ironically is freedom. My desire to love you, please you, pleasure you, cry for you, hurt for you, be tortured for you, kneel for you, kill for you, win for you, live for you and if I have to, I'll die for you."

I cut her off. "Hold on, let's not be so drastic. Let's not speak like that." "Well I mean I pretty much would give and do anything for you Daddy. You're my King, my Master, my most powerful Dominant." I grabbed her. I then said to her, and spoke to her forcefully, but soft...

"Restraints mean shit. It is my words, that hold your mind captive. It is my guidance and commands that bind your body. It is my Dominance and assertion that ensnares your soul." The man that always keeps his cool, while making his women hot. Discipline. Talking shit is an art, now backing it up is a gift. Rope is unnecessary at this point. She has been properly trained to keep her hands exactly where I tell her. Average women should flex with average men. Because people who are not regular, vanilla, or ordinary do not mesh with regular people. Mediocrity craves mediocrity. Phenomenal will always crave phenomenal.

I must control her. Vibrating panties or vibrating toy with the controller in my hand, butt plugs or beads in public, or when she's out with friends, etc. And she won't take it off unless I say so. Because, I say so or I'll starve her. There will be no thick, long chocolate for a week. I won't speak to her as punishment, that's what she likes. I will punish her to obtain better behavior. I thrive to provide Discipline, not punishment. For I always want them to be good. That is what I prefer. Good girls will always be rewarded. Only complete obedience will be appreciated. I do not need props to control her. I do not need threats to control her. She's smart enough to know that I mean what I say, and I say what I mean. I spoke forcefully, yet soft...

"Honestly, I will not give you shit. Only the things you've earned and worked for. Your absolute silence, I am content with for the moment. Now, I properly trained you to fully understand to keep your body, exactly where I say. Moving forward, rope may not be necessary, as you will be fully trained. I am completely capable of handling you with my physical strength, I am that strong. However, rope is just fun and what I love. As you comply face down and ass up, you squirm in anticipated pain and pleasure as you hear the distinct sound as I work the zipper downward, ready to push my chocolate thickness and girth to an unimaginable depth as your dripping wet kitty receives me."

I then pound her flesh, stimulating her erogenous zones as she gushes uncontrollably with ecstasy. I am going to punish her for that, as she forgot to ask for my permission. This rhythm of mine is a deep, vicious, shallow, hard, gentle, slow, fast stroke of a dance that drives her to her madness. She loses herself in my insanity yet finds peace in my chaos. Succumbing to the pleasures of calculated, methodical and meticulous pelvis thrust by me, and roving hands all over her body.

She is pulled, teased, kissed, fucked, loved, destroyed, marked, slapped, man handled, spread apart as if she were being Dominated by multiple lovers at the same time. She's transported to a time and place, out of this world, where the slapping of flesh and wet sounds of our bodies joining, primal grunts and moans are echoed loudly into our stimulated psyche. Massive chocolate man hands reassure her as they grasp her throat firmly. Leave hand print marks on her ass cheeks. Just to hear her deep gasp for air. And my deep, low menacing growl in her ear. Sliding my thick, long muscular chocolate beast, between her drenched feverish and begging lips. Dominating her walls with each thrust, as I place her legs on my big, muscular shoulders. Pinning her thighs to her luscious supple breasts. While my big, strong muscular hands each grasp a cheek of her plump ass.

"Look me in my eyes." I command sharply. Firm gazing, leaving her very damp. One hand grips her throat firmly. Squeezing the flesh around it and her walls begin to do magic. Head swell with power, as I further open her flower. Instant wetness and it sounds as if I am stirring macaroni and cheese down there. Thrusting slow, thrusting quickly, thrusting deep, thrusting roughly. Slapping of flesh sounds as though its background music, as her loud ferocious moans take over. Her hand comes out, as if she is attempting to slow me down. I push it away. She is squirming, and I pause....

" I do not want to utilize rope to bind you up. If you need a break, a pause, utilize the safe word I grant you with, but other than that do not touch me unless I have allowed you to. And stop moving, or it's going to be even worst of a thrust than you thought. Stop running, or I will utilize the rope. You're strong, you can take Daddy. Yes, I am a lot to handle, but you can take it like a good girl. Repeat after me, "I'm strong for Daddy." And she did just that.

"Keep repeating it!" I commanded, now that I have her psyche thrown off of what is at hand, I then thrust and thrust her into a dripping, heaping mess. Focused when I'm stroking, rearranging her cervix and she's now focused only on my commands. She doesn't remember anything else, but, "I'm strong for Daddy, I can take it. I want to make Daddy happy. I'm strong for Daddy, I'm a good girl. I'm strong for Daddy."

We both came, drowned in her pool of lust. Died just to be reborn immortals. After we got it in, she rolled a blunt for me. We both smoked, and we cuddled, and I started to speak with her.

"Do you think there's another world out there? A life of others? I don't know, like aliens, vampires, there's just another world out there, and they can possibly invade our world at any given time?" She looked at me. "Are you hitting that L too hard Daddy? Honestly, all jokes aside, you could be right. Daddy is always right." Precious said to me.

I lit a candle. We burned an incense. "Your eye contact and smile get me aroused. Showing me your mind, make me want to show you mine. But, I'm greedy, I want to see more. Your fears, your passion. Your ideas. Insecurities. Show me everything no one else sees. The side of you no one else knows. Impress me with your honesty, courage, loyalty, your art, your energy, your creativity. However, I can perhaps already read these things from you. But, it does not mean I do not constantly want to know about it. About you. Everyone has a sixth sense. I think I have a sixth, seventh, eighth, etc. Premonitions. Communicating soul to soul. Telepathy, telekinesis, photographic memory, the list goes on. Important encounters are planned by the souls, prior to the bodies ever meeting or seeing each other.

I'm sure, there's a woman or women that have dreamt about me last night, or the week prior and I have never seen them or met them. However, they have seen me. There's probably a woman /women that think about me daily. Or they're wet because of me, and I have never laid a finger on them."

She smiled. "Yes Daddy, I'm sure there's plenty. You are quite a remarkable man." She said. I smirked at her. "You know how I constantly say, 'your mind is your most powerful tool?' You attract what you desire and believe? Allow me to get into depth.

Women and men who have trust issues, always end up getting hurt, why, because they have trust issues. Let's take a woman that is scorned. 'All men are dogs? All men are dishonest, all men are untrustworthy?' This is all you will attract. It's a gift and a curse to feel people, hear things, energies and souls manifesting in your mental so deeply. My brain constantly goes. Dispensing out information. There's so much information. There's things I would love to say but cannot say. Because, there is not sufficient amount of time in the day. I just cannot shut it off sometimes. If I didn't puff cannabis (I'll fuck with indica, because it's like NyQuil. Body high. Pain relief. When I want to write or fuck, I'll fuck with sativa. Head high. Where I can be more alert and creative) once or twice a week or swallow melatonin, I'd never get rest."

One of the things I constantly speak of is soul touching. Most people will think it's crazy or mundane, because they probably never experienced this in their entire lives. Prolonged foreplay. Prolonged sex. Different positions. Rounds and rounds, is the result of having and maintaining an incredibly, deep connection. And that builds a strong sexual chemistry." That's why when I orgasm, I roar and growl in her ear the entire time. I wanted her energy. I wanted her pussy. Not just to have her pussy or not just to be inside her drenched tight hole, Dominating. While her begging lips are wrapped snug around my beautiful chocolate beast. But, I wanted it because, it had intelligence, love, passion, healing, romance, ambition in it. She had the type of essence in her to build my confidence even more. Elevate the King in me. Expand my mind further, and to enhance the man who is the best in the world at what he does.

"Some people are just irreplaceable, and I can tell you these things and you can participate in conversation and you comprehend, but there are people whom are dead spiritually and mentally and look at you like you're crazy."

She touched me. "I know what you mean Daddy, it's like I was telling one of my friends this at work." I then looked into her eyes. "It's because you and I precious, we are ahead of the curve." And by 'curve,' I meant we were ahead of the average. She gazed into my eyes as if she was looking deep in my soul, and said to me, "yup, Daddy you and I are beyond the average." I kissed her on her lips.

"When I first met you, you didn't stare at me in my eyes. In my mind, I thought, 'she's a bitch.' But there has to be more to her than what the outside can see. I knew, If I can touch her pituitary gland, I can change the way she talks. And when I hit her cervix, I can change the way she walks. Your thoughts and beliefs are your single most essential indicator of your state of mind. Your belief and thoughts are hardwired into your biology. They become your cells, tissues and organs. There's no supplement, no diet, no medicine, no exercise regimen that compares to the power of your thoughts and beliefs. If you come to me to boast, you will experience one of two things; you will come humble or be humbled. If you come to me to just fuck, I'll make you fall in love. If you come to give, you will willingly sacrifice plenty. You will give all of yourself. If you only come here for pleasure, I will give you pain. If you only come here for pain, I will give you a psychological lesson."

"Body language is a major component of human interaction. We communicate more of our conscious thoughts and intentions with words. But, when it comes to feelings and desires, a lot of what we are saying is conveyed on a subtler level. Submerged below the level of conscious control and coming out in how we position ourselves, what we do with our eyes and hands, how close we come to another person and many other cues. I believe sixty (perhaps more) percent of human communication is nonverbal. My flesh is on earth. My mind and spirit, they're in the galaxies. Would you like to know what the peasants are doing? Entertaining. The real Kings and Queens are uplifting, elevating and inspiring other Kings and Queens. A King does not have swag, he has essence. When women and men are loved properly, they become five times what they were prior. Whomever said, size does not matter is an idiot. I'll reiterate, an idiot. The larger the vocabulary, the more ways you can seduce her. The larger his biggest muscle in his body, which is his mind. The more possibilities he has to allow her thoughts to flourish and squirt everywhere."

"I looked at you and said to myself…. 'Her mind was deeper than the ocean, most men would drown in. She would scare the average man. Money comes and goes. But, memories are implemented in your mind, body and soul forever. Love eradicates hate. Love, it has the power to heal. A connection is priceless. Some people only know how to love you, the only way they know how. From what they've seen from society, or others. But, it's not sufficient. When you are mine, you will give everything to me. Every cell in your being. Every breath, thought, touch, every inch belongs to me. I can love you with every cell in my being, and still hurt you. Sometimes I will display tenderness, and sometimes I will display 'BEAST.' You need it. You need both. A weak man will never know how to love a strong woman; he won't know what to do with her. He won't know how to handle her. How to love her, or how to fuck her efficiently."

"Many people may be book smart, however, they are inadequate when it comes to life, and people. Have you been with someone, where their chemistry just made you horny as fuck? I do that, and I don't need to take off my clothes to do so. Normal people scare me. Humans scare me. They're weird. They're fickle, they're unpredictable. Normal seems too perfect, and that's what makes me nervous. Because, nothing is perfect. And if it is, it's just fake. Some women preach for a good man, and they're ratchet. Some men preach for a smart woman, and they're stupid. It's like a woman with children, demanding a man with none, and no baby mama. We all want a fantasy. But, what are you willing to do, or give to obtain that? What are you willing to provide or sacrifice to make that fantasy a reality? Your time? Hard work? Memories? Your mind? Your soul?"

"I'm a man that appreciates exclusivity. I usually have women sprung from my personality, and vibes first. I'm at the point of my life right now, where I'm not into the petty bullshit. The nitpicking, and back and forth. That was fun in the past. Because, correcting that behavior was fun. That was fun when I was a teenager. If it's not peaceful, serene, spiritual and emotional, I don't need it around me. I'm at the point of my life where a nice ass, smile, pretty face is not sufficient to move me. You are required to have a little more substance if you want my interest. I'm not asking. I don't wish for this. I fucking demand this. If you can't provide this, step aside. Your openness, honesty, and dedication are not optional when you are with me."

She is a warrior among men, she is a Queen among women. But, she recognizes a King and kneels to only one, that is Discipline. Only mere mortals believe love is crazy, making love is crazier, and they lack passion. Passion changes everything. And when you speak of vibes, they look at you as if you are speaking a language they do not comprehend. Like you're from a different planet. Well, that's true, I am physically on this planet, but my mind and soul are in the galaxies. Connecting on a level many do not understand. Why? Because they are humans, who are slaves to their own limitations. Slaves to the desires of the flesh. Short comers. Pretenders. Selfish lovers. Limited. Unaware there is more to the flesh.

Every cell in your being listens to your thoughts. Atoms and neurons, every synapse. Idiosyncrasies, linked to the stars. I have a question... Kings and Queens, how can you be worshiped, when you do not know, or do not have a desire to worship another? Their body. Their mind. Their soul. To conquer all is incredible. Because, let's be frank here. Plenty of relationships out there, even marriages do not have all three present in their relationship. Here is the truth....Some people are just once in a lifetime, and there's no fucking upgrade from that. It's not sex that induces pleasure, it's the fucking lover. You don't always connect with someone you find physically attractive. This is where true sexual chemistry is a factor. True sexual energy plays a big factor. Sex, it begins in the mind first. And when she is able to orgasm like she does, it's because her mind has been stimulated. Duh!!! You see her shutting her eyes, and she climaxes. Because, it's intense. Men say they have a big dick all the time. I have a big dick as well, but, it's how you use your biggest muscle, which is your mind. This is what allows your big dick to be powerful. I call this, 'conscious dick.' Its intense, and it's healing. You can meet some crazy dick, some devil dick, some stupid dick, but you're still not being elevated. (All those 'dick' references are actually positive, for example, 'stupid and crazy could mean really good, in different demographics, and dynamics).

Conscious dick elevates you. Conscious pussy empowers you. Men really have no idea what it is to have a well fucked woman on their side, what it can do for them. You can give her powers, as she gives you powers beyond your both understandings. When you can touch someone's subconscious. Oh shit! That's a whole different level of intimacy.

She had that "it" factor. That, "Je Ne Sais Quoi." Tan bella, inside and out. She had some special powers. With a gaze she made blood surge south, as my chocolate beast lengthened and grew thicker. I possess a certain type of control. With a word, a command, a gesture, a touch, that ignited that feverish moist flower of hers. Opening, blossoming to my presence. I drink her nectar. I want to put my sting in her like a bee. I enter her cerebral, explore her maze of hidden desires and thrust. Thrusting hard.

Thrusting gentle. Thrusting slow. Thrusting fast. Her mind queefs and she's embarrassed as she apologizes. But I love that sound. It just means, her mind speaks to me, as serotonin is released. Her pineal gland loves me. My goal is never to make her fall for the great things I provide. Those are gifts and should never be taken for granted. However, what is taken for granted, will be taken away.

I am her creator, and her destroyer. The alpha and omega. Her beginning, and I've touched her entire being so thoroughly, that I am her last. There's none like myself. I've imprinted my essence into her soul, and mind. Now, anyone that tries to entertain her after me, will need to know me well. I mean, fucking well, in order to understand her.

"Like a bitch, I'll let you roam. But this is your most familiar bone, and you'll always come home. I allow you to walk the street with no collar, but I keep my invisible collar on your soul. The choke hold I have on your mental. No matter where you are, you know where you belong. I am the most powerful entity you will ever encounter. I will implement training that corrects, molds, perfects your mental faculties or moral your character. No one will ever know you like I know you. And you're so stubborn you won't allow it. If he's man enough and lasts. Has the patience, to explore the depths of your mind, then he deserves all of you. However, I've ruined you. I've Imprinted my essence in your soul, that anyone that tried to entertain you outside of me, would need to know me well, I mean fucking well in order to understand you. I am like your most potent drug. Even if you were to walk away, the urge would keep coming back. A song. Rope you see in the store. A movie. A word. A picture will always remind you of me. You would look for attributes in other men that I already possess. You then will realize it is perhaps a little similar but the feelings will never be the same. I am your guilty pleasure. Your favorite sin. I am your escape. The only place that makes sense to you. I am your stress reliever. You feel the rush. Intoxicated from my touch. Drunk off my gangsta love. This Hennessy thug passion. Long lasting. I own you and conquer you in every way, and in such Dominant fashion. I've put you onto my nasty ways, and you will never care to go back to mediocrity ever again."

I then started opening up to Precious more. "I've walked away from some good pussy in my life. I've rejected many beautiful women in my life. Things that vanilla (average, ordinary) men wouldn't have the strength to do. One thing I'll tell you about a Scorpio, even though there are different levels of the Scorpio, and even though we are the most sexual and powerful sign. One thing I will say about us is, we don't just fuck with anyone. We require some type of connection as we are the most intense sign of the zodiac."

For me, what makes me the best at pleasuring my partner is how well I know her, and how well we connect. Intellectual conversation releasing dopamine and serotonin from our brains. We are engaging in intellectual intercourse. If you are on this level....when you involve yourself with an individual with no vocabulary, you dumb yourself down to their level. This is what happens when you witness the sapiosexuals with the non-sapiosexuals (that's the only way I'm going to refer to them as. I don't want to get extremely derogatory, but you all get the type of men or women I'm talking about). It becomes more difficult as we get older to sustain efficient conversation. And because of this, you have awkward interactions. As a hardcore sapiosexual woman, it is extremely difficult for her to find men that measure up to her degree. I mean women are already emotional to begin with, now you add a sapiosexual to her resume, good luck trying to pursue her. Some of these women, they're in these mundane, mediocre relationships, because they have needs as well, or they remain single.

There's plenty of idiotic and stupid people in this world. Don't underestimate stupid people in large groups as well. You're never going to meet someone on your level. This what makes us all individuals. However, if you elevate each other, or if you elevate the other one to your level, that's a different story. I am a different type of Dominant. Yes I am gangsta, and aggressive, passionate and intense, but highly intelligent as well. Young man with an old soul. Scorpio, wise beyond my years. One of the things that separates me from other Dominants, is I have this Innate understanding of the human's heart and possess the ability to delve in the human mind. I am not smart, I am intelligent, that's a major difference. Two things that bless you; giving, and your genuineness. Authenticity, not counterfeit. Since women are the most emotional creatures on earth, this makes most of them very sensitive. You may say the wrong thing and get them started. Started how? Ball out crying, very defensive or fuel and ignite a large fire. When a woman or man can open up their heart, many good things will come into It. You ever see those women with terrible attitudes? Short tempers? Negative souls? Where does that come from? How do they get them? Past relationships? That negative and bad energy is still in them? Can be many different things. You are the universe. Every cell in your entire being is eavesdropping on all your thoughts.

"Where have you been all my life?" She asked me. I said, "you weren't ready for me yet."

I don't believe in accidents. I don't believe in a coincidence. You create your own destiny. Your own luck. Why is it that the shy girl found that confident Alpha Male? She set that in motion. She knows she craves more courage. Who can help her with that? She knows she yearns more confidence, who can help her with that? She sent vibes to the universe and his soul dragged his body to her. Or she was seeking, and she found him visually. I've said this once in a post, 'Dope souls need Dope souls.' Until a woman, or a man finds themselves, they will ruin everyone they encounter. Or they will just not be ready. Doesn't it feel amazing to be touched by a person who fully understands your mind? A person who acknowledges your flaws, and loves your soul anyways? When there is a deep and genuine connection, you will witness her doing things for you, she will not for another man. This generation is sex crazy and think making love is crazy. He or she is drawn to you in a way that opens his or her heart in absolute vulnerability. Commingled with you in heart, body, spirit. They realize they have nothing to fear. Their flaws, insecurities and secrets are safe with you. They let down their guards. Let down their effort. Surrender in love with you for real without restrictions. It's like when you kiss.... Kissing and sexual energy are linked. Erotic kissing involves the lips and tongue. That is part of love play. When couples kiss with their tongues, also known as French kissing or soul kissing. The tongue reflects and connects their hearts. While their lips give and receive affection between each other. I appreciate sexy lips. Kissing deeply is an exchange of energy. It is emotional. Sexual chemistry is powerful. Sometimes when you are angry with your partner, you may have rough sex to ease the frustration, and once you release y'all think y'all make up. But, I bet you're not kissing, and even if you are it's not sensual. You aren't connecting. It's just all the anger has gotten you riled up, and your disposing that off. That tension. It's not like you're making up, because I promise it will be a reoccurrence of the same shit you were arguing about. It's like a pattern. Patterns turn into habits. Now these habits turn into behaviors. Kissing her while you're inside her is a different level of intimacy. She is more than the pleasure. It is a ritual, where you exchange energy, emotions, thoughts, consciousness. That's why when see girls speaking or behaving a certain way, you can tell who she fucks with, or has fucked with. When you're both engaged in sex, you are one. It's important that your vibes resonate. Each pump and thrust is an affirmation. When a man enters your pussy, what type of vibe and energy is he giving? Is he happy or bitter? Is he a positive thinker? Does he love himself or love you? When a woman makes love to you, is she happy? Is she positive? Does she love herself, and you? She has trust issues? Is she blessing you? Is he cursing you? Is your partner refueling, healing and recharging your soul, or draining the life out of you? Are they dragging you down to low frequency energy, negativity, un-fulfillment, depression? Or are they elevating you? Empowering you? Into the high frequency of love, life and happiness, King, Queen, God, Goddess, immortality?

I say sex is powerful all the time. You need to be mindful. Master how your energy is exchanged, received and returned back to you. Temporary forevers. Pleasures are temporary. But the side effects can last forever. Sex is a therapeutic medicine when done right. When two musical instruments do not resonate to each other's beat, the music is awful, really awful. And so is the sex. Engage in more cuddling. Love. Talking and conversing with one another before, during and after sex. Hugging. Holding hands. These things help with each other being able to orgasm. And when you orgasm, the body and mind start the emotional wellbeing. It's imperative to maintain a healthy wellbeing for emotional strength in today's stressed and negative world. By you choosing who you have sex with, your building a bond to what is conductive to you, and what you desire. That bond becomes stronger through a creation of respect, love. That opens doors to intimacy, trust and loyalty. Respect and loyalty are not upgrades in relationships. They are requirements.

So do I just fuck anyone? No, not only is my sex amazing, but I know what energy you're bringing into my life, and what I'm bringing into yours. It's imperative I know you, that's the only way I'll know how to work you. Physically, emotionally and psychologically.

I always speak of the power exchange relationship, with Dom/sub, and a woman is the most powerful creature on this earth. Dominance is the most prestigious thing on this earth. Similar souls attract, inevitably. I'm superstitious, call me weird, I don't care. But my gut feelings have never proved me wrong. Scorpio intuition. I function based on high vibrations of others. It doesn't matter what type of woman she is, if you're a great leader, she will follow. Men make the mistake constantly thinking, it is money that can woo a woman. To obtain her heart, has nothing to do with superficial things, what it truly is are words. However, what makes these words powerful? Actions, actions, actions that back them up. It is how you touch her emotionally. You can have all the money in the world, doesn't mean her eyes will not wander. Money is great, but it goes as it comes. And if you take it away from many, their Swag vanishes. Their personality is nonexistent. Their confidence has evaporated. It doesn't make you a better lover, seducer or sex partner, and if she meets Discipline, you better pray she doesn't find me or it attractive.

Even physical appearance isn't a huge factor. Because a woman can fall for you, and she may not even know what you look like. I'm a threat. I don't even think God can save your relationship if she met me. Anyways back to the situation at hand. Feminine women are creatures of emotion and feelings. Feminine women gravitate to masculine men. Masculine men, gravitate to feminine women. Masculine men inspire those emotions and feelings out of feminine women as well. Good pussy and Good dick only satisfies basic, mediocre, vanilla(regular) people. Real people need loyalty. Real people desire a connection. Great minds fuck each other. Chemistry allows us to understand words that aren't said. Words that aren't spoken. Mind blown. Body explodes to the point where you lose control of your mouth. Your lips. Your eyes. Your thoughts. Your tongue. Revealing secrets. Giving me the power to connect with you. On the deepest of levels. Stripping away your layers. As you are naked on the inside. Exploring the depths of your mind. You have a taste for my insane, yet busy thoughts. A taste for my intricate mind. Once you obtain this, you will always be thirsty. We need to let it all out, before we get it all in. Get it? Eye contact is a must. So when we fuck or make love, your soul leaves your body.

This is more than sex. This is more than a cheap thrill, more than a cheap friend with benefits or lovers. This isn't about making your blood rush, while we are skin to skin. This is about how I make you breathless, when you're in my presence. How I make your heart skip a beat whenever I speak. I am your prescription. Your most potent medicine. Natural high. Someone who can fuck you dizzy, just by staring into your eyes. Speaking to your mind. Stimulating and seducing your pituitary gland. Ensnare your heart. Piercing through your soul. Now your body is completely mine. In today's world, this is hard to find, people have children as we get older. The responsibilities kick in, the fun comes to an abrupt halt. Then we all become busy. There's no time to invest, to connect, or they don't care to make time to invest in another. Or work hard to know another.

This is your escapism. This is why a relationship like BDSM is so hard to obtain. A lifestyle of this magnitude involves an immense amount of connection, chemistry, and trust. Sex involves the body, but sex that's amazing, great, divine, involves the mind, body, soul. Dominating you completely as you no longer can fight the urge, and you gravitate to me and you are mine. Now your soul levitates. And I feel our souls intertwined. Running up when I am deep inside. We can fuck all day and make love all night. Then talk about the universe, stars, atoms, physics, sports, music, economics, love, idiosyncrasies, human anatomy, etc.

I can explore every crevice in your mental while I sit patiently, and listen, and observe. I play with your mind, and you find yourself masturbating to my words. You can suck my thick, long chocolate Beast, while I watch my sports. Or while I read you my poems. And you can pretend you're listening, or excited to hear it, but you're thinking the whole entire time, 'can you fuck me hard already, with that big ass thing.'

Once the chemistry is gone, the history doesn't matter. I could miss you, I swear you won't ever hear from me. Some men act like they've never had women before. Some women act like they don't know how to treat a man. It's courtesy. You treat people how you want to be treated. Common sense. You pleasure people how you want to be pleasured, common sense. Know why this is different for most? Selfishness. Selfish even subconsciously. Creating a bond takes sacrifice. Something many can't afford. Creating a connection with a desirable woman is essential, as women will be significantly more reluctant to accept your advances if they feel a lack of connection with you. You want to connect with women, then fucking take it motherfucker. Take control. Be a shark. A wolf. A lion. When regular men interact with women, they generally try to compensate for perceived inadequacies. Regular guys generally don't feel worthy of beautiful women (whether they realize this consciously or not), and as a result, they attempt to make up for this by trying to impress women. Vanilla(regular) guys fail to connect with women because they are simply too busy trying to impress her. I know this is going to sound weird, but nice guys are selfish, (I know it's like an oxymoron almost, he's so nice, he's supposed to be giving, and polite, and selfless. That's what makes him nice right)? Anyways, they always appear not genuine. Instead of finding out about women, diving into what makes her who she is, and building a solid emotional connection with her, they instead brag about their job, car, salary, house, and any other achievements (degrees, etc) that they think might help them to attract her. (She doesn't give a fuck about all that stupid shit, if you can't fuck her doggy style and pull her hair at the same time). So seducers generally assume that women already find them irresistible, and so get straight into the action, most guys try to make women gravitate to them by bragging about achievements in an effort to impress.

The nature of the bad boy, better yet a better term I would say, 'seducer', means that he (unknowingly) just jumps straight into connecting and creating sexual tension with women. Because he just gives zero fucks, teases, has fun and just amuses himself. He also asks her deep questions about herself to see if she is 'good enough' for him, not the other way around. He's confident, and knows what he brings to the table, he just wants to see if she's worthy to join him to eat, consequently connecting with her emotionally. If all you try to do is impress women, you seem very unimpressive. If you ask questions and show a genuine interest in a woman in an attempt to see whether she would be any good for you all without even trying to impress her yourself, you automatically seem much more desirable.

When it comes to myself, you see and read my accolades and accomplishments here. I don't speak of them public, you want to see them, be surprised and look at my social medias. I like mystery. I am the embodiment of power. So knowing you will give me that to stimulate in all ways, and we will both be fulfilled. "So tell me about yourself?" "You just need to know the basics, but I'm not here to speak about myself. I want to know you." "Well, I don't know where to start? Ask me questions!" "No, I will not ask you questions, tell me about yourself."

Part of being able to connect with women is engaging in efficient conversation. Women love speaking about themselves, and hearing about themselves. Don't engage in the regular, mundane stuff; "what's your favorite color?" Fucking middle school shit. Unfortunately for regular guys, they are the ones who always feel the need to try to impress women. They demonstrate, they are slaves to women, and slaves to pussy. Therefore, she does deserve to dominate you, you pussy. Seducers on the other hand feel as if they have an abundance of hot women chasing them, and so can be very selective and picky. Once again, this works in the seducer's favor. Him just messing around, amusing himself, having fun teasing her and flirting and so on, all plays into the fact that 'girls just want to have fun'. Because he is a fun guy to be around, even if he is serious or not. He is mysterious. Keep you guessing. A challenge, and women love working for shit. Earning shit. They have egos. Women are drawn to him and want to hang out with him. His excessive sexual teasing and flirting also creates intense sexual tension. It literally drives women wild. Especially with the women with high levels of libido. Having nothing to prove, when the fun dies down, he will most likely begin wanting to find out a bit more about her. Again, this plays into his favor. He both seems impressive, as he has nothing to prove, and is talking about the girl's favorite topic, which is herself!

All in all, without even realizing it, everything the seducer does with women plays into his favor. Women have big egos even if they won't admit it. Men do not get it. You want your ego stroked, you have to know how to stroke ego back. You want to be worshiped? You have to know how to protect and cater. You want to be a boss, you have to be a great worker. It can also be argued that all of the behaviors of a seducer stem from his attitude. The fact that he just gives zero fucks. He does what he wants. Not only do women find this attitude insanely sexy, but everything (behavior) that flows from this core attitude is super attractive to women.

Okay, so let's now explore the two keys to connecting with women. First, look at creating sexual tension, and secondly, we'll have a look at building an emotional connection... when women (especially if they are between 27-45) approach you on some "I want to be friends, I want to get to know you", shit. That's translation for, "I feel strongly towards you, and want you to fuck the shit out of me three times in the day, and give me wild sex all night, but I want to see where your head is at."

Women are never direct with what they say, and you have to pay attention to what they don't say. I've never trusted women to lead, that's one of the reasons I never allow them to. Even if a woman is in control, she's still overly indecisive. Real masculine men are not attracted to masculine women. Women that behave like men, that act like they are not emotional or incapable of loving or etc. Feminine women are attracted to Masculine men, and vice versa. They respect each other, for they play their proper roles. That instills respect and trust.

"Why don't women sexually desire men or care to engage in intimate conversation with, that they place in the friend zone? Or men that do not have it in them to put a woman in their place?" Precious shook her head, not knowing the answer. "Because, women are designed to be attracted subconsciously to the stronger genes. Most women love alpha men and bad boys, you know why?" She shook her head, but said, "wait, is it because, they have stronger genes or at least they appear to exude stronger genes?" I pointed my index finger at her, with a smile, "ding, ding, ding, you're so intelligent, it's one of the things I love about you."

I'm a difficult man. I'm more of a man to please outside of the bedroom than inside it. Pleasing me outside is big points. See, some men stay with women because of what they can do in bedroom. What they can obtain from a woman, or even what the woman possesses. When you don't have sex with your partner, how is the relationship, when you guys go a day, a week, a month and not have sex? Does she become aggressive? Is he disrespectful behind your back? Materials are nice, a big butt is glorious, big boobs are okay, a pretty face is amazing, but all those things lose the interest of real men, if there's no other substance. For the ones that truly engage in BDSM, or the ones that are sapiosexuals, sapiophiles, or the ones that just do not crave mediocrity. We are just a bunch of deep, passionate individuals. We require a connection so deep. We grant each other access into a psychological, emotional, physical space that transcends the parameters of what a basic traditional relationship has to offer. We are simply different.

I know myself; I love hard, I fuck hard, I stare hard, I think hard, I bite hard, I hit hard, I Discipline hard, and I punish hard. I give plenty and I take away when need be. There's a difference between cumin and having an actual orgasm. Sex is so much better when minds actually touch. You can't just be eye candy, you must be soul food as well. Visuals don't last long. Temporary forevers. Pleasures that exceed physical pleasures, for physical pleasures are temporary.

For example, let's say I go for the remainder of the year, and do not post a single image of myself. People will wonder and forget what I actually look like. But, my words, the way I've touched them, the way I've made them feel they will never forget. Food from the Gods fill me with power. Giving me the strength to devour. Pleasures found in the heavens between her thighs transform from physical to spiritual. When two givers indulge in a connection, it's like magic. Alchemy. I water you, and you water me. Such powerful energy, we never drain each other. We simply thrive. Love is the most healing force in the world. The most potent drug is another human being, mortal, God, Goddess, King, or Queen. Nothing goes deeper than love. I'll reiterate, nothing. It heals not only the body, not only the mind. But, it heals the soul as well.

When someone speaks to your soul like no one has ever had.... It's impossible for you not to listen. Sometimes, you just can't explain to someone what you see in another person. Shit, sometimes you can't even explain it to your damn self. It's just the way they take you, or make you lose yourself into a place no one has ever taken you. A place no one can ever take you. High frequency energy is contagious. Those energies always seem to gravitate towards each other like a magnet. Where polarity is a factor, like I say in my first book, "it doesn't matter where you both are in the world, once your souls have touched, they will always be bound to one another.

She can witness what's in front of her, but she knows what's behind her. A woman can bring out the beast in a man. Elevate the King or God in Him as well. A man can lead, heal, love, Dominate and protect the Queen or Goddess in a woman efficiently. And enhance her soul. However, in order for him to do that, he must find himself. For him to sustain this.... Self-development is what it is all about, because, in order for you to lead or develop another, one must be developed, Disciplined, or capable, in order to engage another. Am I ahead of the curve? Well, yes I am and by 'curve,' I am referring to the 'average.' There is the weak, then there is the obsolete. The last of a dying breed. The not enough cloth in the world for all of us to be cut from it. There's nothing about it that's arrogance, it is merely a fact. I view, listen, study, observe meticulously with depth, about life, movements, words, what's said and what's not said, body language, minds, souls, consciousness, subconsciousness, hearts, information, material, negatives, positives and I just see a whole other side to them.

Precious spent the night. I got her way too high from the bud we smoked for her to have a desire to go anywhere. And I wasn't going to let her drive drunk or high. No way. The following day had arrived............

She kissed me goodbye but no Goodbye, just for the moment. She headed back to her place and I had her followed, just to make sure everything was perfect for the days that followed. But I wasn't going to let up on the security shit, think about it, the moment you're not on guard, you will get got so there's no way I'm letting up. She came over to my place, with my permission of course.

"Daddy, I've been so used to being so close to you for the last week, may I stay with you one more night? I'm not used to this yet, but I will be. Just one more night, please?" I nodded my head at her. "Yes, baby girl, of course."

I was not here for any halfway, fairytale, or cute movie fans and neither was she. I was here for a love that a woman had for her man, her King, her Dominant. When she knows that all that she is, is his. Must be his, will be his. When she finds it hard to breath without my permission or when her heart races because I touch her. When she kneels by my side and pledges some endless love and devotion to me. When the thought of another disgusts her. When she only has a mind for serving and the like, when even the breath that she takes seems so right. She kisses the ground I walk on, figuratively. Kisses the hand that punishes, guides, Disciplines and protects her, literally, but if I am her strength and her secure comfort, her lover and protector, what does she owe? The things and ways I need her to step up that are non-negotiable. Where does her responsibility lie, besides being cute and perfecting that whimpering beg I love so much? Honesty, clarity, define her limits, goals. Honesty, not with just herself but me as well. Obedience. There's a difference between a negotiated level of brattiness in a relationship and disobedience. I expect loyalty and I will provide structure. When she's granted structure, she will respond with obedience.

Affection is owed to me, respect is owed to me, but her submission to me is evident that she has granted me, and I've earned her trust and respect. She owes deference. She cannot expect someone to lead if she is unwilling to follow. She must allow me to take the lead by deferring to me. Obeying only when it's demanded of her is not enough. Her understanding has expanded and shifted by meditation and studying my ways and teachings. She was never tired of love prior to me, she was just exhausted from waiting to be loved the way she deserved. The most difficult woman to conquer, admire, the strongest, provides the deepest love. The body is easy to have, for a day, for a night, but the mind, the soul, the heart is a more difficult task. A man who is proudly certain of his own value will want the highest type of woman he could find because only the possession of such a potent drug will give him the sense of achievement. She never needed to be saved or even rescued. She needed knowledge of her own power and how to access it efficiently. Life is denied by lack of attention and proper understanding. You live, you learn then you grow.

The following day I had plans for us. I had scheduled to go to the shooting range. This is going to be an exhilarating, euphoric, orgasmic event. She had on a sundress just as I told her to wear. I was guiding her arm with aim.

"Make sure you aim for the target then run the chamber. Make sure the safety is off and pull the trigger. Eyes on the prize, then fucking get it!! Go to work baby!"

Damn, she was doing so well. She had my big black cock rock hard with her performance. I moved from her side to stand behind her. I raised her sundress up, snuck and pulled her panties down to her ankles. She lifted her feet up off the ground one at a time, one by one, so I could scoop them up into my hand and in my pocket, they went. I unzipped my pants, just to pull out my already erect throbbing big chocolate dick. So discreet, if there was someone next to us, they would never figure out what was going on. I shoved my big thick cock inside her passionate hole, between her begging submissive pussy lips. She knows who she is, when animal instincts take over, and the urge becomes so strong. And I unleash the demon out of her, that was inside her, smoldering desires. My body knew her body well, and her body knew my body well. I always assured no surface of her flesh remained untouched. Selfish I was not, hands touched wherever.

I thrusted, she let out a bullet. Damn, her aim was even better than before. Call that motivation. Our love is strong, our love is weird. Our love is action, thrilling. Our love is always something new and exciting. She was already a beast before me, now I've molded her into a monster. She's the fox to a lot of hound dogs on the hunt, the kush to a lot of kush rolling the blunt.

One of the things I loved about her is she is aggressive, like a lioness who is on the hunt for some zebra to feed her pride. No one can bully her but me. I don't mean it like that, I mean she's an Alpha to most but submissive to me. If she's a bitch, then I am fucking animal cruelty. She cries, moans, whines, and supplicates to me to allow her to gush all over me. I'm her Daddy. I'm her Dominant. She's a Queen only a true King can handle. A beast only a beast can tame. A body like a Goddess only a God can satisfy. A mind only a master can enlighten and penetrate. Pain only a sadist can obtain. She lives to hurt for me, she loves giving me her suffering. She requires my animal at times, but I warn her, he's twisted like a Rubik's cube. I feed her masochist. This love of ours is sadistic, nothing normal. It's dangerous, deviant. It's potent, it's amazing. It's painful, it's tender. It's sweet and it's mean. It's round for round, pound for pound. It's thug passion and gangsta lovin. It's aggressive. It's Dominant and it's submissive. It's bondage, it's Discipline. It's Dominance. It's sadism. All this fancy talk, nice things, do not mean a thing when I'm tearing her ass up and working her like a shift. She gives me all her earth shattering orgasms and they all belong to me. Every last one of them. Her anger, her pain, her marks and bruises. Her insanity, her wetness, her cries, her tears, her joys, her sadness, her arousal, her thoughts, her words, her flesh, her soul, my control.

"Wooooooo, that was good, huh, Precious?" I asked.
"Yes Daddy, definitely relieved some tension and stress.
Very good." I grabbed her hand as we walked side by
side, "let's get out of here."

Chapter 16: Her Body Calls For Me

The following day she's sitting at her desk when all of a sudden, she has to go to the restroom. She calls me.

"Daddy, I'm so wet! Dripping and I can't stop thinking about you. I'm sitting at work, here, and the thought of your touch last night, as I thought and relived your fingertips down my thighs, and traced my lips in a circle. Then you pressed it on my engorged clitoris. Thinking of the moans you created, and brought out of me, as your thick, long chocolate dick entered me slowly. My back arched as I bit my lower lip, images of you breathing heavier on me began to flood my damn mind today. The thought of your voice, subduing my senses until all I feel is the warmth of your cock throbbing inside me. Kissing my sinuously red lips, impairing my touch of sensuality from the breath of your lips in your blissful euphoria. I dream of licking you up and down, from your thick long cock, to your head. Kissing every tattoo, I am so ready for you at all times when you want me. I am at your disposal. My body is burning up, whenever I am in the vicinity of you. I'm clenching my thighs together when I am here. And that does not even help, because my panties just become wetter, and water has soaked right through. I had no choice but to come to the bathroom... I think about you every second, that devilish smile, those sexy beautiful brown eyes., paired with those smoldering tattoos, oh those sexy and hot tattoos of yours. What a girl or woman would not try. I think I have control even when I am away from you, and no, it's like once I get a taste of you, over and over once again, your spirit controls me, when you are not around. You claim all of me, when you claimed me, not just the parts I chose to show. You will not allow a wall to be between us, you see all of my demons wrapped in a bow. You see right through me, you know my true thoughts, my true feelings, and my true face, not the face that I display to the world. I heard about this stuff, I read about men like you. But I never believed it was true, because I never felt it actually existed. You made my body melt, until I had nothing left but my soul merging with yours."

I then cut her off. "I have other subs, but you and I connect on such a different level. I am successful. I have everything I want in life and if I don't have it, I work hard to obtain it. I see it, I want it? It's already mine. I was content with my life. But there was that one percent . . . That one percent that told me I was an utter and complete failure, or better yet something I was missing. Lacking, something perhaps I have not yet conquered. That I was surrounded by hundreds of people but known by very few. That my lifestyle was not acceptable. That I would never find someone I could love and who would love me in return. I never regretted my decision to live the lifestyle of a Dominant. I normally felt very fulfilled, and if there were times I did not, they were very few and far between. I felt incomplete only until I made my way to the public library and caught a glimpse of you. In that moment I knew you would be mine. I set my mind on you, my thoughts, I knew somehow the universe would work in my favor and bring you back to me. I knew if you came to me, you would be mine forever. I knew our worlds were so far apart, they could not and would not collide. But if you were a submissive and wanted to be my submissive, you would feel like the luckiest woman in the world. And I knew I would have the most precious thing in the world. I ran through images of you in my mind, at that moment I first met you. Naked, and bound on my bed. Begging for my power. Begging for my hand. My whip. My Dominance. Vaginal sex, masturbation, blindfolds, spanking, swallowing my semen, hand jobs, and sexual deprivation. I wanted to be your Dom, I wanted you to give in to your natural submissive. I wanted to think to myself, could I put my thoughts of Mia away, and have the submissive Precious?"

I never call her by her first name. Her government name.

"Damn Daddy, you haven't called me 'Mia,' in quite a while." I laughed over the phone. "Yes, you are right. But, I knew I could have Precious. I have Precious. Then I pictured you as I would now allow you to—as my submissive, ready and willing to service me. Craving you to obey my every command. I would say to myself, 'you've done this plenty of times Discipline. She wants to be your sub. You are a Dom. She's nothing new. Nothing special. It's very, very simple, so stop trying to make it complicated. Give her what she wants. What she needs. Take what she'll give. And some of what she doesn't even know she has to offer." Precious was just listening to my words.

"Man, I just knew you would be here. I knew this wasn't a fad. Just an experience. Just a weekend thing or a flavor of the month."

Yes, I thought, when her eyes met mine once more. We were going to move forward. I had her in my hands and I would not let her go. She then asked me...

"May I please touch your pussy?"

I wanted to see it.

"Show me, I want to see you and my pussy when you touch it."

She had her own bathroom where no one else would go into. She took down her bottom attire and started touching her clit.

"Slowly... now rub that clit in a circular motion. Stick that finger inside that damn hole. Stroke that shit back and forth like you're imagining my thick, muscular, chocolate dick Dominating that pussy. Fucking you so good, you want to scream out to God." I guided her through it all. "Wet enough my pet? How wet is it for me my doll? She gasped, "Oh Daddy, so wet." She lifted her hand from out of her pussy to show me just how wet. Her finger was dripping.

"I didn't tell you to stop fucking yourself, did I? Put your finger back in there, now put two fingers in. Fuck yourself harder!" She began to thrust harder and faster with her two drenched fingers in her wet, tight pussy hole. Her mouth was opened wide, her eyes staring at me through the phone, in deeper love and ecstasy than ever before. Her pussy was so wet you could hear it through the damn phone on my side. Music to my ears.

"Cum for me, cum for me baby." I reiterated. Her lips part and her mouth opens wider. She then began to soak her hand with her juices. Cuming to my every command, cuming to my deep and masculine voice. Cuming to the idea of me having her body soon. Her body calls for me. Her body needs me, her body adores me. Her body empowers me. Her body motivates me. Her body waits to be devoured by me. Her body is trained by me. Amazing how I touch her body without touching her body. My mind touches her body, my soul touches her body. My heart touches her body, my words touches her body. My presence touches her body, my guidance touches her body. My will and empowerment touch her body. My Dominance touches her body, my distance touches her body. My intellect touches her body. I constantly seduce her mind; therefore, I will constantly seduce her body. The real orgasm of hers is being desired. She does not crave to be handled delicately. She wants to be passionately desired, chased, pursued. She wants to be the object of a man's unbridled lust. No, not just any man, but me. She wants to be conquered. Love is the strangest thing, it can make the strongest person weak and the weakest person strong. You become each other's addiction. I fucked her mind and spoke to her pussy profoundly, now her body calls for me constantly.

"I want to see you later on." I demanded from her. "Yes Daddy." She's like a drug, I swear, her body keeps calling me back.

I met up with her later that night. As she stepped through the door I grab her towards me. I didn't speak, I didn't say hello...I know right, so disrespectful. I pulled her towards me and tossed her on the bed. She was an adventure, her body uncharted territory to which I was irrevocably willing to lose direction. When my lips taste her skin, every blind curve seemingly better than the last. This was not a time for gentle discoveries with one destination sight. Such burning desire, it's time to cut the bullshit, no teasing, no foreplay. No time to waste.

Once I pushed her on the bed, I ripped her clothes right off her. I tore her panties off of her and fucked her senseless until she was trembling uncontrollably, screaming my fucking name, 'Daddy', and creaming all over my big chocolate dick. Cuming on my dick like she has never done before.

"Taste yourself off of me like a good little slut you are for me." She licked off all her cream from my dick.

"Back down, as matter fact, turn around for me. Face south and your ass north." I spread her ass cheeks wide open, shoving my big fudge cock so deep inside her. Her pussy spits on my cock once again. Such a pretty sight from the back. Her ass looks so good in my massive hands. Pussy so wet it didn't stop dripping. She polished my dick perfectly, nice and shiny. It just looked so lovely. I grabbed her hips bouncing her on me. Her moans became louder and her breathing changed. The slapping of flesh was like background music as her moans continue to take over the entire room.

"Take that dick and show me why you belong to me. Give me my pussy and I'll show you why I own it." I pushed my palms down onto her lower back, making her arch a lot more for me, then I started pounding into her. Ass claps so loud, louder than an Oprah ovation.

"Daddy, can I cum please?" I allowed it. "Yes, cum for me, cum nonstop for me. Let me see what belongs to me, let me see what I provide you." Her pussy soaked the sheets. Dripping on my dick on a whole other level. Her pussy screaming, squirting on my big cock. My dick is potent, more potent than cocaine. She adores the pain. Ferocious sweat pouring, going hard like it was game six and I was Michael Jordan. I get her wild, fucking her crazy, making her pussy smile. Yanking her hair, smacking her ass, I'll make sure I'm her first in everything and her last. She has so many orgasms in her and I haven't had my first yet. Sea shell pussy but a v-12 dick. I ride her Ferrari like a wild horse, then I put her on top and let her ride me around like I was a mob boss. Dick just opened her right up. I pause and take it out just to look at that pussy and the huge gape I leave. That hole is definitely open wide for me now. I placed my cock back inside that begging hole of hers. Her pussy queefs.

"Yessss!!! Talk to Daddy." That pussy is talking to its owner. I take care of her body like I should, I take care of her body the way I know how. I take care of her body like no one has ever taken care of it. I take care of her body like no one ever will, she is mine.

We went to take a bath, I told her, "go run the bath I will join you shortly. She ran the bath, I could hear the warm water running. I yelled out to her, "make sure that shit is extra bubbles baby girl!" she yelled out back to me, "yes Daddy, I will do that! She calls for me. "Daddy, the bath is ready for you and me!"

I walk into the bathroom with her. She waited for me completely naked, and she was waiting for me to enter into the tub first before she got in. I walked over to her and said, "go ahead baby girl, get in there." I stared at her ass cheeks as she walks in front of me. "Don't shake that sassy ass in front of me, baby!" I then slapped her ass right cheek with my massive right hand, and then I slapped her left ass cheek with my massive left hand, just in case the left cheek was jealous.

She slowly gets into the tub, one leg at a time, and I follow after her. We lather each other up, we kissed. I grab her luscious breasts and cup them with my massive hands, sucking on each one, because if I just sucked on one, the other one would be jealous. My deep eyes hold her stare as I smirk, and thread my big arm around her waist. I slowly pull her in towards me, into my muscular chest, and her body molds perfectly. Her heart pounds. I said to her...

"Can you feel it Precious?" She nodded at me, indicating 'yes.' Her breath quickens, and her skin is so sensitive to my touch. She is tingling all over. I move my face closer. Blood pulses through her body, her clit is throbbing. My dick is hard, I grabbed her and placed her on top of me. "Get on top, put your arms around my neck." She did just as I commanded her to. "This is going to be a bumpy and rough ride, it will be fast, it will be slow. It will be climatic, it will be euphoric."

I grind her on me, I push her downward, I pull her upward. Her begging lustful pussy lips wrapped around my fat, long, muscular, chocolate dick so tightly. There is much greed in my hunger, the appetite I have for her is insatiable, one time is just never enough. Lick, suck, touch, play, kiss. I grasp her hips tighter, and grind her into myself harder, I grind her right into me deeper, I push her down, and I pull her up slightly. She rides my big dick now, how I want her to ride my big dick. I stare into her eyes, I bring her closer to me, I press my full lips against her full lips, her lips part, and mine does as well, and now our tongues begin to wrestle with one another. She moves her head sideways, so she can moan. How dare she, I was not damn near finished kissing her, I didn't care how good I made her feel.

She moans as I grind her into me harder, and faster. But, I then shut her up, when I press my full lips against her and now my left hand grips her right waist a little tighter. My right hand leaves her left waist to grab her by the jaw and bring her face to face with me, once again. I kiss her while I am inside her. I go harder, I go faster, we created a wave in the fucking tub. She then hums melodies into my mouth, she hums melodies into her moans. Melodies of pain and pleasure, we now breathe into our noses. She then begs me to cum, she speaks into my mouth.

"Papi, can I cum? Daddy, may I please?" I allow her to cum. "You may cum now, cum now for me baby. But, you are going to cum many more times after this, I'm not fucking finished with you yet." She let out a big gasp of air, and screamed, and her walls became so tight around me, I had to stop grinding her, or she was going to make me cum as well, and I did not want that yet. I wanted her a little more, I wanted her a little more longer. I bit her bottom lip, she let go of her walls, her pussy was so open for me, her walls were begging for more.

The buildup increased, I slowed it down, then I worked her up again, I started to grind into her once again. I was growling in her ear, kissing her sloppy in her mouth, hands slapping, balls deep slapping, that ass bouncing up and down on these big balls of mine. She was creamy, on my big dick, and the water from the tub washed it away clean.

One of the greatest things a couple could have is an insatiable, savage, raw, craving, hungry, animalistic sexual appetite and chemistry. I told her...

"Let us get out of here." She got up and waited for me to get out. I lifted her up off her feet. I put her over my shoulder, and I tossed her onto the bed.

"I want you on all fours." She replied, "yes master." I then grabbed a towel for each of us, and I wiped her down, and I then wiped myself down. She remained on all fours, face down, and her ass up. I took a pair of rope, I then bonded each of her wrists to her ankles. I moved in closer to her like a predator and she was my prey. I maneuvered my body downward, and I placed my massive hands, and my palms touched the top of her back. Her rear deltoids. I then stuck my face into her pussy, her juices conditioned my goatee. I stuck my tongue into her asshole, then into her pussy hole. Then I sat my big tongue on her clit and rubbed her clit with my tongue back and forth, clockwork, and counter clock work. I then repeated those steps back and forth again. Her moans were loud, her eyes were rolling in the back of her head. Right when I felt her walls closing in, and she was about to beg me to cum, I stopped, and said...

"Hold on, don't cum yet, I want to be inside you when you do, I want you to cum on my big dick instead. I want you exploding on my fat, long, chocolate muscular dick. Polishing and blessing my cock with all your lustful juices, all your lustful desires." I shoved my massive cock into her, then I began to thrust, I didn't take my time, I wanted to get her right back to the point of the edge, right back to the point of climax. Right back to the point of when I take her to another world. Right back to the point of no return. When I take her soul, out of her body, and it leaves and wanders, right when she goes into sub space, then I must bring her back down to earth again, she begs, and she begs.

"DAAAADDDDDYYYY!!!!! PLEAASSSSSEEEE??? Can I cum, please?" She was whining and moaning at the same time, this climax was bigger than in the tub, bigger than when we went into the tub, I wanted it, I wanted that cum. "Give it to me, you know I want to see it." She released all over me.

"UUGGHHH, thank you!" It was beautiful, cream all over my big dick, her ass looks so amazing.

"Now, turn around and come lick yourself off of daddy's cock." I commanded, I grabbed her body, she could not do a lot of moving as her wrists were still tied to her ankles. But, she licked off all her cream from my dick. "Turn around, Daddy wants to cum."

I moved her body back away from me, where her ass was facing me, her head was down. And I then shoved my big throbbing dick back into her dripping pussy once again, her ass looks so good, I had each hand on an ass cheek of her, each massive hand of mine spread each cheek apart. I spread her left cheek opposite of the right cheek. I took my big dick out just to look at that gaping hole of hers for me. It looked so pretty. "Looks nice baby." She begged me, "Damn daddy I wanted to see, can you record it?" Shit, my phone was on the other side of the room, I was not fucking up my rhythm for that. "No baby girl, next time." I held her cheeks still spread apart, and I went inside her balls deep, I slap each cheek with each hand. I saw my massive hand print on her ass, love changing that ass a different color, I was stroking so fast and just the sight of her bruises turned me on even more.

"I'm about to cum baby girl!" She begged, "Yes Daddy, please, cum inside me! Please!" I let out a big load, and I roared. I grabbed her hair, and leaned in towards her, just to bite her on her shoulder. "Damn, I love you, but damn I sure love this pussy."

Her body will always cum for me. Her body will always come to me, her body will always cum because of me, and that's why her body will always call for me.

Chapter 17: Fuck Her So Good, She's Wet Thinking About It The Next Day

I then untied her wrists, that I had tied to her ankles. Now I usually tie the rope two different ways. The noose tie; the overhead knot is a very basic knot. I mostly like to use it as a stopper to prevent the end of the rope from passing through another knot or grommet. This knot is the basic for many other knots as well. Then there is the square knot; that knot is tied by first tying a right hand overhead knot and then a left hand one. This knot works best if both ropes are of the same diameter. Or you are tying the end of the same rope together. The square knots can be used as to tying, or securing a rope around something such as a belt, or around your waist. Tying a bundle of sticks together or holding a dressing of a wound. Or can also be used to extend a section of rope with another rope.

She never needed to be saved. She needed to be discovered. By a man, whom would bring out of her what was already inside. There's no turning back for her now. There's no going back to normalcy for her now. After all that sex, I was hungry.

"I'm hungry." I said to her. She replied, "let me make you something Papi? Let me cook you something my King, please?" She looked at me with her puppy eyes, but I wasn't falling for those eyes. "No, I want to be out, get dressed, get nicely done, go back to your place, I am giving you two hours tops, I will come by to pick you up in exactly two hours, be ready for dinner. I want you to wear a nice black dress, I want your hair down, no ear rings tonight, yes wear makeup. Let's show you off to people. With your sexy and pretty self."

She got dressed and headed home. I fixed myself up and was getting ready to pick her up. I wore a nice satin suit I had not worn in months, I wanted to match with what she was going to wear tonight, not the material of our attires, but the damn color. 'BLACK,' because it was going to be a funeral of a night, we were going to kill it tonight. I picked her up, and I grabbed her hand and led her to the car, we sat in my car.

"You look sexy tonight." I said. She looked at me. "Thank you, but only tonight? What about the other nights, or am I just sexier when you're hitting it from the back?"

I gaze into her eyes, and she does mine, we do not exchange words, and then a second later we both start laughing.

"That smart mouth of yours will get you punished, smart ass!" I grab her by her throat. "You know you look sexy to me every day, you beautiful bitch, you." She replied, "your bitch, your beautiful bitch, Papi." Yes indeed, she was my beautiful bitch. But in public, she was my Queen. We arrived at this restaurant, and everyone there was staring at us, I could read their minds. They probably thought, 'who the fuck are they? Are they people of importance? They stopped eating their food just to stare, I mean people just loved to stare at anything, but they stared tonight, because our energy Dominated the entire room, and they all could feel that shit, that is why. The waiter sat us down, I said...

"No, I don't like where we are, move us to a booth, I want a booth." He nodded his head at me, "uh, yes sir, I can arrange that."

Fuck yeah, you can arrange that buddy, we are spending money in here, you could arrange whatever we wanted. I thought to myself. He then sat us at a booth, and I allowed Precious to step inside, and I remained on the outside. She brushed her sleek long Latina hair back over her shoulders. From her right side, as I was sitting on her right side, so she brushed her hair away, so I could get to her however I wanted with ease, also so I could see her face. I mean, you know when women get dressed and dolled up, they want us to notice, especially if they are doing it for us, she must have spent like 45 minutes doing her make up alone, she was sexy. I whispered in her ear...

"You do look so beautiful tonight, my love. I know I didn't tell you, what color to wear, but what color do you have on?" She looked confused. "You always do that Daddy, I think you do it on purpose, just to see if I am reading your mind." I smirked, "what do you mean?" She shook her head. "You know exactly what I mean, okay, I'll play along, but I am a step ahead of you." I looked at her, "how so?" She smiled at me. "So, you want to know what color? It's not my dress, because you know you picked this one out, the color I am referring to."

I knew she would know, I will just give her some time, perhaps she gets it right she would earn her pleasure tonight?

"The color you are referring to is, the color of my panties? Right Daddy?" She was so intelligent and so smart. "Ding, ding, ding, you are so intelligent." She leaned in, "can I kiss you?" I nodded my head, 'yes.' And she pressed her lips against mine. "Nope, I'm not that intelligent, well I am, but I am not all that, it's just because I know you Daddy, that is why." I leaned into her earlobe, "so, you didn't answer my question, still." She smiled, "oh, sorry, yes, I am wearing blue Daddy. I mean, you could take three guesses Daddy and you would get one right. I wear your favorite colors; black, red, or blue. My lipstick is Dominant red, my dress is authoritative black, and my panties are passionate blue. See, you taught me so well." I smiled, "that I did baby, that I did. Tan Bella, baby." She stared into my eyes, "gracias, Papi bello. Esta noche, eres guapo, mi amor." I lean in closer, "oh, only just tonight, I look handsome, huh. Yeah, I got you back, smart ass. All jokes aside, give them to me, take them off now." She hiked up her dress to her knees, and then past her knees, as she reaches with her hands to grab her panties. She slid them down to her ankles. She lifted up her stilettos, and she took her blue panties in her right hand, and she handed them to me. I took them with my right hand, and I put the panties in my right pocket. My right hand pushed her thighs apart. The waiter came back.

"Are you both ready to order?" I didn't take my eyes off of her, when I ordered, nor did I take my hand off of her thigh. "I will have a steak, the 24 ounce steak," before he could ask, how I wanted it done, "how would you like.....?" I cut him off. "I want it medium well, with broccoli and asparagus on the side." The waiter was writing down my order, "and for you miss?" Precious, ordered, "I will have a filet mignon, please?" As we shut our menus and give it to the waiter, I whispered in her ear, "yeah, I'm about to filet mignon that pussy when we get the fuck out of here," she giggled.

The waiter left, my right hand was still on her thigh, and it moved her thighs to spread apart. She was already wet, I did not even need to get her started. My two fingers; my index and my middle finger moved the pussy lips apart so, I could get to her clit. I rubbed on her clit, and she was moving all hot and bothered. She whispered in my ear, "oh fuck." As she grabs my shoulder firmly for dear life. "I have never been this wet in my life, what have you done to me? I just get wet for no reason, all the time, I can't control it." I stuck my finger in her pussy hole, and she was moaning in my ear while gripping a hold of me. "Don't fucking cum, save that shit for me later, I know you are going to bust a major load, and I want that, I want to feel it, I want to see it. So, don't cum."

She did as I commanded her. The food came to us, and we ate, but before we ate, the waiter brought us the food and my hand was still in her pussy, and as soon as he left, I took my hand out.

"Taste yourself off of my fingers." I ordered her... she shut her eyes and tasted herself off of my fingers. My index and middle fingers were drenched prior to going into her mouth, but she sucked her juices off of them dry. "Now, let us eat!" I commanded.

I ate all my steak, and she had a good portion of her food, and she wrapped it up to go. I said, "you were not hungry huh?" She said, "not that much, I have a major appetite to eat your big meaty cock, but not so much food, plus, we can wrap it for you later, you might get hungry again, matter fact, I know you will get hungry again." Yeah, she fucking knew me well, it was kind of scary, and kind of good. "Let's get out of here," the waiter came back to us, "will you be ordering dessert tonight?" I looked at her, then I looked at him, "no need, she will be my dessert tonight, I'm going to eat her." He smiled, she smiled, and I smiled at her. "Okay, I will bring you both the check."

The waiter brought us the check, and I grabbed it, then she grabbed it from me. "Precious, what are you doing?" I asked. "Papi, I want to pay it, please mi rey? Please Master?" I allowed her to pay the tab. We went home, we went to my place, and as soon as I got into the door, I lifted her up off the ground, and I walked us both over to the bed and I threw her onto the bed. I got on top of her, I pinned her wrists down with my massive hands. I gazed into her eyes, and I kissed her lips passionately, I kissed her lips savagely. I yanked at the fabric of her dress, and I took it off swiftly and threw it on the ground. I did the same thing with my clothes, onto the ground they went, I slid my big head of my erect chocolate cock into her pussy, she gasps so loudly, oh how I love that gasp on the first thrust.

She has that right amount of pressure on my cock, she squeezes that shit with her walls and her begging pussy lips. She loves to strangle my big dick, and I love to place my hand on her throat and squeeze the flesh around it. It's ironic, the tighter my grip, the more she lets go. She lets go of the hold she has on. The hold of her pussy walls on my massive cock, and she lets go of her mind. She is so wet now, she's so open now. I slide back and forth, easy, her pussy stretching out for me, I mold myself in her pussy. Pussy so wet, it sounds as if I were stirring macaroni and cheese down there. It sounds like kids smacking water down there. "

"You hear that baby girl?" She is like, "yes, I do, damn, I'm so wet daddy." I grab her head, I curl my strong finger inward into her hair, grabbing a fist full. I anchor her head towards me, "look at that fat, long chocolate cock going inside you." She looked at it, I then reached on the ground where my phone was in my left pocket, and her blue panties was in my right. I grabbed my phone, and opened the screen, I was then recording that pussy, just like I promised I would do, the next time.

"Turn around, "I ordered her, "I want to see that ass bounce on this cock." She turned around. "Face down, ass up, and put your hands behind your back!" I grabbed both her hands, with my left hand, and my right hand was recording, I was multitasking like a beast. Dick was penetrating, left hand was grasping, right hand was directing a movie. A movie for just her and I to see.

"Damn, baby, that pussy creaming on my cock, like crazy, bounce that ass back towards me, yeah, just like that, like the sound of that ass slapping on my cock, baby." I talked dirty, she just screamed, moaned and whimpered, "yes, there you go, my slut, my nasty fucking bitch, my fuck toy, daddy fucks you just how he likes. That pussy, shining daddy's cock, for him huh? You love that fat, long cock Dominating your walls, huh?" She was breathing heaving, her voice changed, she was moaning, groaning, crying, "yes, yes, yes Daddy." She was speaking a different language, that's when you know it's so good. "damelo duro, por favor Papi ? Ay Papi, que rico. Mas, mas, mas. Me encanta, es tuyo papi. That's your pussy Daddy."

I then stopped recording, and I tossed my phone, in front of us on the bed. "Now I'm going to really fuck you." I grabbed her waist with each hand. My fingers were on her waist and my thumbs were on her lower back, I pulled her into me, and thrusted powerfully, that is double the trouble for any woman. I started going harder, pull her firmer into me, and thrusting firmer into her, both at the same time, she was louder, her moans and screams were now ferocious, just like my dick game. It was potent, sweat was pouring, I go hard like I was Michael Jordan in game six.

"Papi, can I cum, please? Her pussy was squeezing me, I was not about to hold out, "yes baby, I'm about to cum with you. "Oooohh, ugh." She moaned and "grrr," I growled as we both came together. We drown in her pool, just to be reborn once again, so powerful. I sink myself so deep inside her, she will feel hollow when I am not around.

We cleaned ourselves off, she could not stay, she had to be at work the following day. The next day she was at work and she just could not seem to concentrate. She was constantly texting me. 'I'm having mini orgasms when I think about last night. What got into you my King? You were like a demon, an animal that was unhinged.

Devilish and out for destruction. We fucked so much, I lost count. You were like a madman or lion seeking prey, then when he found it, nothing was going to get in his way of devouring it. It was completely scary... Please do it again Daddy!' I sent her the acronym, 'lol' (laugh out loud) back after reading her text, it made me chuckle a little. I texted her, 'if I wasn't tied at work, I'd be there at your office with some rope, tying you to the fucking chair you're sitting on...having my fucking way with you as we speak.' And so as we text, she became wet once again. 'Daddy, you're making my pussy wet again, I mean, your pussy.' 'Get back to work,' I texted her back, 'You have a job that isn't a regular type of job as everyone else has. You are required to focus, you're dealing with people's lives here. We will text later.' She pouted, I'm sure. 'Awwww but Daddy, I miss you already.' I texted her back instantly, 'but nothing Precious.' She and I were in complete agreement, 'Yes Daddy.' I then texted back, 'Good girl.'

She could not stop thinking of me, however, she did exactly what I asked, exactly when I asked, or I demanded rather, which was to always be on top of her game. To focus at her job and be the best. Men and women, as human beings, are such different creatures. When shit is going on in a relationship, women tend to have an issue focusing at work. When work is an issue for men, they seem to be unable to focus properly on the relationship. It's because, we men, pride ourselves on being the fucking providers, the Alpha of the pack. The Dominant one in the relationship...speaking of, she texts me, 'Daddy, I want to take you out tonight.' I respond with, 'What?' She sends back question marks and I text her, 'We will discuss this a little later on.'

Later on arrived and I called her on facetime right away. "So, what were you asking me via text?" She replied, "I want to take you out for once." I laughed, "So all the times we've been out, you and I, have not been "out"?" She shook her head, "You always make things so technical Daddy. I mean take YOU out and cater to YOU. Treat you, pay for you, etc." "I'm not looking for that baby girl. That is not something you are required to do unless I specifically demand it of you, understand?" She was compliant. "Yes Daddy." But she was also persistent. "I know I don't have to, but I want to. Please let me treat you, let me show you how much you mean to me." "Okay, you can take me out." She was filled with extreme joy. "Yayyy!!!" But there was a catch with me.

"You can take me out, but it will be a place of my choosing, and not a place of yours. I will give you details regarding that later on during the week or day." She had no choice but to comply. "Yes, Daddy."

Later that week, I reminded her the conversation we had regarding her taking me out but how the venue had to be of my choosing.

"So, Precious, I thought of a place where you can take me." I said to her. I sent her information on it and gave her directions on how to get there. She asked me, "wait, a gentleman's club? Like a strip club?" I smiled my devilish yet handsome smile. I then said to her, "yes, I mean, you said you wanted to take me out, right?" She nodded her head vigorously at me in complete agreement. "Yes Sir, I did say this. Yes Daddy, whatever you want my King." So I then continued on how the night would go.

"Okay, I will be working a little longer than normal that day so we can head there after. I'll arrive at your place when I can, but I will keep you updated on the schedule so that you can get ready for the night as well." She was in accordance with the plan. "Yes Daddy. Do you want me to wear anything specific for you when we go to the gentleman's club Sir?" I put my finger (the index specifically) on my temple for thought... "Well...no, nothing too out of the normal from what I like. Just a dress and some nice heels for Daddy."

The following day had arrived, and it was the day we were to go out. Work was hectic for the both of us. I had worked so many hours this week already, but we had plans tonight, and was not letting a little fatigue or exhaustion stop that at all. I got home and did about 50 pushups and 45 pull ups just to keep my blood pumping. I jumped in the shower, got out, got dressed and was ready to go. I headed over to Precious' place and walked up to her door. I rang the doorbell and texted her, 'Outside, now!!' She opened the door and allowed me to come in. "Hi Daddy." We embraced and kissed each other hello. "Listen, I want you to drive tonight." I said. She looked confused. "Is this a test, a trick or something?" I shook my head no, "It's not a trick or test, I'm tired. I don't feel like driving." "But Daddy, you know where we're going and you're the man. Don't you prefer to drive?" She's good.

"Precious, you have the directions from when I sent it to you, but you're right." If you want to get a stubborn Alpha female to do something...just tell her she can't do it, or she doesn't know how.

"Look, I'll drive," I said forcefully, "I know I'm a better driver than you anyway, matter of fact, men are better drivers than women period. You can't drive better than me!! No fucking way in hell!!" She put her hand out as I

turned my back headed for the door. She snuck in front
of me with her hand out. "I'll take the keys and show you.
I will represent all the women today and prove you wrong
Daddy." She was handed the keys by me with no talking,
no argument. I then got into the passenger's side and she
got behind the wheel. I reclined my seat back and
meanwhile she's thinking she's proving something to me
while I'm resting and getting her to do exactly as I
wanted. Reverse psychology. I was smirking but the
entire time she believes she was proving me wrong.

We arrive at the club and she asks, "so what did you
think?" I laughed. "Look, you did great like you do
everything else. You're a phenomenal driver, perhaps
better than me but, how else would I have gotten us here
without me driving?" She pouted at me. "Damn Daddy,
you are so bad. You're so mean." I started to laugh,
"Let's go throw some money at these honeys."

I took her by the hand and we walked up into the club.
I ordered us both some drinks. They had some pretty
faced women there.

"You like her Precious?" She looked over to where I
was nodding to. "Ohhhh, Daddy, she's cute." I grab her by
her hand and we sit close to the stripper, in the front row
where she was dancing. I watch her open her purse and

take out these large bills. I place my big massive hands on her wrist. "Baby, look, you can't throw these big bills at these women like this so fast. They are the workers, you are the customer, so make them work!!! Think about it, if you don't make them work and you give them all of it, they won't need you any longer. A hungry bitch will always come back for food, it's when she's no longer hungry that you need to worry about, so keep her hungry baby girl." I said.

She's learning alright. I was molding her into something very special. She was smiling and laughing, just having a blast, and all I could do was stare at her. That smile could light up a room, make the stars in the sky jealous. It could make a blind man see. I've been through a lot with this woman already. She needs to know more about me, she deserves it. She's earned it. "You're getting a little too intoxicated my love, we are limiting your drinks as of now." She lowered her bottom lip and gave me those puppy eyes.

"Don't do it, that look won't work with me. I could love you with every fiber and cell in my being and it still won't change my decision. It won't make things easier."

We had a blast here, I can't lie. We both got some great lap dances. It started to get late.

"Get on top, come here. I need that pussy on my cock right now baby." She came over to my side. I reclined my seat and pushed it backwards. She got on top as I grabbed onto her hips and slid her wet pussy on my erect chocolate cock. It felt so damn good! Sliding up and down on me, I started to bounce her up and down on me using my strong massive hands. Her moans became louder when I began to do that. The slapping of her body against mine became background music as her groans got louder and louder.

"Can I cum please, you feel so good inside me Daddy. Can I? Pretty please Daddy?" I growled at her. "Yes, cum on my big black dick my love. Cum on it like you need to cum in order to live. You need to cum on that big fat long cock to remain sane. You need to cum on that dick like it was the last steak dinner and you've been fiending. Like you have been starving all fucking day long." She was cuming so damn much on me and then I told her. "Get off and lick those juices off of Daddy's big chocolate dick baby girl. Yeah, there you go, suck that cum off my dick...like you need it for energy. Suck that cum off like it's the greatest thing you've ever had."

But it *was* the greatest thing she's ever had, so what was I saying? That didn't make sense. "Good, now get back on that cock. I want to cum." She continued to ride me and I grabbed her hips so she would go at my pace, my time, to move just how I wanted her to move. I control her moves, I control her speed, I control how she grinds on me. I move her on me faster, bouncing her up and down, riding that cock like a roller coaster. Her flesh slapped down hard on me with every thrust. I felt it coming, the feeling was getting so damn strong. Yes, I was about to cum, bust more powerful than my desert eagle magnum.

"Here it comes baby, get up!" She got up off me. I grabbed her head and directed her towards my lap. "Jerk that big dick into your mouth and swallow these Dominant juices of mine!" She jerked that big dick like her life depended on it, because she knows I mean what I say, and I say what I fucking mean. "Grrrrr," I roared so loud, cum shots into her mouth. "Swallow every fucking drop, every damn last one bitch." She did just that until there was no more cum dripping from me. She sucked me off clean. She wiped me off well. "Now, let's get back on the damn road and get you home and into bed baby." The next day came and there was so much I've been waiting to tell her and share about me. I was just looking for the appropriate time to do it. We've been through so much in such a short time and I just feel she's earned it, and her loyalty is not ever to be questioned.

"So Precious, there's something you must know about me." She looked at me and nodded. "Okay Daddy." "Well, you know I am a polyamorous Dominant and you know I have other subs, but not to what extent. So the other subs, different subs have different purposes. Some are long distance, some we engage in play, some we engage in Discipline..." She then cut me off.

"Hold on, so what we do, you do with others?" She seemed so damn shaken up and why? I mean she knew I had other subs. "You know and knew beforehand that I had other subs." She shook her head. "Yes but not the real extent of them and the relationship you have with them." I continued. "Some, we engage in play, Dominance and just submission, but I don't see them as much because you and I spent the most time together lately." "You have other things with subs, what we share. I don't know if this is for me." I grab her firmly. "You're not leaving." I push her up against the wall. "You're here. You're here for all of me and everything in my life. Not just the good but the bad as well. You are my sub, you're not my girlfriend or my wife. You want a vanilla life? Go find a vanilla man and engage in vanilla things, but you're not leaving. Even if you were to walk away, the urge would constantly come back. I'm more than breathing to you. I am intoxicating, your favorite sin, your guilty pleasure. Your Alpha and your Omega. Your first of many things and your last of many things. You will not find a better connection, love, sex, Discipline, guidance, pleasure, affection, Dominance, chemistry and bond stronger than this and I will love you better than any vanilla man could ever dream of. They are incapable. Why? Inadequacy. They lack so many things you required as a woman. You are not a regular woman; therefore, you will never desire a regular man."

She knelt before me. Instead of running away, she knelt. "You're right my King, there is none like you. None with your power, your soul, your knowledge, your grace, your ways. Dominance, connection, sex, love, protection, affection, pleasure, pain, your insane or bond. None like you, you're right. No one will ever know me like you do. I'm too stubborn to let them as well. You have me, I'm sorry for the outburst. I remember who I am, and you will always have my devotion, no matter what my love, my King, my Dominant, My Daddy. Thank you for your time, energy and your honesty."

I place my big strong hand on her head and I begin to stroke her hair slowly and gently. "Good girl, that's my good girl." She smiled, her head and eyes to the ground. She loved when I said those two words, it made her wet. It placed her mind at ease, calmed her spirit and more and more importantly, it pleased her. It pleased her to know I was pleased with her because we both knew, when I say, 'good girl', I'm completely happy or pleased with her.

She was still in the kneeling position, hands came up to touch my thighs. I grabbed her chin. "We're good now but, your little outburst, jumping out of character, you will be punished Precious."

And just like that, I had her wait for me for about fifteen minutes, on her knees. I brought out my thick belt. I haven't used it in a long time because I haven't punished someone this severely in a long time.

"Hands out in front of you. Remain kneeling forward and do not move your hands. Don't run, or we will start all over again. Every time I lash you, you will fucking count out loud. You miss, we start over again. You move, we start over. You are not granted to use your safe word either. We stop when I say we fucking stop." I lashed her hard, I lashed her quickly, I lashed her for a good period of time. Welts and red, so much red on her sensitive skin. "You're not getting any good dick afterwards either. Your main and only job is to please me, whether that's through pain or pleasure. Get up on your fucking knees and do your whorish best…."

Chapter 18: Daddy Can We Keep Her?

I cuddled her gently and kissed her passionately. She said to me. "Daddy, I've always been bi-curious." I raised an eyebrow. "Okay, and what happened with that?" I asked her waiting patiently for a reply. "Well Daddy, I never had the chance to experience it." I cut her off. "Listen baby girl, just because I am poly doesn't mean you need to engage. It's not something required of you. I have always respected your hard limits and I will always respect them." She nodded her head at me. "Yes Daddy."

The night would soon give way to daylight. "We both have work in the morning. Let's get some rest." I brought her home and I left for my house. I showered then jumped right into bed and got some sleep. We both woke up early and texted each other, 'good morning.' I went to work, and I know she had an even bigger, busier day herself. I felt the day went by so fast, maybe because I was so productive but I'm always productive. It just felt like the day was moving faster than normal. Precious texts me, 'Daddy, I have a surprise for you, nothing too crazy. Can you come over to my place after work to see it?" I agreed and head over to her place. I arrived at her house and rang the bell.

"Hi Daddy." She met me at the door and kissed me on the lips and hugged me. I already knew something was off. "What have I told you about surprises?" "Yes Daddy, you don't like them, but you so deserve some fun." I looked confused. "What the fuck? Fun?" She took my hand and guided me into her bedroom where I find a woman there on her knees.

"What the fuck is going on here?" I asked forcefully. "Daddy, this is your surprise! Isn't she cute? Daddy, can we keep her?" I didn't know if I should be furious or be glad. Furious because she brought someone into our world without my permission, glad because she wanted to engage and experiment like this. I mean how many men could be this lucky? Fuck, how could I punish her? But if she was going to embrace this, she was going to see the responsibility of it.

"Can you even trust her?" I asked. "Yes, I know her, and I can trust her." I smirked, "trust is very expensive. Loyalty and devotion follow. Let's see how those factors come into play here. I am placing you in charge of her. If she fucks up, I am holding you personally responsible. You will train her on my ways. What I like and love and how to please me the way I expect. If you fail to train her properly or if she fucks up, I will punish you then I will punish her. When one fucks up, both of you get fucked up. This will teach and assist you both on teamwork. How to band together and come together for a common goal...pleasing me!!!" She smiled. "Thank you, Daddy, you won't be disappointed." I smirked, "I'm not saying we can keep her and I'm not saying we can't. All I'm saying is She Will Earn It and You will be her teacher. Now, let me watch you Dominate her."

She took off her clothing and placed them on the bed. She handcuffed her to the bedpost. I had my arms folded across my chest and nodded my head in shock. I was impressed. She started to eat her pussy, sucking on her clit. Damn, she made my dick so hard. I took my pants down, hand on my cock, jerking my dick. I then moved closer and put my big erect cock in Precious' pussy. She was so extremely wet from eating her new slave's pussy. I then released the slave and ordered her to sit on Precious' face.

"Precious, eat her kitty." I laid Precious on her back and had my massive cock going in and out of her begging moist pussy. The slave was aroused from the devouring of her pussy by her new Mistress. I grabbed the slaves head and pushed it downward towards Precious' pussy. "Lick my baby girls' clit, bitch. Lick that shit good and please your Mistress!!" I demanded. She was sucking and licking her love button while I continued fucking the shit out of Precious' creamy pussy. She was in heaven. They both begged me to cum at the same time. I allowed it. I was impressed, not by the fact that they both wanted to orgasm at the same time, but the fact that the slave was already put on to my ways.

"I see you taught her well Precious." "Yes Daddy, I told you, she's a good girl." "Okay, go clean up, the both of you. We will go over some stuff afterwards." After cleaning up they came to speak with me. "You both are in charge of each other, well actually, my fault, Precious is in charge of you." I pointed to the slave, "and I am in charge of Precious, therefore, I am in charge of you as well."

The slave never looked at me in my eyes as I spoke. "Look at me when I speak to you, at all times. The only time you have your eyes down is when I'm not addressing you specifically, other than that, all eyes on me, understand?" She nodded her head. "You will address me as 'Mr. Discipline', you haven't earned a prominent name yet to call me, but you will address Precious as Master or Mistress"

She nodded once again. "Yes Mr. Discipline. Sir." I looked at Precious. "You have your hands full." As I begin to walk away to go home, I stop to mention one last thing. "And by the way, do not play without my permission!" I pointed to Precious' slave..."and YOU, do not touch MY pussy without my permission. I don't care how frisky you become, you will personally answer to me and I will not take that shit lightly." I gave her my darkest stare of all time. Then I walked out of the room and left the house and headed home. Precious reassured her.

"He's really a good Daddy, he's just overly protective. You'll get used to that, just stay on his good side and you will be fine."
The following day I had plans with Precious. We had a specific time to meet and she was late. I called her, "Precious, what's taking so damn long? You're not just five minutes late, you're twenty minutes late! And we had dinner plans." She gasped, "I'm so sorry Daddy but I was getting dressed and we had to make sure the house was tidy and etc..." "WE!?!" I said sharply then calmed myself. "I'm sorry Daddy. I'm coming, I'm almost there, Daddy."

So I waited another fifteen minutes. It was a total of thirty-five minutes that I waited for my Precious. She finally got here and we hugged and kissed hello. I then asked. "How was the drive?" She was out of breath from rushing to come see me. "I was hurrying to come see you but I had a great drive." I nodded my head. "That's good, now you can have a better drive back home." She looked very confused at me. "What?" I smiled at her, "I didn't stutter, you can go back home. We are not having dinner together tonight. I don't need you tonight. You could not make time a priority, therefore, dinner is not a priority. I'll see you tomorrow."

I took the dinner napkin from my lap and placed it on the table and waited. I waited for her to leave. "You may leave now." "Yes Sir." She then got up and turned to me. "I'm sorry to have disap…" I cut her off. "We will speak tomorrow. You're dismissed for the night. You may leave my presence, thank you." She walked away.
The next day I called to have a meeting with the both of them, Precious and her slave, at her place. "You were late yesterday Precious, was she here? Is she the reason why?" Her silence let me know it was. "So you didn't prioritize and she didn't help either. I told you both, you were supposed to start looking out for each other and ya'll didn't listen, so appropriately, I must teach you both a vital lesson."

I sat down in a chair and made them both stand. Both, standing in my presence, in front of me so meek. Supplicant when they are in my presence. "So who's going first?" I asked and they both stared at each other. "Whether you both need to participate in rock, paper, scissors, someone is fucking going first. So who's it going to be?"

This was a huge test. I was interested in seeing who was going to throw who under the bus. I also wanted to grant them some type of empowerment and authority. I really didn't give a fuck who went first. None chose, pretty good. I thought one of them was going to throw the other under the bus. I was wrong. I could see in their eyes, they wanted me to be the one choose. I fucking tired of this quickly. Now let's up the damn stakes.

"Okay, allow me to rephrase things. The one who chooses to go first will receive the least." But, I didn't mention the 'least' of what. Now they both look at each other as they both want their turn to speak. The slave steps forward. "Mr. Discipline, I'll go first." "So be it." I said, "you will receive the least...amount of spankings for the majority of the time." "WHAT?!?" she replied. I grabbed her by the hair and anchored her head downward toward me. "Who the fuck do you think you are saying 'what' to?"

Precious tried to chime in, "Daddy, she doesn't know, forgive her." She, the slave, was apologetic, "I'm sorry Sir, Discipline. I'm not saying "what" to anyone, Sir." I then continued. "Allow me to reiterate. You will receive the least amount of spankings, with the crop, for a larger amount of time, which will be five minutes." Now I pointed to Precious.

"As for you, the "most" spankings for the least amount of time. The belt for four minutes and forty seconds. No safe words and we will only stop when the time is up."

I finished handing out the punishments. Their asses were bright red and welts blessed their flesh. "Since there was a twenty second difference between the two of you, I will use twenty however I want. Now I want you both to kneel for twenty minutes. If you both choose to get up before then... well let's just say, you don't want to get up before then."

I've put them both in a psychological bond. I sense the bickering will commence the second I leave. As I shut the door I can hear them bickering back and forth, just as I anticipated. "It's your fault he's angry." "No, it's your fault!" I go make a sandwich, watch some television and the twenty minutes are up. I go in the room. Such good girls as they are still on their knees.

"So ladies, what have we learned?" Here comes the blame game. "Well, she was the reason" ...Precious started the blame. "No, it was her that..." I'm shaking my head back and forth as I cut them off. "Silence!!!" I roared the command at them with precipitation to be obeyed. "Ladies, ladies, ladies, I am so fucking disappointed now. I really thought the both of you would be able to create a cohesive unit and come together to solve this little problem. Instead of blaming each other, take responsibility for your actions and your punishment would've been over. All three of us would have some fun. I would've allowed you to fuck her, as I watched and then I would fuck the both of you, very hard!!" They both gasped at the same time.

"But unfortunately, you both need more Discipline." Precious spoke first. "But Daddy, we have learned our lesson, please?? We can coincide and work together." I laughed, "I'm sorry ladies but I do not concur." Even though in my head I knew they could. "You two haven't learned your lesson, however, you WILL coincide as I tie you together." I grab them both and toss them onto the bed. I begin to bind their bodies together in the 69 style. Precious' ankles were tied to her slaves wrists and I grabbed another set of rope to bind them both, stomach to stomach. Over one, under the other I was tying. Such intricate tying styles. It may, perhaps, take them a while to get out of this. "Now ladies, two heads are better than one."

Let's see if they work together to help each other get out of this bind. I gave them a hint already, let's see if they actually take the hint. Before I walk away I say, "remain trapped or you can escape. The choice is yours, ladies."

I walked out, and they speak among themselves. The slave asks Precious, "how is he? Tell me about him. Do you love him? Is he this cruel all the time? What type of man is your Dom, Master? Master, will you tell me? All those questions and Precious only says, "yes, I love him." and then stops talking. They worked together and got out of the rope. I came back and gave them a round of applause with a smile on my face. I shouted, "Progress!!" They were free.

The following day I told Precious to meet me at the park so we can chat. "Hey baby, take a seat. Look, something about your slave doesn't sit right with me. I feel something is off with her, like she can't be trusted." She looked at me confused. "Why do you say that Daddy?" I then continued. "She just seems like she can't be trusted. How do you know her again?" I asked her. "Well, she's like a distant friend. I met her after you and I became real close. I told her about you, how I feel and everything. She's constantly MIA (missing in action) so I don't see her every day. She does a lot of traveling Daddy." I stare at her then said, "You need to let her go. Something is off and I'm not going to have a person we're both unsure of, whether she can be trusted, to come into our world." She was sad, but compliant with my decision.

"Yes Daddy, you always know what's best and your gut instinct is always right." The following day she told her slave it was over and that she could no longer keep her. "So he's making you throw me away? Throwing me away in the damn woods or to the wolves or something?" Precious defended me. "This is between you and I and I don't trust you. You're asking way too much about Daddy. You are MY slave." "Fine, I'll leave but I won't ever really leave." As she left, Precious calls me.

"Daddy, that was hard, letting her go." I then spoke some clarity to Precious so she understood the magnitude of this. "Listen, you need to watch it. Anyone you bring into your space, your home, life, mind, body and spirit you better and need to trust. You're giving them information and space that they can ultimately harm you with or worse. Don't be so trusting, not everyone wants peace and not every person is your friend. Some people just want what you have. They see how happy you are, and they become greedy. Just be careful. I'm not paranoid, baby girl, or even crazy, I'm just ahead of the curve.

Chapter 19: Good Girl, Dirty Mouth

I wanted her right then and there. I could not wait. I didn't use any rope, I put her on her back and took all of her clothes off, down to her panties. I slid my chocolate beast into her supple, drenched pussy hole.

"Fuck!" came out of her mouth. "Oh fuck, mmm, shit, you're so fucking deep Daddy. Yes, fuck that pussy like I know you can. Stab that nice cock inside my tight pussy. You like stroking that fat long chocolate dick inside this tight pussy hole, Daddy?" What's gotten into her today? She was extremely talkative. I put an end to that.

"Shut the fuck up!" I slapped her face hard. That made her shut up, but it also got her wetter. "You're so mouthy today and demanding. Don't tell me how to fuck you, when to fuck you, how it feels or where to put my cock. Perhaps you had some fun Dominating your ex-slave, but don't get carried away. You know who you are what you are to me. Don't forget it." She was apologetic.

"I'm sorry Daddy, my King. You're right." I fucked that pussy harder and I placed my massive hand over her mouth. I just pounded even harder and when I'm finished, she's going to feel like a newborn baby deer, struggling to walk. Hurt so good, body screams for more punishment, more torment, more Discipline, more limits. "I won't hold your hand, I will feed you my energy and corrupt your sensibilities. I will challenge any notion of pleasure you've ever known."

I will dismantle the preconceived notion she's ever had of me. I will shatter every boundary she thought she wouldn't cross. "I will always be your first of many things and your last of a few." Right before I can begin talking again, I feel her walls closing in around me. "Cum for me!" I command. "Cum for me right now. Cum for me and let me feel those lovely juices release out of you onto the sheets, all over me. Let me feel that pussy." Her walls clinch and choke my big fat muscular cock. Her back arches up, here It comes...EXPLOSION..."Yessss!!!" She cums, she releases, her orgasm is violent like a hurricane hitting the shore. Her body rolls and conforms and she is helpless to stop it. It's such perfection. Her thighs vibrate. Her fingers and toes go from stiff to curled and back again. Her breath comes out staggered and pulsating. Her ears are ringing from her own deep scream of passion. My bite on her flesh made this orgasm so much more intense. It was a trap, she was devoured, and she couldn't contain it. It isn't until she inhaled deeply that she realized just how loud the orgasmic scream she let out had been.

Bad girl with that filthy mouth. She should be punished but now, she couldn't move. She lay there breathless and convulsing. Such a pleasurable moment for a bad girl. I'll remember this shit and next time I'll make sure she's fucking gagged. This time I don't even waste too much time. I go get tape. I don't get the gag ball, I get fucking duct tape and I tape her mouth shut. I shove my erect, throbbing, massive cock into her slick pussy hole. Thrusting so hard into her. Back and forth, so deep, so rough. How sweet it is, the little taps on my skin from the quickening pulse. How wet she becomes from being taken and feeling helpless. Wet for Daddy, when she caresses my strong fingers as they squeeze her fragile throat. She loves every fucking second. The dark kiss on her cheek as she begins to fade. The warm buzzing that slowly creeps from her head and then covers her entire body like a blanket. My thick chocolate dick sliding in and out, singing her pussy that sweet lullaby... slow, fading, so good.

My hand momentarily leaves its perch from around her neck and swiftly snatches her back to reality. The cold hard slap on her cheek, to bring her back in the fucking moment. Her mouth is wide shut, her eyes wide open, breathing heavily through her nose. Her pussy begins to gush around me. I mean, she can't even beg for permission to cum. Fuck it, I'll give her a pass this one time. I'm just going to fuck her until she cums, cums, cums, cums and cums over and over until she can't cum anymore tonight. She loves that just as much as I do. The whip of my strong fingers across her face to remind her exactly where she belongs, to whom she belongs to and where she is. In my zone, at my mercy. In my presence, and she is perfectly made for me. Taking big dick like the slut she is for me. My grip tightens, and I can see it in her eyes. I can feel it between her damn thighs as she releases again. Her eyes shut as she squirts so much on me, fireworks like it was the fourth of July. Eruption like a volcano, she cums all over my dick and down her thighs like a good girl. She hums so loud at me it's like a monsoon is due. I lean deep into what becomes a raging river of her. Those eyes pop in deeper love than ever before. The oxytocin and dopamine dripping from her brain driving her insane. I rip the tape quickly off her lips.

"Say it, say it!!, cum, beg!!" She took a final breath of air and, "please, please, please Daddy, please can I cum for you?" I allowed it once again. Splish splash was right here and all over the damn sheets. Her eyes roll back, her limbs go slack. She arches her back right before it all goes black, before she loses her mind as quickly as she loses her breath…. She whispers. "Thank you, thank you, thank you my King."

I go downward, and I go head first for her pussy. "Oh fuck," she says, and she caught herself with her good girl, dirty mouth. She covers her mouth with both her hands. Her body trembling in the wake of my talented tongue. I meet her lips with mine now just so she could taste herself off of me.

"My turn to show you exactly what this mouth does, just in case you've forgotten." I move my head back downward towards her wet pussy. The look I gave her, she already knew what she was in store for. I take my big hands and slid them underneath her butt. I cup her ass cheeks and push her butt upwards, towards my face. I take her into my mouth and now I start to work her like that. My tongue is like a fucking motor, nibbling on her clit and sucking her pussy lips. I hear her moans through her hands that she had covering her mouth. Her body explodes.

"Daddy, please, can I cum, please? I can't..." I say "Yesssss, let me feel it, let me taste it." I can taste her deliciousness. I love to take all of her in, not a drop to waste. I treat her good, I treat her bad, but I always eat and fuck her better. My big tongue strokes deeper and deeper. Tougher directions than they initially sounded like as I pull her further out of her body with each roll around her clit, with each dip inside her walls. I take both my hands and spread her pussy lips open as I feel her juices come to me. I shoved my big hard dick inside her open and waiting pussy and suffocated her walls with all my thickness. I fill her up and her pussy wraps around my girth like never before. I put that pussy to sleep. My thickness sings lullabies to her drenched walls. It sees and feels me in its dreams when I'm not around. I take my dick out and go back to sucking her pussy again. With each long slurping suck on her beautiful hood that simultaneously vibrates her clit, I push her completely over the edge. I slide two fingers into her while continuing to dance the tip of my tongue around her wet little pearl. Her eyes shut completely as her mouth opens wide. Her head falls backwards into the natural holster between her shoulders that's created when you lay on your back with her elbows on the bed. "Open your fucking eyes." I growled as she forces her soul back into her body long enough to pry open her eyes and watch me licking her pussy. Juice dripping and streaming down her thighs rushing down towards my waiting eager mouth.

She waits for my touch, my mouth. She stares down at me, deep stare into my eyes as I look at her while I eat her and she is watching me while I eat her. I love watching her eyes and mouth beg, but the words just don't come out to ask me. Love watching her submit, watching her surrender. Waiting to give her what she needs, spreading her gaping hole even further. Giving her what she's earned and what she deserves. Loud moans and relief escapes her soul.

"Daddy, oh god, can I cum... again?" New heights and journeys begin... "Yes, baby, you may cum." Huge gasps of air escape her lungs. She bites her bottom lip. "Don't worry Precious, Daddy knows what to do with you always. Daddy knows how to handle you, always. Daddy knows how to do your body like no one will do your body. That moment when I feel your legs start to shake, your moans get louder, and I push harder. Whether that be with my mouth or my massive cock, hitting your clit faster and your juices blessing and cleansing my soul. You start to cum and your legs convulse. Your hands attempt to push me away, but I push them away and grab both your thighs harder and tighter as I growl loud into your pussy. I suck and fuck the shit out of MY pussy, hitting your clit harder and faster. You don't push me away and I don't let go!!!"

Chapter 20: This Is Exactly How I Want You

I tied her wrists to her ankles and gagged her mouth with the gag ball. I didn't say much. I walked around the bed, stalking her like she was prey, and I was like the most fearsome Dominant lion in the jungle and my prime incentive was my hunger.

"This is exactly how I want you. I will always want you bound by me, whether that be by my rope, my mind, my physical strength, or my words. You will be bound to me in all ways possible. Physically, emotionally, psychologically. This is how I want you. This is exactly how I will always want you."

I continued to walk around the bed, but she didn't know what to expect. Her eyes followed me wherever I moved to. I wanted to tantalize her with my most darkest desires.

"I do believe you have your own dreams, hopes, desires, wants, opinions. You put those things aside and you have submitted to me. You've given me your precious gift. To put yourself in such a position like this takes a lot of trust, strength, and it demands respect, and I do respect you. Everything I do, I keep you in mind. My rules on clothing, foods, exercise, people you allow in your presence and energy. I have certain expectations of my submissives. As you know this. My chastisement is for your betterment." She licked her lips, her pink tongue running around the edges of her mouth. I ran my fingers through her hair then moved them to her erect nipples on her breast.

"And any pleasure or pain I give you." I then continued to run my fingers downward until I slapped her clit hard. "Ahhhhh." She gasped. I then continued. "Any pain or pleasure I give you, you've earned and deserve, and you have no qualms concerning them." I Dominate her intensely, passionately, roughly. She felt every powerful thrust into her yielding wet pussy with my big dick. Every delicious impactful slap, every intense bite until she was a puddle, a dripping mess of cum.

The following day she texts me, 'Daddy, I'm so sore!' I smirk before I reply to her. 'That's how I want you.' She texts me again, 'I don't know how I made it up the stairs here at work. Every step felt like I wore iron shoes.' I replied back to her, 'I want to fuck you tonight. Not just any fuck, I want to fuck you nice and hard tonight.'

I don't care how sore she is. I will have her sore, ready, willing and able. 'Yes Daddy,' she replied back to me. I said, 'I'm coming to see you later after work. I want you to wear one of my favorite lingerie's, the blue one baby girl, the blue one.' She replied, 'yes Daddy.'

I planned a surprise for her. Earlier that day, I went to my favorite jeweler to have something specially made for her. I glanced over the offerings in the necklace display. My previous submissives had worn plain silver chokers, but I wanted something more for Precious. I wasn't impressed with anything I saw.

I saw the manager and looked at him and said, "I'm looking for a choker, platinum, with diamonds, perhaps?" The manager's eyes lit with excitement. He responded. "I have just the thing. It arrived this morning, and I haven't had a chance to put it out yet." He scurried off, then he returned moments later with a leather-covered box. Inside was an exquisite choker made of two rope-like platinum bands, intertwined with diamonds embedded throughout. I could easily picture it on Precious. Yes, this my collar for her. My submissive. My slave. She is my slave.

"Perfect," I said to the manager. "I'll take it, I love it." As the night arrived and I went over to see her, she greeted me at the door and knelt immediately after. She stayed sitting with her juicy ass cheeks resting on her heels. I walked around her and watched her every curve so meticulously, then meeting her back at the starting point. Face to face. I grabbed her by the jaw and kissed her lips so passionately and roughly. I ripped that lovely lingerie right off her body.

"This is exactly how I want you." I watched her exposed, free, ready and willing for me just because she was ready for me. I ripped the remainder of the lingerie off, I pulled it over her head and watched it flutter to the floor. "Look at me." I commanded. She did just that. I waited until her gaze met mine and I slowly removed my belt. I raised her up. "Get up." I walked from behind her and explored her once again, slowly.

"You crave me don't you? You're sore. What would you prefer for tonight?" Honestly, her answer didn't matter. We would engage however and do whatever I wished, I just wanted to see what she would say to me. She then responded, "whatever you wish my King!" I smirked at her. "Whatever I wish, huh?" I reached in my pocket of my pants. I took out a fancy looking box. I opened it, and I pulled out the diamond platinum choker I bought earlier for her.

"One thing I must tell you before you and I do anything, this is aside from my lifestyle. This is aside from Dom and sub dynamic. This is aside from play or the other physical activity that we engage in. This is, about your dedication. This is about your hard work. This is about your loyalty. This is about your devotion. This is about your love. This is about your strength. This is about your willingness and your service. This is about worship and appreciation. This is about trust, respect, and your New life. This is about you now becoming my slave."

She had a huge grin on her face. Her head is normally down, and she lifted her head up to look me in my eyes and to witness what I had in my hand. Her eyes were wide with shock.

"Wow, Daddy, it's so pretty. I love how it has rope and everything on it. It's nothing I've seen before." I smirked, then I said, "I had to get you something special. I had to get you something that is like us. It's not much, but it's a lot to me. It's now a lot to you." She then said, "yes, I will wear this everywhere I go, I never want to take this off." Which brought me to my next thing.

"That brings me to my next thing, it's like you could read my mind. I want you to wear this at all times. I understand your workplace and the medical field is a little bit more delicate, but, other than that, I want it to be worn at all times. Work will be the only exception." She replied. "Yes, my Master. Yes, my King."

I then unbutton my pants and push them down to the ground. "Now, we got that out of the way, get on your fucking knees!" I demanded. She dropped to her knees once again and glanced at my magnificent, long, thick, hard, chocolate cock. "Open your mouth and do your whorish best!" She leaned forward and took the tip, the big tip of me past her lips. Slowly she moved to the rest of me. My dick was throbbing in her mouth. It was like it grew bigger in there. I could imagine how wet her tight little pussy was, not only because of how great I feel in that drenched pussy hole, but she was wondering how I was planning on fucking her tonight. My big tip touched the back of her throat.

"Relax your throat." I ordered. "Yes, just like that." She made herself breathe through her nose as I was now thrusting into her mouth. I then said to her, "you're ready for this dick inside you, Precious?" Her pussy was so wet, if it were a pool we would need goggles. I said sharply, "get on the bed, get on your back and spread that pussy open for me, ready to take all of me inside you!"

I loved it rough and hard. Fuck that, I loved it brutal. I grabbed a fist full of her hair anchoring her head towards me, so she could watch as my big dick went in and out of her delicious looking pussy. I spoke to her sharply once again, "hold on tight baby."

I pulled out and put my cock in her mouth, riding her face while she was on her back and my other hand reached around to play with her pussy. I pumped in and out several times and I returned to that luscious hole. She gasped as soon as I slid back in. She took a deep breath with every thrust I made. I growled into her ear and she moaned, "yesssss." I pounded into her harder. She started to twitch while I was inside her. I grabbed her butt cheeks with my massive hands, pushing her ass towards me as my dick kept pounding into her.

I then commanded her, "bring those fingers in front and rub that pretty clit while I fuck you senseless. Rub that shit now!" I was driving her crazy. She asked, "can I cum now Daddy?" She then begged, "Please?" I didn't answer. I put my hand on her breast and leaned forward. Precious' warm breath brushed across my ear as my hand closes around her throat. "Cum for me!" I told her forcefully. She was needy, and I was what she needed. I was fucking hungry and she was the only thing I wanted to consume. I leaned forward once again and rolled the tip of one nipple then the other with my tongue. I then bit her breast. She needed me, she wanted me. She craved me. She was spread before me in complete and utter offering. I filled her like she had never been filled before. Her heart beating frantically as she waits for what I do next.

I fucked her harder, I fucked her deeper. I pushed deeper until I could feel her cervix. Stretching her out with my thickness. Her legs tightening, and a low groan escapes her lips.

She then asked once again, "can I cum again my King? Please?" I allowed it once again. There is not a time I don't let her cum, only time is if she's been a bad girl or I just love watching her suffer. But today and tonight, I wanted to watch her leave the sheets soaked. She released and came all over. Her breathing returned back to normal. I thrusted harder, I was ready to cum. "Grrrrr," I growled as I filled her pussy with all my cum. She was my submissive. A woman that submitted to me in all ways, not just sexually but emotionally and psychologically. She was completely mine. SHE WAS MINE.

There was no explaining the number I'd done on her. I had her off kilter, off balance. She is my woman. Submissive to my Dominance. She exists for my convenience, but she was more than a body to warm my bed, more than a fuck toy. She didn't care about others.

She just wanted me. Our connection and dynamic, heightens everything. Perception, arousal, it was all of it. That's one of the reasons the orgasms are incredible. How much she trusts, how much I trust. How much love we have for one another. That kind of need and satisfaction flowing through two people was a rare and 'precious' gift indeed. She said to me...

"Daddy, may I make you something to eat?" I didn't answer her right away. She requested, "so, perhaps I'll make you some steak?" My eyes light up, "you know I really love steak!" She smiled, and I nodded. Cooking is what she wanted to do, and she cooked a really good steak. My stomach was full, and my balls were drained. Such a good girl but a better woman. We relaxed a bit and watched some sports, football, wrestling, basketball. She loved the things I loved and if she didn't, she knew not to bother me. Because she knew I loved them, and she wanted me to enjoy them. I would watch my sports while she sucked my dick or massage my massive muscular, tattooed back. As we were sitting there she asks a random question...

"Daddy, can I ask you something?" I nodded my head and said yes. She turned to face me. "Why can't I ever get on top? You love when I please you, I can do that when I'm on top riding your big dick as well Daddy." I laughed.

"So you want to get on top? Are you sure?" She was so good, I wanted to reward her. Normally it's rare I allow a woman to take the top position. I enjoy being on top, but she doesn't know how hard it is and I'm going to teach her a lesson now.

"You will get on top." I grabbed her, and we went to the bedroom. I'm going to make her work, 'be careful what you ask for, you may get it'. I growled at her and allowed her to get on top and ride this prominent cock. What was the catch? Her hands and wrists bound to her lower back? My massive hand on her fragile throat? My other hand grasps her waist, perhaps? I would be controlling her movements. Now she moves how I want, her body not her own, her movements not of her own. Even though she's on top, this is exactly how I want her, bouncing her up and down like a hydraulic impaler. Low riding on my thick chocolate cock. Slapping of flesh turns into background music as her breathing and moans take over. She whines, cries, whimpers for the dick. My thick long dick whips that pussy in shape. It perspires on my chocolate muscle and I leave it so sore. I usually drive her Ferrari like a wild horse but if she's good, sometimes I kick back, relax and let her chauffeur me like a mob boss.

My enormous hands grasp her ass cheeks, spreading them apart, driving her into me. Then my hands grab her throat, now she can't focus on riding and stroking. Then I tell her to squat on it. My massive hands grab her ankles just to hold her in place as she continues to bounce up and down like an elevator on that strong big dick. Moans become ferocious, eyes roll back, and her breathing begins to change significantly. I further open her flower. Dripping wet on my ample dick, she feels her walls contracting on that big chocolate muscle of a dick. Her quads begin to fatigue, she's feeling the burn.

"Keep squatting on that cock, that fucking animal." I ordered her. "I didn't tell you to stop!!" Her breathing was heavy. "You wanted to be on top." I said so fiercely. "It's not as easy as you thought, huh? I don't care if it hurts, I'm not trying to hear that. This is what YOU wanted. This is exactly what you asked for." She replied, letting out deep breaths and a gasp of air. "Yes Daddy, yes."

I pound her down into me harder. Such barbarity, such power. "Then fucking work whore, work slut. Work that cock, work that pussy, work hard for that dick. Work that animal inside you, work that animal you're riding."

I fuel her voracious appetite. She paused, she shouldn't have asked to get on top if she knew she couldn't handle it. I'm going to put an end to this 'pausing shit.'

"If you stop one more time without my permission, I'm going to reach for my thick, large wooden paddle and that's going to keep you locked the fuck up baby girl." She started riding that cock again like her life depended on it. "So giddy up baby, let's see and feel what your body is made of."

After that I flip her over, face down, ass up and I blow her back out like a pickup truck. I hit it and make her ass shake like a bowl of jello. The ass claps so loud from my pounding, it sounds like an Oprah ovation. I grasp a fist full of her hair and anchor her head back towards me. Her eyes are to the ceiling as if she is calling out, 'Oh God'. Not even HE would save her from this Discipline, this devil dick. Her legs burning, her pussy throbbing. "Daddy, can I please cum on that dick? Can I cum all over it, please Daddy, please?" Oh yeah, I wanted that cum all over my dick. "Yes baby, get that cock wet. Let me feel it on me."

She started dripping down on my dick, cream all over my cock, my pelvis. She couldn't stop cuming for me, she couldn't stop cuming for that dick. There was cum on the sheets, dripping down her thighs, from her pussy, to my dick and onto the sheets. What a wet puddle we have here. Such a mess. A dripping, breathless, motionless mess.

I walked to the bathroom to clean myself off. When I came back she was laid out on her stomach, still lifeless, going through the motions and the aftermath of Discipline. I walked over to the bed with a smile on my face, looking at how I destroyed her. I get on the bed and my massive hand kisses her flesh hard. *Smack* her ass cheek jumped, and she let out a big gasp of air.

"Go clean yourself up baby girl." We were both going to get cleaned up. "Listen, I want to take stroll in the park. It's a night full of nice blissful starlight and I want us to be in that atmosphere, walking in the park, watching the stars and being about us. Let's talk and get in a different vibe or energy, a different environment. Just dress in something casual, some jeans and a tee shirt, no makeup, comfortable and free." She smiled at me with love in her eyes. "Yes Daddy, I love that idea."

Before we left, I cooked us both dinner. I led her into the house. "We'll have dinner tonight at the kitchen table. You can consider the kitchen table your free space. You'll take the majority of your meals there, and when I join you, you may take it as an invitation to speak freely. Most of the time, you will serve me in the dining room, but I thought we should start the evening on a less formal basis. Is all this clear?" She replied, "yes, Master."

I took her to the kitchen and waited for her to sit down. Her hands trembled when she pulled out her chair. I went over to her, and pulled out her chair some more, and made sure she sat down. She was nervous; that was all. I could understand that. She did not know what to expect. This was a different approach. A little bit more into me. Into my world. More access inside of myself. My privacy. But she was here. Here in my kitchen. My slave.

"Understand, you are no longer a submissive. You are no longer my submissive. You are my slave. You are already in the mentality of slave; therefore I don't need to educate you on the requirements." She nodded her head, "yes Master. You are right. I would do anything for you. I have no limits. No safe word. You have all of me, for the longest." She was accurate on that one. We ate in silence for several minutes. She devoured the chicken. I shifted in my seat at the sight of her at my table, enjoying the food I'd made for her. "Did you cook this?" she asked. She speaks. Finally. "I am a man of many talents," I said. Then said, "haha, trying to be funny." She shook her head with a smile. "No, I thought maybe you had a maid do it, or something. I know you cook Master, but you don't cook everything or every day. I would love to cook for you, like every day if you would allow me?" I didn't answer her. But, we had a good dinner.

"So, how was it, Precious?" She smiled? "It was delicious, it was very good." I was pleased. "Okay, now, let's go for a stroll in the park!" She was ready to go, it was a very warm summer night.

Later that night we went for a stroll in the park, it was really late. We talked at a park bench and she was asking me some questions. "So Daddy, what's next for you? You've done plenty, my dear King. Traveled the world, written books, you have your submissives. What's really next for you, my Master? Mr. Discipline, the movie?" I laughed. "No, no, no. One day, I will own a few clubs, a few fitness clubs, some night clubs. Perhaps some casinos. One day, I care to have children, I mean, I'm not going to be ninety years old still tying women up. I will always be Dominant, that's in my DNA and that won't ever change, even if I wanted to run away from that, I could not. It is who I am. But, I would love to give this greatness off for them, which would be my children, to carry on my legacy. I will die one day, we don't all live forever." She smiled at me. "Daddy, you will live forever, no matter what, your soul will be around and everywhere. There are so many more lives to touch, so much more things you can and will do. You work so hard, you are so amazing, and the world needs to catch up. They need to know how special you are. Watch, you will get everything you want, you're too great not to. You're like an immortal Daddy."

I then ask her what her dreams for the future are, her goals and desires and her aspirations. She paused and was in deep thought, then she said, "I love to serve you, it makes me happy and I've accomplished all my dreams except one." I asked her. "And that would be what?" She replied. "To have a child or children!" My face lit up and I believed now that we both had a similar interest for the future.

"That's a good goal, for the future, if that." I said to her. Then she said, "what if I told you the future could be now?" I looked at her confused. "What the fuck do you mean?" She smiled. "I can give you something sooner than you thought." I was beginning to become frustrated because I hated riddles, I hated hidden secrets and surprises were the fucking worst. "Well, I know I might get punished for this, but I had every intention on telling you my King. I'm giving you something you eventually want in the future but it's happening now...I'm pregnant!!!" She covered her mouth and her eyes after telling me. I guess believing I would become super angry. "Pregnant?!" I smiled. "Ha, that's amazing!" She uncovered her eyes. "Amazing?" She asked with a flat stare at me on her face. "You're not angry with this, you are not angry with me?" She asked me. Then I laughed. "Well you will be punished but no, I'm excited! You're having my child!!! You're going to be a good mother and I'm going to mold our child into a prominent individual in this world. But you will be punished for keeping this from me." I smiled. She frowned. "But Daddy, it's good news, you said so yourself." I smirked again. "So, it still doesn't change the rules or how things go on with us." She then cut me off. "I just found out like yesterday morning. I was going to have an abortion, I really didn't know how you felt and didn't want to bring any distraction or stress or unwanted desires into our relationship."

I put my index finger up and that silenced her immediately. "Yes, I was not looking to have a child at this moment but if it's here now and not later, that's not a bad thing." I rubbed her belly so gently and then I kissed her lips passionately prior to my massive hand touching and grasping her throat firmly. We got up.

"Let's go. Let's walk over there." I grabbed her hand and we clasped our fingers together and walked side by side. We watched the stars as we walked.

Suddenly, I felt a change in the air. It was a warm summer night and all of a sudden, the air changed. I stopped moving, Precious looked at me frantically.

"Daddy, what's wrong?" I started looking around. "Something is not right. I feel off balance tonight. You feel that?" She looked around. "What do you mean?" she asked. I stared at her. "There's a change in the air."

Precious never questioned my instincts. She never called me crazy. She knew if I said something was off, then something was off.

"Look, forget it. Let's keep moving baby girl." I grab her hand and we begin walking a little faster. All of a sudden, I hear a noise, like a branch fall or something. "You heard that?" She looked confused and scared. "No Daddy, I didn't hear anything." Damn, was I going nuts? I mean was I just hearing things that weren't actually there to be heard? Fuck! What the fuck? "Let's keep moving baby."

Suddenly, something jumped from behind us and bit the side of my neck. I don't know what it was, but there was major struggle with some sort of being. Precious got involved, and I began feeling weak. She was struggling with this thing, this creature, as it threw her to the floor and stood over her. I found the strength to run over to them and fight this being off. It was a woman! Such strength and speed. I yelled out for her.

"Precious!!! Hey, you get away from her!" I lunged towards the woman and she ran off. We were in an area where people could hear us from afar, but no one was around. I grabbed Precious' limp body. The damage that was done! She was motionless and not responding to my calls for her.

"Precious!! Wake up baby!!" I lifted her body and held her in my arm. I walked with her for not even a mile when I collapsed and dropped to the ground with her. The bite on my neck got worse and I was extremely weak. I yelled out "help!!" We were in an open area now. I reached for my cell to dial 911 and the operator answered.

"911, what's your emergency?" I lost consciousness, but my phone remained on. The operator asked once again, "what is your emergency? Hello? Hello?"

Someone found us and brought us to the hospital. They were saying Precious didn't make it. Myself, the doctors asked themselves, "how can this man's body be so cold but his heart remains so warm?" They couldn't figure it out. "What's this bite mark on his neck? They're two deep bite marks. I know this sounds weird but, it looks like fangs." The other doctor said, "no it has to be something else. You're talking about fangs, like vampire? Supernatural or something?" The third doctor said, "let's figure this out."

All three of them went into the other room to discuss the situation and how they were going to move forward. The woman or creature that attacked myself and Precious in the park came back. Shit, I thought she was coming to finish the job but instead, she helped me out of there. Then she said to me...

"These mortals are not about to work on you." I looked at her with mixed emotions. "Who are you? What are you? How do you know Precious or myself? Where is Precious? WHERE THE FUCK IS PRECIOUS??!" I demanded. This woman was some supernatural shit! We teleported out of there. She took me to her lair.

"I'm going to teach you how to do that one day." I thought, what the fuck is going on here. "Fuck that, where is Precious?" I tried to swing at her, but she was too fast and I was too weak still. I managed to catch her by the throat but she just shrugged it off, smiled and tossed me around the room.

"Silly mortal! You can't overpower a vampire! A supernatural." "Ugh," I brushed myself off. "So that's what you are?" She raised her hand and I lifted up off the floor. She brought me to her with just her eyes and hands. "Have you ever been handled so violently by a woman before? Perhaps not, but I am not a woman. I am a God. I chose you because you have such extraordinary powers of a mortal. Precious, didn't seem like that. This is what I saw, and what was left of her." She opened her hand, and it was the jewelry I gave precious to wear at all times. She handed it to me. "In all of my two thousand plus years of life, I have never seen a human like yourself. You impressed me. I am going to mold you into the most elite supernatural to ever exist. You will stand by my side and we will take over this world."

I had other plans. I still don't know what happened to Precious. Where was she? I buried my face in my hands, raw agony clawing at my fucking insides.

"I fucked up, Precious. But I'm coming for you. So, help me God. I know I failed you. I let you down. But goddamn it, I will not let you go. I'll never let you go. I'll fight for you with my last breath."

The only woman I had allowed to see me at my fucking lowest, unguarded. Vulnerable. Nothing mattered to me. Not exposing my weakness. Not allowing my iron control that had maintained me through most of my life to slip. But then I never had to raise my voice to make my point. When I spoke, others instinctively ceased talking and listened to me. I was a man who commanded authority and respect. She didn't suspect what Precious was to me. What she meant to me. Suspected nothing of how I felt for her.

"I'll never forget. As long as I live, I'll never forget that night." My tone grew savage, fury radiating from me like a beacon. "She could be anywhere out there. Alone. Afraid." I said. "She put Everything on the damn line for me. I was supposed to protect her." This woman, creature I don't know then started speaking to me again.

"You've protected her at all turns, kept her secret, her doubts. She was weak, something or someone that could be used. If someone wanted to get to you, they could through her. And afraid she would be used against you. Which is why you had to do what you did when things changed and there was no other way to protect her."

What the fuck was she talking about? "You are making me furious, lady, or creature." She continued, "you shouldn't have gone public with that woman. It's damn near dangerous." She clearly wasn't making sense, but I had to educate her. "Are you just trying to get her raped, tortured, killed?" She asked me. "No, you don't hide her," I said forcefully. "You make her your fucking Queen. You let the goddamn world know she is yours and that you'll kill anyone who so much as look at her wrong, threatens her, tries to use her to get to you. Let me ask you a question! Let's say, you are the most feared man in the city. Do you honestly think they would be fool enough to go after what you value the most?" She nodded her head, "yes, no mortal would dare, but what about a beast? What about a vampire? What about an immortal?" I charged at her quickly, I just wanted to knock her the fuck out, but I was stopped quickly in my tracks, and she was protected by a forcefield she created over her. She spoke to me.

"Even if you doubled security, when have you ever publicly laid claim to a woman or made it clear that anyone harming her will die a long, agonizing death? I mean, I saw what you both did. Well, what she did, and how you covered it up. I mean, I could ruin your life." I gazed into her eyes, "what are you talking about? I haven't done anything. Ruin my life? How?" I asked. She then said, "I saw her shoot that man, and you covered it up. Don't play dumb."

She had me, I had to play ball. I then paused, pondering the conversation, lowering my head in thought, so much rushing through my mind. I who was always in control of any situation. Every possibility accounted for. Now find myself being controlled. Find myself in a position to compromise or make a deal.

"She's your woman and you've given her no reason to believe she matters as more than a body to warm your bed, a submissive to your Dominance. She exists solely for your convenience." She said, and then I cut her off, "what did you know about our relationship, you are assuming." My voice raises loudly. "Perhaps, But, were you planning to marry your sub, were you both even living together? Exactly, you mortal, are very unusual creatures, but I'm the creature right? I'm the monster? I'm not the monster here, I am just ahead of the curve. I've been around for many centuries. Many decades. Many eras. I've seen the ways. The mortal women act so much different in this era here. You're going to have to prove with actions and not just words that she is more to you than a woman who will warm your bed for a few nights and be sent on her way with an expensive gift for her time, if you found her again that is." She said to me.

"She hated to take things from me." I told her. She then asked me, "and why do you suppose that?" She asked. I then told her, "because, her only desire was to please me. Her only desire was me, nothing more. Nothing less." She laughed at me, "hahah, you damn fool, yeah, you. She wanted the lifestyle. She wanted the idea of you. You are a high ranked, Powerful man. A Dominant man, in a world full of pussies, and submissive men. What woman would not want that? Discipline, she didn't love you. She loved the idea of you. She loved, your alias, 'Discipline.' She loved to be owned, she loved the control. She loved the Dominance."

I see this woman was attempting to fuck with my head. She didn't succeed, and I wasn't going to go back and forth with her, on something she knows nothing about.

"For a woman of great power, you sure are stupid." I guess she didn't like that, she grabbed me, and she placed her hand around my throat, and lifted me off the ground. I was choking. "You know, I could easily snap your neck, with one hand."

I didn't say a word, I was still choking from her grasp. "Haha, look at you, have you ever been handled by a woman before? Weak mortal." Technically, she wasn't a woman, but I was going to find out, who or what she was. I was determined. So, I put both my hands up, showing signs of surrender, she then released her hand from my throat. And I then dropped hard to the ground. I placed my hand on my throat and begin coughing and gasping for air. What a grip this creature had, but, it or she was not going to kill me, she has some type of purpose with me, and I was going to find it out.

Perhaps I should play the game with this woman, this creature, or this beast for now. When she makes a mistake, I will use that to my advantage and take her out. She will make a mistake, she fucking talks too damn much, she will make a mistake. I don't know, I had so many emotions running through me. She finally let me down and I passed out.

"You need to feast. She said to me. "You're not strong enough yet. When you feed, you become stronger after each time. You need blood." She then began to say, "you can't beat me, so you might as well join me. I need someone like you by my side. A man of your caliber can do so much damage and you don't even know the powers you possess. You can either hunt or be hunted, the decision is yours. Do you want mediocrity, or do you want immortality?"......

To be continued in my fourth book...The Immortality of Discipline.

About the Author

Born and raised in New York, E.L Discipline is educating the masses on the true form of spiritual connections and knowledge. He is the author of The Seduction of Discipline, and The Importance of Discipline. With his third book, Discipline's World, E.L Discipline is breaking barriers in the world of seduction and sensuality. His reputation for being known as the king of erotica is widely spreading and is changing the way we view relationships forever.

Also, as a certified fitness trainer, he mentors and teaches about endurance not only in the body, but the mind as well. His will to dominate has pushed him to master a variety of enterprises. His books are taking the world by storm, and his education speaks volumes. His goal is clear, as he has one main purpose in mind: To change the world, one reader at a time.